S0-ACO-352

STRANGLED INTUITION

CLAIRE DANIELS

BERKLEY PRIME CRIME, NEW YORK

If you purchased this book without a cover, you should be aware that this book is stolen property. It was reported as "unsold and destroyed" to the publisher, and neither the author nor the publisher has received any payment for this "stripped book."

This is a work of fiction. Names, characters, places, and incidents either are the product of the author's imagination or are used fictitiously, and any resemblance to actual persons, living or dead, business establishments, events, or locales is entirely coincidental.

STRANGLED INTUITION

A Berkley Prime Crime Book / published by arrangement with the author

PRINTING HISTORY
Berkley Prime Crime mass-market edition / January 2004

Copyright © 2004 by Jaqueline Girdner.
Cover art by One By Two.
Cover design by Erika Fusari.
Interior text design by Julie Rogers.

All rights reserved.
This book, or parts thereof, may not be reproduced in any form without permission.
The scanning, uploading, and distribution of this book via the Internet or via any other means without the permission of the publisher is illegal and punishable by law. Please purchase only authorized electronic editions, and do not participate in or encourage electronic piracy of copyrighted materials. Your support of the author's rights is appreciated.
For information address: The Berkley Publishing Group, a division of Penguin Group (USA) Inc., 375 Hudson Street, New York, New York 10014.
Visit our website at penguin.com

ISBN: 0-425-19463-9

BERKLEY®
Berkley Prime Crime Books are published by The Berkley Publishing Group, a division of Penguin Group (USA) Inc., 375 Hudson Street, New York, New York 10014.
The name BERKLEY PRIME CRIME and the BERKLEY PRIME CRIME design are trademarks belonging to Penguin Group (USA) Inc.

PRINTED IN THE UNITED STATES OF AMERICA

10 9 8 7 6 5 4 3 2 1

To my readers: past, present, and future.
Thank you for giving my characters a home.

PRAISE FOR
BODY OF INTUITION:

"Fans of Jaqueline Girdner's Kate Jasper series will relish Claire Daniels's new Cally Lazar series. Cane-wielding Cally and the rest of the cast are a delight."
—Jan Dean, editor of *Murder Most Cozy*

"Prognosis: original, innovative and unique. Don't miss Cally Lazar's fresh approach to problem-solving. Claire Daniels creates an 'energetic' plot with captivating characters. *Body of Intuition* will open up your mind to new perspectives."
—Janet A. Rudolph, editor of *Mystery Readers Journal*

"A riveting plot. Absorbing and endlessly entertaining."
—Lynne Murray, author of *A Ton of Trouble*

"Whether your aura is serenely silver or your karma needs a tune-up, you'll enjoy following intuitive healer Cally Lazar as she uses her unusual talents to find a murderer at a Love Seminar."
—Kate Derie, editor of *The Deadly Directory*

"Daniels's portrayal of the New Age milieu is both realistic and a bit tongue in cheek."
—*The Drood Review of Mystery*

"Hilarious and outrageous . . . Murder is no laughing matter, but in Claire Daniels's capable hands, catching a murderer has never been so amusing."
—Sandie Herron, *I Love a Mystery*

"Claire Daniels has written a creative New Age psychic mystery starring a heroine that it is impossible not to like."
—*Midwest Book Review*

PRAISE FOR
BODY OF INTUITION:

"Fans of Jaqueline Girdner's Kate Jasper series will relish Claire Daniels's new Cally Lazar series. Cane-wielding Cally and the rest of the cast are a delight."
—Jan Dean, editor of *Murder Most Cozy*

"Prognosis: original, innovative and unique. Don't miss Cally Lazar's fresh approach to problem-solving. Claire Daniels creates an 'energetic' plot with captivating characters. *Body of Intuition* will open up your mind to new perspectives."
—Janet A. Rudolph, editor of *Mystery Readers Journal*

"A riveting plot. Absorbing and endlessly entertaining."
—Lynne Murray, author of *A Ton of Trouble*

"Whether your aura is serenely silver or your karma needs a tune-up, you'll enjoy following intuitive healer Cally Lazar as she uses her unusual talents to find a murderer at a Love Seminar."
—Kate Derie, editor of *The Deadly Directory*

"Daniels's portrayal of the New Age milieu is both realistic and a bit tongue in cheek."
—*The Drood Review of Mystery*

"Hilarious and outrageous . . . Murder is no laughing matter, but in Claire Daniels's capable hands, catching a murderer has never been so amusing."
—Sandie Herron, *I Love a Mystery*

"Claire Daniels has written a creative New Age psychic mystery starring a heroine that it is impossible not to like."
—*Midwest Book Review*

ACKNOWLEDGMENTS

To everyone who inspired, incited, and abetted the writing of this book, including Bill Girdner, Carol Straus, Lynne Murray, Dan Paul, Eileen Ostrow Feldman, and Greg Booi. Thank you.

CAST OF CHARACTERS

THE PARTYGOERS:

Cally Lazar: Medical intuitive, recovering attorney, and reluctant finder of dead bodies.

York Lazar: Cally's brother, a teacher of martial arts.

May North: Our party's hostess. She is also York's student and Cally's client, a former madam, and a current affront to the city of Mostaza.

Gerry Cheng: May's husband, a prince of computer software.

Becky Cheng: Gerry's adult daughter. She doesn't want to call May "mother."

Eric Ford: One of May's boarders, a bankrupt physician.

Ian Oxton: May's second boarder, a "resting" actor who doesn't mind playing butler for May.

Phil Morton: May's third boarder, a minister who struggles for finances as well as souls.

John Turner: May's neighbor. He deals in furnishings from around the world.

Julie Turner: John's wife. She'd rather stay home and rule in Mostaza.

Zack Turner: Julie's fourteen-year-old son.

Sarah Quesada: May's neighbor, realtor, and member of Mostaza's planning commission.

Dutch Krentz: May's neighbor and town gossip.

Francie Krentz: Dutch's wife and backup gossip.

CALLY'S CREW:

Roy Beaumont: Cally's sweetie . . . as long as the "dark forces" aren't present.

Warren Kapp: Cally's friend most of the time, an octogenarian attorney and know-it-all.

Dee-Dee Lee: Cally's friend, a vegetarian hypnotist.

Joan Hussein: Another friend of Cally's. She's an attorney, too, but she doesn't pretend to know as much as Warren Kapp.

Virginia McFadden: Yet another friend of Cally's and a longtime client.

Pete: Roy's roommate at Glasse General Hospital.

Geneva, Melinda, and Arnot Lazar: Siblings to Cally and York.

THE POLICE:

Chief Upwood, of the Mostaza Police Department.

Sergeant Verne, Officer Daly, and Officer Affonso, also of the MPD.

ONE

"Do you have kids?" asked the silver-haired woman who lay faceup on my massage table. She smelled of a perfume that tickled my nose. I suppressed the urge to sneeze. Sneezing on clients was definitely in the code of "modalities not to be tried" in my energetic healing practice.

"No," I answered her question briefly. I could have said more. I am, after all, all of thirty-six years of age, well into the range of child-bearing potential. But how could I explain to a first-time client that the one man I loved was no more fit to be a father than I was to be a mother. In polite conversation, I would have asked May North if she had children herself. But that Friday, I was working. Or maybe I should say that energy was working through me. After all the seminars I'd taken on energetic healing, and all the clients I'd had on my table (once I'd recovered from my attorney phase), I'd concluded that I wasn't the healer when I "worked." The client was the healer. I just enabled the healing.

I traced the edges of May's energetic field with my hands and gauged her sadness as she spoke. My own eyes felt a sudden pressure of tears behind my glasses. The sadness, grief, and longing were a surprise. I'd met May in one of my brother York's martial arts classes. She was witty, ribald, and aggressive on the surface. Her imitation of the mayor of her hometown, Mostaza, had made me laugh until my face hurt. Anger, now *that* I'd expected to find. But this extreme of sadness? I shook my head. I could see it, too, in the blue aura of mourning that surrounded her and in the green of frustration and loss. These colors might have meant something else in another client, the blue of truth or the green of healing. But in May, they were clearly sadness.

"You oughta think about kids, Cally," she suggested, her voice harsh in tone, but kind in undertone. "You've got the heart for it."

I nodded, barely hearing her words as I concentrated on imagining May loving herself, imagining May accepting compassion, and imagining May filled with joy. I gently touched the two points on either side of her nose and ran my hands all the way down to the ends of her index fingers. I could feel the grief following my touch to her fingertips and out. I breathed in contentment as May smiled, her face pinkening as her aura gentled into softer tones, and as a corresponding sense of warmth spread through my limbs. May was a client who was able to accept the gifts of energy work. And quickly. Not every client was this open. Actually, very few were.

"But you have animals," May continued. "Now cats are sneaky little sweet-talkers. But they're cute. And goats. Whooee! What a trip. It's nice here, Cally. Nature's damn near to heaven as far as I'm concerned, and you've got it all around you."

My cat, Leona, purred in approval from the bottom end of the massage table. I felt like purring a little myself. My small house was a stucco minimansion of twelve hundred square feet in the town of Estados next to May's town of Mostaza in the county of Glasse, a small county sandwiched between Marin and Sonoma in northern California. True, the house was located on a slope of land that was impossible to garden, but I had three goats to keep the vegetation down, and my pride and joy, a lattice-surrounded deck overflowing with flowering plants that my goats, Moscow, Persia, and Ohio, would dearly love to trim for me but never would. And no, I didn't name the goats. They'd come with the house that I'd bought in the days when I'd worked as an attorney. The rooms of the house were necessarily small, but all filled with custom-made floor-to-ceiling bookshelves. I blessed the bibliophiles who'd built it. "Damn near to heaven," was right. Even on this cold January day, it was cozy in the former living room that now housed three stuffed chairs, a massage table, and endless books on healing esoterica.

"I've got lots of critters myself," May went on, and her sadness seemed to lift a little more. "Dogs, cats, a parrot. The parrot talks dirty," she whispered, then cackled. "Can't imagine where the little nitwit got that habit."

I chuckled. There was something about May that was impossible not to like. May was a beautiful woman in a big-boned, Germanic way, with a lush mouth in red lipstick, overly made-up saucer blue eyes, her skin delicately wrinkled below her silver hair. Even her clothing, tangerine-and-chartreuse plaid with a gold necklace heavy enough to pay a ransom, couldn't quite overshadow her beauty.

She'd approached me in York's class, complaining of unexplained digestive and respiratory disorders. I was glad to take her as a client. It was so easy to see the goodness and light in May. Anyway, she told great jokes. At least, sometimes.

"So, you name yourself Cally?" she demanded suddenly.

"Nope," I answered, certainly not for the first time in my life. I'm Cally Lazar, the fifth child of the Lazar clan, recovering attorney, and energy worker. Some people would call me a "medical intuitive," but I prefer "energy worker."

"Your parents named you Cally?" May pushed.

"My parents named me Calypso," I explained. My parents were dead, killed in an accident when I was a teenager. I didn't like talking about them very much. "I shortened it to Cally."

"They like that Belafonte guy?" May plowed on.

"No, not Harry Belafonte, not Jacques Cousteau's boat," I said, covering all the bases. "They named me for a classic sea nymph." I sighed.

May laughed. "Calypso! Whooee, shake your mermaid tail! That's one helluva name for a kid. But don't feel bad. I named myself. I won't even tell you the god-awful name my parents saddled me with. My parents never really got the drift of things." She shook her head. "Good hearts, but no brains. And I was one raggedy-assed kid. So anyway, once I was old enough to vote and do a few other things, I decided there was no reason on this green earth that I couldn't have a better name. I found out that Mae West was taken, though, so I named myself May North."

Now it was my turn to laugh—and to wonder what May's original name had been.

I ran my hands lightly from a point on each collarbone down to May's thumbs and felt a little more grief let go. And then I felt the pressure of the small-intestine meridian, the pressure of secrecy, all tied up with her grief.

On an impulse, I asked May to turn on her side with her back to me.

"So, does your stomach feel any better?" I asked quietly.

She didn't answer.

I asked again, turning up the volume on my voice ever so slightly.

"What?" she shouted, rolling over on her other side to face me again.

Well, there was one secret, one that didn't surprise me. May was deaf, or at least partially deaf. She had to face me to hear my words. She was reading my lips.

"How's your tummy feeling?" I tried once more.

"Better," she said slowly, surprise on her face. "When your brother suggested you, I thought you two might be hustling this old lady, but I'm feeling really good already, hungry enough to eat grits." She paused for effect, and added, "And I hate grits."

"Well, good!" I grinned at her. Her spirit was infectious.

"And I'm breathing better, too," she told me, holding one hand over her ample bosom. "Hot damn, this stuff really works!"

It was time to wrap up the session for the day. I had a feeling May North had a lot more to reveal, but I was going to quit while she was feeling good.

"You may find that some difficult feelings crop up after today," I began my postsession lecture. "Call me if you need to, but just as long as you know that feelings can be a natural outcome of the work—"

"Just a natural outcome of life, if you ask me," she interrupted.

Twenty minutes later, I'd finished my lecture, and May was still smiling. The room felt warm, but maybe it was really the warmth of a newfound friend. Because May felt like a friend now, not just a client.

"You want to come to a party with that gorgeous brother of yours?" she asked when I was finished. "I figure Mostaza needs a little scandalizing, so I'm throwing a shindig to-night. Champagne, good eats, the works. York already said he'd come."

It took me more than a minute to switch gears.

"You got a boyfriend, or a girlfriend or whatever, you can bring them, too," she added.

"York's going?" I asked stupidly.

"Yep, I hornswoggled him yesterday."

I thought about it. I didn't have any plans. Maybe Roy . . . I decided I'd think about Roy later.

"Why not?" I said to May, and she hopped off the table and gave me a hug that imprinted the contours of her gold necklace onto my minimalist chest and the imprint of her perfume into my nostrils.

After May left, I picked up the cane I used to support my weak leg and crossed the hall to the tiny dining room that I used for an office. I made out a file for May enthusiastically and wrote up some notes about the session. I was sure May would be back. Then I walked through my kitchen for an early-twilight view of my deck garden, which shimmered with the pink, yellow, and blue of primroses, the orange of Iceland poppies, and the purple of pansies. I stepped out the back door onto the deck, cold air chilling my face immediately, and waved at my goats. They were white LaManchas, with sturdy bodies, elf ears, and straggly beards. Ohio bleated at my wave, and the world felt perfect. Then I remembered Roy.

Roy. What can I say about Roy? I went back into the kitchen to put the kettle on the stove for tea. Roy was the man I loved, an accountant originally from Kentucky, with an endearing drawl, a weedy body not unlike my own, red-dish brown hair, and intense golden eyes. We'd been lovers for about seven years when he'd started in about the "dark forces." Dark forces were what appeared when he looked at me. And being the sweet man he was, he figured that this darkness meant that our being together was somehow harmful to *me*. How's that for a Rorschach? Criminy, he could have *blamed* me. But he did worse, especially when I started getting stomachaches. He avoided me entirely. Somehow, though, neither of us could manage to stay apart, and we'd been seeing each other again . . . cautiously. Well, Roy was cautious anyway. Even my healer friends could see the darkness around us when we were together. Even *I* could see it. No one knew what it meant. All I knew was that Roy was a good man, even a sane man, despite the dark forces. How could I think otherwise? I saw colors when I looked at people. Roy saw darkness. But still—

The teakettle shrilled.

I poured the boiling water over a bag of peach tea, inhaling its scent, and made up my mind. May said I could invite a boyfriend or "whatever" to the party. I'd invite my whatever, Roy.

As soon as I heard his voice on the phone, I knew Roy wouldn't go to May's party with me. He already had the dark forces for company.

"Cally, darlin'," he breathed. "I was about to call you. Something's wrong. I can feel it—"

"No, Roy," I begged. I didn't want to hear it. "Please—"

"I can see it, Cally," he insisted. "There's a terrible evil near you—"

"Roy, you know I don't believe in evil. Remember, I believe in light—"

"Don't go to the party," he interrupted.

Now my cozy house felt cold, because I hadn't even mentioned the party yet. Had York told Roy?

I opened my mouth to ask, but I was too late.

"Please don't go, Cally," he whispered, and hung up the phone so gently that I didn't even hear the click. It was only when I heard the clanging signal and automatic phone message instructing me to hang up that I knew he was gone. I hung up.

Then I walked around my little house, trying not to cry, trying not to be angry, trying not to feel foolish. I leaned on my cane more heavily than usual. My leg had buckled for no reason when I was fifteen, the day my parents had been killed in an explosion. But the weird thing was that it had buckled before anyone had told me about their deaths. And it'd remained weak all of these years, except when I was doing energy work. So, go figure.

Once I got to my bedroom, everything felt lighter. And it looked lighter, too, with the last twilight flowing through the panes of the funny little windows over my double bed. I drank in the blue light and decided what to wear to May North's party that night. I was going to have fun, Roy or no Roy. I refused to believe in his prediction of evil.

By the time my brother York came up my driveway in his Subaru, I'd fed the cat, walked down the back hill and given the goats their goat chow, eaten a light dinner of cheese and bread and fruit, and fussed, rebraiding my long hair in the back and fluffing the short curls in the front. I was dressed in a fluid, purple pantsuit with a Mandarin collar that my sister Geneva had designed. It fit like it had been made for me—which it had. That was the nice thing about having a clothing designer as a sister. Like all the Lazars, I'm small, dark-haired, and fair-skinned, with razor-sharp features. A very, very past boyfriend had once asked me if I used a pencil sharpener for my nose every morning. Hardee-har-har. There were worse fates than the dark forces.

York stepped out of the driver's side of his car. He was wearing a fluid, black pantsuit with a Mandarin collar.

"Son of a lizard!" we both yelped simultaneously.

Have I mentioned that all Lazars use their own private language under stress? "Dack," "son of a lizard," "criminy," "midgin," "keerups," "ratsafratz," "snerty," whatever.

"I thought you wouldn't wear Geneva's clothes," I accused, noting that he might have looked a touch better in his pantsuit that I did in mine. York was lithe and handsome, with compelling dark eyes and long hair pulled back in a ponytail. And the pantsuit had a certain martial arts flavor that he carried off well—being a real live martial artist.

"Criminy," he breathed. "She said she designed this exclusively for me."

"Well, the exclusive must have been the color, because she told me the same about mine," I argued, tapping my cane in irritation. It was cold out, too, but I hadn't wanted to spoil the look of Geneva's creation. I guess York hadn't either.

Then York gave me one of his rare smiles. "I suppose we'll be midgin twins tonight," he offered, and opened the passenger door for me. Pantsuit or not, York was cool.

I asked York what he knew about May on the way over. He countered by asking me how my "cane-fu" practice was going. York didn't gossip. Lazars aren't all *exactly* alike.

In a few minutes, we were turning onto one of the more exclusive drives in Mostaza. The homes were all earth tones here, with subtly landscaped yards and quiet gates. Except for Citrus House, as the sign on a very unquiet gate labeled the last home on the block. Citrus House was a tangerine-colored giant of architecture, jutting with Greek columns, turrets, and random balconies in lime trim. The yard was filled with plaster dogs, cats, horses, and birds entwined with overgrown roses and berry bushes, all of the plaster animals placed as if looking upward at the three stories of moneyed, unsubtle taste.

York slowed and turned his car onto the driveway to Citrus House.

"This isn't May's house, is it?" I breathed in awe.

"This is it," York answered briefly.

Citrus House was dressed like May, I realized, with a little spurt of affection for the place. It looked as appropriate in its surroundings as a circus in a zen monastery. Just like May.

"She's a good student," York growled once he was parked in the circular driveway, as if he felt the need to defend May.

"She's a lovely client," I assured him, and the two of us got out of the Subaru and walked to the front door.

From the moment the man in full butler regalia opened the door to Citrus House, time seemed to speed up.

"Ian Oxton," the man introduced himself, sticking out his hand to be shaken. He had a long, lean face with high, expressive eyebrows.

"Cally Lazar," I greeted him, shaking his hand. I'd decided that if he was a butler, he hadn't gone to a traditional butler school. "And my brother York."

"Cute outfits," Ian commented, turning to York. York's face reddened.

I closed my eyes. York was a top martial artist. He could turn Ian into a heap of broken bones if he felt like it. I reminded myself that York had ethics, and I opened one eye. Ian was still standing. I opened the other eye.

And then the dogs arrived: a black Labrador retriever jumping happily, paws first on my "cute" outfit; a dachshund nosing my boot; and something that looked like a mop, yipping and hopping.

"It's the welcoming committee," Ian confided in a stage whisper. "At least, the parrot didn't see you yet." Then he swiveled his head, and bellowed, "May!"

"Cally, honey!" May shouted back happily. "York, sweetie!"

May hustled up to us, holding the hand of a kind-looking Asian man with gray hair and a thin-lipped, shy smile. The animals turned their attentions to May and her companion.

"This is my hot honey of a husband, Gerry Cheng," she introduced, and wrapped her arm around Gerry's waist and squeezed. Gerry was wearing a plaid jacket in shades of orange, brown, and yellow. I wondered if May had picked it out. "We're still just honeymooners, really," May purred.

"Good to meet you, Mr. Cheng," I tried. "I'm Cally—"

"Just Gerry, please," he murmured, looking at the animals at his feet as York identified himself.

May let go of Gerry for a moment to give me and York a couple of perfumed hugs. She wore a multicolored concoction that combined netting, jewels, gold flakes, and silk in a way that would have made my sister Geneva gag. But May had her own style. Her dress was consistent with the rest of her outfits, not to mention her house. And she was still wearing the gold necklace.

In seconds, May was pulling me and York around the room to meet the others, throwing out their names and descriptions as fast as an auctioneer, while the dogs noisily followed in our wake.

A thirtyish, nicely dressed, tall man with skin the color of cloves was, "Phil, a preacher, you know, he lives here." A fortyish, not so nicely dressed, bearded man with skin the color of blanched strawberries was, "Eric, a doctor, lives here, too." We passed heaped platters of food on a huge buffet table, way too much food for the small gathering. I saw some prawns that seemed to beckon. But May was still showing us around.

"My neighbors, Dutch and Francie," were a tall man with widely alert blue eyes and a smiling woman with dripping curls and layers of scarves and skirts. The man looked near to May's age; the woman a little younger. "And John and Julie Turner, more neighbors." John was good-looking in a bland, symmetrical way, and his wife, Julie, was downright gorgeous, with her bee-stung lips, big blue eyes, and fair skin under dark hair in a short, high-priced style. "Sarah Quesada, a friend and a joy, most the time," was a friendly looking woman with an overbite and warm brown eyes that were endearing. "And Becky . . ." May's voice slowed here. I guessed Becky wasn't a friend and a joy. Her plain, oval face looked hostile behind her glasses. I wondered how old Becky was. She looked about my age or older, but she was acting like a sullen teenager. "Becky is Gerry's daughter," May finished up diffidently.

Becky crossed her arms over her chest. Gerry murmured, "Now, honey . . . ." I'd almost forgotten he was still with us. I tried to remember the people I'd been introduced to as May moved on and left us.

May said something to Dutch that sounded German, or maybe it was just all the noise in the room. And then Julie, was it Julie?, stomped up to May.

"Stay away from my son," the beautiful woman said, her voice tense. Julie, right. "That's the only reason I came, to tell you that."

But May just grinned.

"Hey, so I'm the crabgrass of life," she told Julie. "And you're a PTA mom. That's the breaks. I know you want to run for school board—"

"So, what's wrong with that?" Julie demanded, her voice cracking on a higher note.

"There's nothing the matter with it, Juliette, but when the chips are down—"

"Don't call me Juliette," the younger woman yelped, and retreated to her bland-looking husband's embrace. What was his name? Jack? No, John, I remembered.

"Hey, sailor!" someone called out, and I looked up to see a parrot on its perch in a high window. A cat sat in the next window over. Well, the window wasn't quite over, more over and down. All the windows in the room were randomly placed, as if they had been thrown there as impartially as the varied decorations on the orange walls.

At least York seemed to be enjoying himself. He was talking to the scruffy-looking doctor we'd been introduced to. Eric? Had May actually said he lived here?

"Please, honey, just try," I heard Gerry Cheng say to his daughter.

I couldn't hear her muffled answer, but I could see the anger in her face.

"So, you're Cally," a voice said from behind me. I whipped around and saw Ian Oxton's lean face, his brows raised even higher now. He was definitely not the butler, I decided, despite his clothing. "May says you're not as boring as the rest of them," he went on. "Whaddaya say—"

But the doorbell rang then, and Ian went on alert.

"Duty calls." He sighed and stepped toward the door. Okay, maybe he *was* the butler.

A boy who looked about fourteen stepped through the door when Ian opened it. He was a good-looking boy with large blue eyes. I figured out where he got the blue eyes when Julie charged through the room.

"Zack, what are you doing here?" she demanded. "You're supposed to be doing homework."

"Mrs. North invited me," the boy explained, exchanging a long blue-eyed wink with May.

Julie threw up her hands and turned to her husband. But I couldn't hear what she was saying because Ian was back.

"Gawd, the neighbors." He sighed theatrically to me. "They're simply barbaric."

"Are you May's butler?" I asked.

"Looking for a good time?" the parrot asked above me.

"I'm not her butler," Ian answered, ignoring the parrot. "I just live here, and it amuses May for me to dress the part, so—"

"You live here?" I asked.

"Now, Zack," I heard Julie say, and saw her son leave by the door he'd come in. Julie's husband returned, his face somber.

"I'm one of May's boarders," Ian explained.

I looked around and spotted May speaking to Dutch and Sarah.

"Hey, Sarah," May cawed. "How's about I build another house like this and make it an apartment?"

"You can't do that," Sarah answered, her warm brown eyes looking panicked.

"But—" May began.

"No more favors, May," Sarah said quietly. "I mean it."

"Hey, don't worry, sweetie-pie," May told her, patting her cheek affectionately. "I'm just playing with you."

"I'm a resting actor," Ian said, and I remembered who I was supposed to be paying attention to.

"Resting from what?" I asked politely. I was sure Ian had good qualities, sparkling qualities. If I could only listen to him.

Out of the corner of my eye, I saw May join her husband again where he stood talking to his daughter.

"Oh, commercials, small theater, you know the drill," Ian answered languidly.

I focused on Ian and tried to remember why I came to parties. People, conversation, fun. Right. I stretched my face into what I hoped was a smile. Suddenly, I wanted to be back home in my cozy little house with my cat in one arm and a book in the other. Dack. Was it because Roy wasn't here? Was it because—

And then someone screamed. It took me a moment to locate the sound, but when I saw Gerry Cheng with his arms wrapped around his daughter, Becky, holding her back from May, I was pretty sure I'd found the source.

Then the scream turned into words.

"You are, too, a gold digger!" Becky shrieked. "I won't let you do this to Daddy!"

And then the room was finally quiet.

TWO

But the room wasn't quiet for long.

"I might have been in Alaska a few too many years," May announced, placing her hands on her multicolored hips emphatically. "But I wasn't any nitwitted gold miner."

The dachshund at May's feet yipped in agreement.

"You know what I mean," Becky insisted, ignoring the scattered laughter that May's announcement provoked. "Anyway, you were worse than a gold miner. It makes me physically ill just to think—"

"Really?" May interrupted, widening her already impossibly large eyes. "It never makes me sick to think."

The laughter was even louder then.

But Becky wasn't laughing. Even May noticed.

"Listen, honey," she said to the younger woman seriously. "I know you're never going to accept me as a sweet little old mother substitute, but don't accuse me of things that aren't true. I worked damned hard for my money. I bought this house with it." She waved her hand around her. "Do you really think I would marry your father for his money?"

"But—" Becky tried.

"I married your father 'cause he's a goddamn sweetheart

of a man, and if you're too blind to see the truth of that, then you aren't much of a loving daughter."

"Daddy?" Becky whispered uncertainly, turning to her father.

"Oh, Becky," Gerry muttered, shaking his head and looking at the floor.

"You know I love you, Daddy," Becky said quietly. Then she shook her own head in a way very much like her father and looked at her own spot on the floor. "I'm very upset. I've said untactful things. But it doesn't mean that I don't understand why someone might want to marry you. I'm . . . I'm sorry."

"That's okay, Becky," Gerry said, and gave his daughter a hug. He looked over at May, as if hoping that forgiving his daughter didn't overstep some line.

But May just smiled.

"Hey, it's just fine, kid," she told Becky. "Nothing to have a coronary over. Reminds me of a night in Alaska. There was this drunk who was meaner than a polar bear—"

"May was a madam of a house of ill repute," someone whispered in my ear. I turned my head and saw Francie of the dripping curls and scarves and skirts. Her round face was animated, her small eyes lit up maliciously.

"What?" I asked, not sure of what I'd just heard.

"You know." Francie winked. "She ran a bordello. Would you believe it? But all you have to do is look at her clothing. I mean, really, she can be so awful."

I turned and looked back at May, who was still immersed in her story.

". . . and this little gal, no taller than five feet, and skinny, too, threw him across the room. Got me interested in martial arts right then. . . ."

I looked back at Francie. Could she be right about May?

"You telling May's little secrets now?" Francie's husband, Dutch, asked from behind us, his voice low and insinuating.

Francie turned quickly his way, visibly startled.

"Not that they're really secrets," Dutch went on smoothly. "Most of the people in this town know what May used to do for a living. That's why they didn't come to this party. They think May's a bad influence. Or else they're just jealous that they didn't make as much money as she did in their boring lives—"

The doorbell rang again, cutting Dutch off.

Ian did his door duty, and Zack came stomping back into the room, his adolescent face sullen.

John was at Zack's side in an unexpected burst of speed. "I thought you were going home," John reminded the boy.

Zack opened his mouth, but before he had a chance to say anything, May spoke.

"Aw, come on," she prodded. "Let the kid stay. When the chips are down, kids are safer where you can see them."

John turned to Julie. Julie shrugged her shoulders and averted her face, but not before I'd glimpsed the frustration in her big blue eyes.

Behind me, someone laughed at something. And someone else was talking in a low voice. But I was watching the Turners.

"You can stay, Zack," John said quietly. "But this is an adult party, remember that."

"Sure, dude," Zack shot back.

John fixed his gaze on Zack, not exactly glaring, but Zack still turned away after a few moments.

"Sorry, Dad," he apologized in a low voice.

John put his hand on Zack's shoulder. It might have been an affectionate gesture, but it looked proprietary. Zack waited a few breaths, then slowly moved away from John, away from his hand.

May turned back to her captive audience and began to talk again.

"People are always asking me about Alaska," she began in the age-old comedic rhythm of someone about to launch into a long joke. "I suppose they want to break the ice, so to speak. Well, Alaska's a strange place, all right. You know what they always say about the place: If you're a woman, the odds are good; but the goods are odd."

There was more laughter in the room, and Ian Oxton shouted, "Bravo!"

May turned to Becky.

"I had to come down here to find a good man," she finished. "And I damn well did."

"How about a good kid?" Zack asked, smiling. "I wouldn't mind going to Alaska with you."

May took a few steps toward the boy, put her finger under his chin, and gave him a light kiss on the cheek.

I was trying not to peek at auras, but I couldn't miss the sparkling green of love and healing around May's heart. It was good to see.

Zack laughed. "Are there really polar bears—" he began, but Julie had grabbed him by his arm before he could finish.

She led the boy to the other side of the room, her finger raised in lecture mode. I couldn't make out her words, but I could hear her tone. Criminy, I was beginning to feel sorry for Zack Turner. And for May. The sparkling green had disappeared along with Zack.

"Kid, are there polar bears?" she tried. I wondered if

Zack could even hear her over his mother's lecture. "Is a cow's behind beef?"

"You tell 'em, May!" a new voice shouted. It was Eric, the scruffy man who had been talking to York. But Eric's face was reddening above his beard now that he'd shouted. I had a feeling Eric wasn't a shouter by nature.

I felt something damp push my hand, and I jumped. But it was only the Labrador retriever making friends.

"Polar bears are some shrewd operators," May went on. "Now, the tourists are another thing. Always want their pictures taken with the polar bears. So here are these polar bears minding their own bees wax, and these half-witted tourists come running up—"

I didn't hear the rest because Francie was whispering in my ear again. I looked her way. Her husband, Dutch, seemed to have wandered off again.

"Not only was May a madam," I heard, "but she still has no morals at all. She sunbathes in the nude. At her age."

"So this jackass tourist shoves his wife at the polar bear—"

"And," Francie cut back in, "May waved at the Turner's boy, Zack, from her balcony, stark naked. Do you believe it?"

Actually, I did believe it. For all of her lack of "morals," May seemed to me to be an innocent in her own goofy way. She probably thought no more of her naked body than her animals did of theirs. Still, Zack's mother must have been shocked by the scene. I looked across the room where she was still lecturing her son. No wonder she was so angry with May. One person's innocence can be another's evil. I sighed. The Labrador licked my hand in sympathy.

"Then, kaboom, the nitwit hits the flash on his camera," May was saying. "That bear whaps the wife away with one paw and goes for the tourist with the camera. Hooeee! Little bits of that guy and his camera were flying everywhere. Then the bear dusts off his paws and leaves in disgust. Can't say I blame him. Like I said, bears aren't stupid. People are."

"Madam," Ian Oxton purred, bowing. "Then you must be a polar she-bear."

May threw her head back and laughed. Gerry Cheng smiled at her fondly. I was glad to see he was smitten by his own wife. He stroked her back, probably unaware of his own gesture.

But there was something about the way Ian had pronounced "madam" that made me certain that Francie had been right about May's former occupation. I thought for a moment. Madam could cover a lot of ground, ethically speaking. Had she been a good madam or a bad madam? Was there such a thing as a good madam? I told myself I'd think it out later. For the moment, I'd remain cool, nonchalant. Because I had a feeling I'd probably been one of the few people in the room who was unaware of May's Alaskan adventures. I glowered over at my brother York. He'd known. I was sure of it. He saw my glower and shrugged in return. There are times when Lazars don't have to speak to communicate.

"So this Texan comes to Alaska," May started up again. "Says he wants Alaskan citizenship. The good ole boys tell him he's gotta do two things, kiss an Alaskan maiden and wrassle a polar bear—"

"She's probably having it on with her tenants, too," Francie whispered in my ear.

"So the guy comes back all beat-up. He says, 'Well, I kissed the polar bear, when do I get to wrassle the Alaskan maiden?' "

I laughed along with everyone else, actually everyone but Julie, John, and Francie. Even Becky was smiling by then. May knew how to tell a joke. I didn't care what Francie whispered in my ear.

"Wanna kiss an Alaskan she-bear, sweetheart?" May asked, turning to Gerry.

And he did. May and Gerry embraced the way they did in the old movies. I didn't even have to peek at their auras to see the passion there. And May didn't mind us watching. It was easy to imagine her nude on her balcony.

Then May bowed, still squeezing Gerry's hand.

"Gotta go upstairs and freshen up," she told him in an overloud aside. She turned to the rest of us. "Enjoy the party, kids. Don't do anything I wouldn't do."

"Humph," Francie snorted, as May opened a door leading to a stairway. "There isn't anything that woman wouldn't do."

"Yeah, she's pretty impressive, all right," I agreed, purposely misunderstanding her.

"Oh, but I—" Francie began.

"Hey, sailor!" the parrot squawked.

I felt hot breath on my neck. Too high for a Labrador retriever, I decided, and turned carefully around.

Ian Oxton stood far too close to me.

"Perhaps a kiss for an Alaskan he-bear, mademoiselle?" he proposed, his breath alcoholic enough to drink.

I didn't even open my mouth. Because I wasn't sure what to say to this man who May obviously liked. There had to be some good in him somewhere. But all I could think was "yuk."

"Ian," another voice chimed in. It was a good voice, deep and quiet, but forceful. I shifted my gaze and saw Phil, the black minister who May had introduced to me earlier. He put his hand on Ian's arm gently. "Are you behaving yourself, Ian?" he asked, a touch of humor in his serious question.

"Why, of course I am, my man," Ian answered with an exaggerated wink.

Phil looked deeply into Ian's eyes, and Ian seemed magically to become sober.

"It's hard to have any fun with a man of God around," Ian grouched. "Can't you save the preaching for your church?"

Phil looked embarrassed. He wove his hands together and cleared his throat.

"Are you making fun of Phil?" yet another voice demanded of Ian, female this time. Sarah, I remembered, Sarah Quesada. Her brown eyes didn't look friendly anymore as she glared at Ian.

"*Moi?*" Ian objected, rolling his eyes under raised brows. "Would I ever say anything about the man who can do no wrong? Especially in front of an admirer like you, fair Sarah?"

Sarah's skin pinkened. I looked at her more closely. Sarah was a few sizes more than was fashionable, with fair skin under a black pageboy. Her overbite gave her face a certain sweet quality. Or maybe it was her obvious crush on Phil—and his uncertain reaction to it. Or was Ian's influence causing me to read more into the behavior of the two than existed?

"Um . . ." Phil said.

"Uh . . ." Sarah responded.

Ian laughed. This was getting too painful to watch.

"So how do you two know May?" I intervened brightly.

Sarah's head jerked up as if she'd forgotten I was there.

"I'm one of May's tenants," Phil finally answered. "The

church hasn't found a place for me to live yet. But obstacles can be blessings—"

"Oh, pleeeze," Ian objected. "No more positive stuff, okay—"

"What's wrong with positive?" Sarah cut him off. "Gotta be positive or you're sunk. Shoot, some people!" She shook her head briefly, then stuck out her hand to shake mine. "I'm Sarah Quesada, local Realtor. If you ever gotta make a sale, I can help you."

"Cally Lazar," I shot back, shaking her outstretched hand. Her skin was soft, but her grip was firm. I hesitated, then spilled the rest. "I have a healing practice."

"Oh yeah," Sarah acknowledged. "May told me about you. She's all excited. You're good for her."

"Yes, indeed," Phil put in. "We all care a great deal for May."

Then there was an uncomfortable silence over our little group as three of us tried to think of something more to say while Ian grinned a snerky little grin. I would have preferred the Labrador retriever for company, I thought, and once again reminded myself that Ian must have his good points.

"Cally," a quiet voice beckoned from my side. It was my brother York, and was I glad to see him.

"York!" I greeted him, as if I hadn't seen him in years.

"Thought you might want to see May's garden in back," he suggested. "She's got some interesting topiary."

"Topiary," I said, my legs already moving. "I love topiary. Nice meeting you, Phil and Sarah."

As it turned out, I wasn't even lying. The topiary was pretty spectacular even in the cold, night light. There were no neat, little poodled bushes behind Citrus House. Instead, there was a whole zoo of trimmed hedges in shapes of tigers and lions and, of course, bears, with a couple of giraffes and other animals just to round things out. York and I floated around the moonlit yard, admiring the green animals . . . and having a little family discussion.

"Why didn't you tell me that May used to be a madam?" I demanded.

"Why does it matter?" York answered.

I moved on to a leafy gorilla, considering his answer.

"I'm not making a moral judgment," I said slowly, wondering if I really was. "I just don't like getting blindsided by people like Francie what's-her-name."

York leaped to my side, and I was already turning with my cane in hand, even though I knew I had no actual hope of ever landing a blow, or even a tap. York was the one who'd taught me cane-fu in the first place. Just as my cane might have touched him, he was behind me.

"If you can't be blindsided when you're fighting, why allow it in conversation?" he said. "Do you really care about Francie Krentz?"

"No. . . ."

"And you know May," he plowed on, ever the teacher, ever the big brother. "Is she a former madam or the person you know?"

I didn't have to answer. However aggressive and lacking in subtlety, May was still a warmhearted, funny, sad woman. A woman I'd already come to like very much. Her past didn't matter. I answered the only way I knew how when I was wrong. I changed the subject.

"So, do you know Eric?" I asked.

"He seems familiar," York answered, frowning. "He's a doctor. But he's telling everyone he's a bankrupt doctor."

"Dack," I said, surprised. "I thought doctors made good money."

"Not necessarily, according to Eric," York told me. "It's

all got to do with insurance companies or something. But they don't always make big bucks anymore."

"Wow, and I thought it was bad news that my clients couldn't get insurance to pay for them to see me."

York just shook his head. Out of his teaching persona, York was generally a quiet man. I gazed at him in the moonlight. He looked good in Geneva's pantsuit. It was something about the way he walked, with confidence and precision. My brother was a very sexy man. And very gay, something few people ever guessed. Not that York was in the closet. He had too much integrity. I smiled in the darkness. I liked my brother. I put my arm through the crook of his as we passed a green buffalo.

"Thanks, York," I whispered, glad for his lecture about judging May.

He just shrugged, and said, "Hey, you're my sister."

I was still smiling as we made our way back into the warm house through the kitchen. People were good, especially my brother.

May still hadn't returned to the living room when we got there. In fact, the room seemed nearly empty. A few people were still there. Francie was. And the dachshund yipped a greeting.

"How can you say a madam is a good person?" Francie was demanding of Phil, as they stood in front of the still untouched buffet.

"Would you sit in judgment of this woman without knowing anything about the actual circumstances of her past?" Phil returned her question quietly.

"Anyone who lives off the earnings of other women is immoral," Francie argued.

"Shopkeepers, factory owners?" Phil questioned. "Is divine grace suspended in their cases?"

"Now, you know what I mean," Francie insisted, her face reddening. "I'm very sensitive, and the very thought of what this woman did is disgusting."

Phil opened his mouth, but didn't get a chance to voice his thought. Francie's husband, Dutch, was back from wherever he'd been.

"The thing that really bothers me about May," he declared, facing Phil, "is the way she keeps you boarders captive. Does she get you to sign a contract or what?"

"No, she doesn't have us sign contracts," Phil answered, his quiet voice a little angry now. "May is a fair woman. Excuse me."

Then he turned and left the room.

"Loser," Dutch offered, once Phil had left.

"All the boarders are losers," John Turner agreed, suddenly joining the conversation. "I don't know what I'd do if she trapped me into living here."

"And the house," Francie threw in, shuddering. "What a disgrace."

John nodded his agreement. "How'd she ever get the planning commission to approve her house?" he asked. "That's what I'd like to know."

Dutch laughed heartily and slapped John on the back. "Connections, my boy, connections," he answered. "See Sarah over there, talking to Becky?"

John nodded. Dutch went on.

"She and May are close, you know what I mean, real close. And Sarah's on the planning commission."

"But so are you, honey," Francie piped up.

Dutch glared at her.

I turned my attention away from the threesome. I was tired of hearing May bad-mouthed. And Sarah Quesada.

I found York again, talking to Zack Turner.

"So what would you do if someone attacked you?" he asked the boy.

"Oh, Dad would take care of anyone who bugged me," Zack replied.

So much for that martial arts sale.

Suddenly, the living room seemed full again. Or maybe it was just that Ian was back. As he walked toward me, I saw Gerry and Eric in one orange corner, Sarah and Phil in another, and Becky now talking to Julie. Dutch, Francie, and John were busy laughing at something, something I didn't want to know about. And York continued to quiz Zack about martial arts.

"Where's May?" I asked once Ian reached me. I'd come to this party to get to know May better, and she wasn't around. And it had been way too long since she'd gone to "freshen up." Dack, if she didn't come back soon, I'd try to get to know the parrot.

Ian frowned. The expression looked strange on his face.

"May?" he called out. But no one answered.

Gerry turned around. "Oh dear, is my May missing?" he asked.

"I'll go find her," Sarah offered, and turned to the door leading to the stairway.

Gerry followed her, apologizing to the rest of us.

Then Ian turned back to me.

"So, Cally," he murmured, standing way too close to me. "May says you do voodoo." He rolled his eyes in mock fright. "She says you've got second sight—"

And then a scream came vibrating down the stairway and flooded the living room.

THREE

All my muscles clenched, and I felt my leg buckle. So much for second sight. Because something was wrong, and I'd never had an inkling.

The scream that still echoed in the room wasn't angry. It was a scream of pure terror.

And by then someone else was shouting.

"No!"

And then the Labrador began to howl, and the dachshund yipped, and cats meowed while the parrot squawked.

Something was *very* wrong, I amended, my mind kicking in before my feelings could. I made my way to the door that led to the stairs as fast as I could with my cane supporting me. York was there before me. I stepped through the door into a chartreuse staircase with lime carpeting.

And then it seemed as if the staircase was filled with everyone who'd been at the party, shoving and shouting to push their way to the top. I could smell fear, and alcohol, and something else. Bitterness? Anger? And the smells were all around me, pushing like the people. I took a deep breath and wanted to spit it all out.

At the top of the stairs, I was swept by the crowd to a doorway halfway down the hall and inside a bedroom

with flocked paisley wallpaper in all of the shades of a
fruit basket. I'd wanted to turn aside at the doorway, but
the push of bodies around me had made my entrance
inevitable. And even when I was inside, I thought of closing my eyes or at least keeping my gaze on the wallpaper.
But the need to see was as inevitable as the push of the
crowd. So, I looked.

I saw Phil first, with one arm around Gerry and the
other around Sarah. And then I saw York and Eric kneeling
on the floor, and May . . . May. May was lying on her back,
her lively face horribly distorted and her gold necklace bit-
ing into her neck. Her feet were almost touching an ornate
antique dresser piled with jewelry, her head resting a foot
away from a bed covered in plump, colorful pillows.
Finally, I turned away, sudden tears in my eyes. May!

"No!" I heard again.

I jerked my head back. Gerry was howling as Phil tried
to comfort him. I wanted to howl myself. And Sarah
looked like a person waking from a nightmare. But the
nightmare was real.

My own reason was giving way to a sickening mixture
of feelings, and foremost among them, guilt. Because Roy
had warned me of this, or at least of something. Should I
have listened? Should I have warned May? I knew the guilt
was unreasonable, but I felt it anyway, along with anger
and fear and sadness. Dack. Why May? Death was one
thing, but this death was . . . was . . . And then I allowed
the truth slowly into my mind. May had been murdered,
strangled with her own necklace, most probably by someone in this room.

Then I wanted to shout myself. Because I didn't believe
in evil. I didn't want to see what was in front of me. In time,
maybe I'd be able to know May's death to be something

more complicated than something as easily labeled as evil, but now—

York stood up suddenly, his face pale.

Seconds later, Eric stood as well. "She's dead, I'm afraid," he declared quietly. And I remembered that Eric was a doctor.

"Dead?" Julie said from across the room. Her large blue eyes were round and glazed. "No, she can't be. She—"

"You'll be all right, honey," John murmured from beside her, his hand on her back.

Julie turned to him and pushed her face into his chest as if trying to blind herself. John held her quietly.

"Mom?" Zack questioned.

Julie turned back, her eyes wet, and threw her arms around her son. "It's okay," she tried, her shaking voice belying her words. "It's okay."

"But Mom—"

"Everything will be all right," John pronounced.

Zack looked at John's face, then at Julie's. I hoped he'd get some kind of therapy after this night. Because if I was feeling what I was feeling, what would a fourteen-year-old kid be feeling? Criminy.

"She's with God," Phil threw in, still holding on to Gerry and Sarah.

Gerry closed his eyes and nodded almost violently when he heard Phil's words. Was he praying? Or maybe just spasming?

"Can someone call the police?" Eric asked quietly.

York said, "I will," and left the crowded room quickly.

My mind was returning. If someone in this room was a murderer, could I see it? I looked at Phil, Gerry, and Sarah. And all I could see was a gray mist. I shook my head. The mist had to be coming from my own mind. Then I looked at Eric . . . and saw a gray mist. John, Julie, and Zack, gray mist. I looked past them to Ian, who seemed to be drinking from some kind of flask, to Dutch, whose face was angry, and Francie, who looked as confused as Zack, and to Becky, walking slowly toward her father. And still, I could only see gray. No! I clenched my fists. What was going on? Was this like the blackness that Roy saw? I closed my eyes for a moment and took a deep breath.

With my eyes closed, my sense of smell grew stronger, and what I smelled was May's perfume. The scent pervaded the room. My eyes popped open. Whoever had killed May must have gotten her perfume on them. Maybe I could find the killer by smell alone.

"Daddy?" Becky asked softly.

I looked over and saw her put an arm around her father's waist. Gerry looked in her direction, his eyes blank. Phil murmured what sounded like a blessing and relinquished May's "sweetheart of a man" to his daughter. She led him toward the door, unresisting. I placed myself in their path and sniffed. Yes! I could smell May's perfume. The scent lingered on Gerry heavily and slightly on his daughter, Becky. But, of course, May had been touching her husband all night long and had probably hugged Becky hello.

I walked toward the Turners and once again, I could smell May's perfume. But she'd probably hugged them, too. Keerups, she'd probably hugged everyone. I turned to Dutch and Francie, ambling their way.

"But I don't understand," Francie was saying, her voice high and childlike. "This is so terrible. How could May—"

"Just shut up for once in your life!" Dutch hissed. And I thought I saw a flare of red anger pulse through the gray mist. Not that I needed to see that flare to know he was angry. His square features were clenched so tightly,

I thought the bones of his face might actually fracture.

Francie flinched at his side, temporarily silent.

As I got closer to the couple, I sniffed the residuals of May's perfume. Yup, everyone in the room probably smelled of May, not to mention the room itself. I gave up on playing bloodhound.

And with that thought, a dog howled from downstairs. At least, I hoped it was a dog.

Then I smelled May's perfume from behind me. I turned quickly, cane in hand, and saw Phil holding Sarah's elbow.

"Ms. Lazar, how are you doing?" he asked quietly.

I looked into his intense, dark eyes and wanted tell him everything: about Roy, and Roy's call, and my guilt.

"Fine," I offered instead. Did I mention how articulate we Lazars are?

"Well, ma'am, I know you can't be fine, any more than the rest of us, but are you well enough to take care of Sarah for a bit?" he asked seriously.

That was the best therapy he could have given me. Maybe he knew that. Because Sarah needed someone to take care of her. That was a fact. Her pale face looked entirely drained of color, her black hair disheveled, and her eyes wild.

I reached out, and Sarah placed her icy hand in mine.

"Thank you, ma'am," Phil whispered. "Thank you for your kindness."

He started to turn away from us, then turned back.

"Sarah," he blurted out, "you know I'm not abandoning you. There are just some things I have to see to, that's all."

Sarah nodded. I could see her trying to mouth the right words, but no sound came from her lips. Then she nodded again.

"Thank you," Phil repeated, and he turned away for certain, walking back to where May's body lay.

"I . . . I found her," Sarah told me so softly I could barely make out her words. "I came upstairs to see what she was doing, and I saw her on the floor. She . . . she . . . See, I loved that old lady. I loved her, and . . ."

Sarah blinked back tears, and I put my arms around her in a full body-to-body embrace. Then she cried, and I felt some of her tension lift. I even saw drifts of colors swirling around her and dissipating ever so slightly. Fear and grief, and something that looked like secrecy. No gray mist. Phil had done his double therapy well. I leaned into her, willing both of our fears away, smelling not just the hint of May's perfume but the acrid scent of sweat. I wasn't sure if the scent was coming from my own body or Sarah's. It didn't matter.

"She was good to me," Sarah's muffled voice said. "She teased, but she was good to me. Always up, always positive. I just can't believe . . ."

And then she was crying again. I cried with her, and for that short time, we might have been the only ones in the room. But we weren't.

All around us people were whispering, arguing, even whimpering. There were probably only a dozen people in the room, maybe even fewer now that Becky had led her father away, but the chorus still seemed deafening.

"If you'd all do me the kindness of listening for a moment," Phil interjected, raising his deep voice now. "We have a terrible situation here, but we can make it through if we all hold on. We must cooperate if we are to find out what happened here tonight—"

"May was murdered, that's what happened," Dutch shot back angrily.

"Yes, it appears so," Phil agreed slowly. "We must be ready to help when the police arrive. For May. I believe the best thing right now would be for everyone to go downstairs and wait for them. I'll stay with May—"

"Who made you God?" Dutch demanded. "Why you?"

"Dutch could stay as well as you could," Francie chimed in. "He's a sensitive man—"

"Phil's the man to stay," a new voice put in. I turned, surprised to see that Ian Oxton was speaking. All his mannerisms were gone. His skin was ashen. "Phil is a minister. He can deal with this. Who else—"

He broke off as he looked at May's body. Green tinted his ashen face. He put his hand over his mouth and ran from the room. The sounds of his retching echoed back down the hallway.

"Would you like me to stay, too?" Eric asked.

Phil nodded without speaking. He lowered his eyes for a few breaths as if seeking guidance. But he still had more to deal with.

"Well, we're going home," John Turner pronounced, his left hand on Zack's shoulder and his right on Julie's back. "My wife and son have had enough for the night."

"Sir, I don't believe that would be best," Phil answered him. "The police will want to talk to everyone who was here tonight."

"Oh, but not us," Francie piped up. "This was May's affair, not ours."

"Yeah, buddy," Dutch tossed in. "You can't hold us all here. And as far as I'm concerned, the party's over."

"No," Eric argued, his face reddening. "The police will want to see everyone. Phil is right. Everyone can go downstairs and make themselves comfortable. We all have a responsibility to May—"

"Are you going to make me stay?" Dutch blustered. I wondered how old he was. He looked somewhere between sixty and seventy. Fit, but not fit enough to take on two younger men—

"Mr. Krentz," York said, his voice steady and menacing, even in my ears. I jerked away from Sarah. I hadn't heard York come back in the room. "Phil or Eric could hold you here. But I don't think they should—"

"I told you—" Dutch began.

"I'm the martial artist in this room," York went on. "I'll make sure that you stay. Or anyone else who wants to leave. This is no joke. A woman has died here. If you leave, the police might assume you have something to hide."

I wasn't sure which argument had worked, but Dutch closed his mouth. And John Turner stood stock-still.

"So, I'll go downstairs first," York offered with an overstated bow. "And the rest of you will please follow."

York scanned those of us in the room quickly before turning to the doorway. He wasn't looking for auras. He didn't even look like he was checking for possible sneak attack. In that quick scan, I had a feeling he was weighing his own actions, wondering if Phil and Eric were the right people to leave with May's body, wondering if they were murderers, because if they were, they would be left alone to tamper with evidence. Or maybe it was only me who was wondering if they were murderers. I looked at Phil and Eric and saw only two shaken men doing the best they could. But that didn't mean that either one or both of them hadn't killed May. I shook my head hard to clear it, took Sarah's hand, and followed York as he exited the doorway. Maybe I'd never know.

Sarah held on to my hand all the way down those stairs.

"Someone killed May," Sarah whispered, as if we were

the only ones who knew. "Someone strangled her with that goofy gold necklace she always wore. I always told her it was too heavy. But she wasn't into dress-for-success, you know what I mean? I'd tease her about her clothes, and she'd tease me about my love life. She invited me here to get to know Phil better. Jeez, Cally, why would anyone want to kill her?"

That was a good question. And my mind was supplying possible answers far too fast. May had been abrasive. In the short time I'd been at her house, Becky, Julie, and Francie had already been angry with her. And what was all the stuff about her keeping her boarders captive? And Sarah and the planning commission? And her husband. Husbands could kill. I didn't even want to think about it.

"Oh, Cally, do you think the police will investigate?" Sarah asked.

"Of course they will," I soothed her.

But Sarah didn't look soothed. If anything, she looked even more pale. What was it May had been saying to Sarah about building an apartment? Something that had upset Sarah, I remembered.

Finally, back down the staircase and in the living room, I saw Gerry and Becky. Becky was urging her father to sit, but he didn't seem to hear her.

"Daddy, please," she begged.

But Gerry Cheng looked stunned beyond thinking, catatonic. He didn't even seem to notice the Labrador retriever staring up at him and whining or the dachshund sitting on his foot. Or the mop dog yipping.

Sarah and I took seats on a short yellow sofa near the buffet. Sarah was quiet again. But Francie wasn't, taking a chair next to Dutch across from us.

"I told you I didn't want to come to a party at her house,"

she began. "That woman was always nothing but trouble—"

"Stop right now," Dutch warned her.

I saw fear in her face as Francie slumped down, looking lost in her scarves and layers of skirts.

"Mr. Lazar," Julie said softly, approaching York. She looked as shaken as anyone else but Gerry, her face wet and makeup smeared around her wide blue eyes. She clenched her shaking hands together. "Do you really think Zack needs to stay? He's just a boy and—"

"Mom, I want to stay," Zack interrupted from her side. "I liked Mrs. North. I want to help."

And he wants to take care of his mother, I thought, as Julie put her arms around the boy and held on.

When Julie began to sob, Becky and Sarah joined in.

"Daddy, please come back," Becky implored, her voice thick with tears.

I turned to Sarah to ask her if she was all right, and before my lips could form the words, the cat landed in my lap out of nowhere. Charcoal gray with large coppery eyes, he looked up at me as pleadingly as Becky was looking at her father. Then he flipped onto his back and offered up his belly to be stroked. I stroked it, the feel of warm fur flooding my body with sensation again.

"Wanna have a good time?" the parrot squawked.

"Tomato," Ian murmured from a pear green ottoman in the corner.

"What?"

"May called the cat Tomato," he said a little more loudly. There was nothing arch in his tone now. Gone was the Oscar Wilde of the heterosexual set.

"How about the other cat?" I asked, wanting to talk about anything but May's death.

"Catsup," Ian answered, a small smile leaking onto his face, brightening it.

But before I could ask him anything else, the doorbell rang.

Ian blinked and seemed to age ten years. He rose slowly from the ottoman and walked to the door.

The first one in was a woman, blond and haggard in a business suit.

"I'm Sergeant Verne of the Mostaza Police Department," she announced as two uniformed officers came in behind her, a dark-skinned woman and a dark-haired man. "These are Officers Daly and Affonso."

Last in line was a man with the handsome, heart-shaped face of a two-year-old. He beamed at us.

"And this is Chief Upwood," Sergeant Verne finished. I thought I could hear her sigh as she pronounced his name.

The chief spread his arms as if to embrace the orange room and all of its inhabitants.

"You may be feeling a little down right now," he declared. "But I'm sure we'll all feel much better if we talk about this." Then he lowered his arms and beamed at us again.

FOUR

"Chief, this is murder!" Sergeant Verne hissed.

"Of course it is," Chief Upwood murmured sympathetically. "And you have every reason to be upset—"

"We have to secure the scene," Sergeant Verne insisted, adding "sir" belatedly as she pulled at her dry blond hair.

"Yes?" the chief inquired, tilting his head.

"The *body*, sir," she whispered, all too audibly in the silence. "Where's the *body*?"

"Ah," the chief said like a zen master. Then, "Would someone be good enough to escort Sergeant Verne to the . . ." He cleared his throat. "To the deceased."

We all looked at Ian. But he didn't seem to be jumping out of his chair to do escort duty.

"I'll go," Gerry Cheng offered in a raw voice. He was still standing, and the shock hadn't left his face yet, but there was a hint of life in his eyes.

His daughter, Becky, just stared at him for a moment where he stood, then jumped in front of him.

"No, Daddy, no!" she ordered. She turned to the police. "I'll take you," she offered.

Gerry began to object, but Becky was too fast for him.

"I'll go," she insisted, and pushed him gently but firmly toward a chair.

Gerry collapsed into the chair and put his head in his hands. Becky took one look back at him, seemed to steel herself, then walked toward Sergeant Verne.

York jumped in just as I was ready to open my mouth. He was always just a little faster than I was.

"Becky, you don't have to—" he began.

"Yes, I do," she declared. "Just take care of my father till I get back."

York bowed his head in acknowledgment and walked over to the older man, tentatively putting his hand on Gerry's shoulder. York probably would have preferred escort duty. In-depth counseling was outside of his martial arts training.

Becky said, "Follow me," to Sergeant Verne, and the two of them disappeared through the door to the stairs, trailed by Officer Daly.

Chief Upwood took a seat on a lemon yellow wing chair and folded his hands peacefully in his lap before smiling at us all some more. I began to twitch in my own chair. I was postadrenaline by then: tired, shaky, and impatient. I wondered if the Mostaza chief was trying to drive someone into a confession. Or maybe he was studying us. Or maybe he was just meditating. I turned to look at the door that led to the staircase. I wanted Sergeant Verne.

"Chief Upwood," a voice boomed out. I swiveled my head back around. Dutch was on his feet. "I'm Dutch Krentz. This has been a most upsetting night for my wife. I'd like to take her home now. We wouldn't want to waste your valuable time. We only came here as neighbors, and we live in Mostaza."

"Then I'm sure you'll be able to offer something valuable

tonight," the chief answered blithely. "It's amazing how group energy can turn a bad situation around. Even in a situation as difficult as this one. If we all cooperate, well, who knows? So, do stay, Mr. Krentz. I'm sure you'll be glad you did." Dack, this was Mr. Rogers at a murder scene.

As the chief paused in his lecture, I heard a sound I didn't recognize at first.

Dutch was sitting back down, red-faced, but that wasn't what I heard. It sounded like a man choking. And it was coming from Gerry Cheng. York paled as he looked down at his charge.

And then Ian Oxton rose and strode toward Gerry. He knelt by the widowed man and put his arm around his shoulder. York stepped back quickly, his hand off Gerry's shoulder a millisecond before Ian's had touched the man. Martial arts in action.

"Gerry, we're here," Ian said simply. "We'll try to do what we can. You're not alone."

Sobbing aloud, Gerry lifted his head and held on to Ian like a drowning man. Finally I'd found a reason to like Ian Oxton. But at what cost?

Even the Labrador seemed to realize Gerry was in good hands. He trotted over to Chief Upwood and sniffed him. He must have liked something he smelled because he lay down at the chief's feet. All the chief needed was a pipe and bedroom slippers to be completely cozy.

"Well, what I'd like to do now is to get to know all of you a little better," the chief announced. "We'll go around the room, and each of you can tell us your name and a little about yourself. Maybe you could start, Mr. Krentz?"

Dutch clenched his fists, but he answered. "Dutch Krentz, retired." The chief continued to stare at him. Dutch added, "I live in Mostaza, dabble in real estate."

Chief Upwood didn't remind me of Mr. Rogers anymore. He was scary.

"And you, ma'am?" he asked, turning his stare on Francie.

"Oh, my," she burbled. She blinked her eyes in a way that might have been flirtatious, or maybe just confused. I figured Chief Upwood didn't scare her. "I'm Dutch's wife, Francie Krentz. And, well, I'm an artist. I've always been sensitive to beauty, you know, so I try to bring a little into the world. Our surroundings are so important to us, don't you think—"

"Quite so," the chief cut her off. His delivery was so friendly that Francie smiled at him. He returned her smile and turned his head a little.

"And you?" he asked, his mild eyes on me. Only they weren't really mild. There was an intensity in the irises that didn't match the softness of their shape. I saw a faint haloing of purple at his temples. Telepathy maybe? I couldn't tell. But there was something about him—

"Maybe you could start with your name," he nudged.

"Yeah, right," I agreed hurriedly. "I'm Cally Lazar. I'm an energy worker. I live in Estados."

The chief was still staring at me.

"With my cat and my goats," I added. Criminy, what did he want from me?

Finally, he switched his gaze to Sarah next to me. She was looking a little better. There was some pink in her pale skin and her warm, brown eyes were alive again.

"I'm Sarah Quesada," she offered. "I'm a realtor here in Mostaza. I'm . . . I was a friend of May's."

The chief nodded. Maybe that's what he wanted from us, our relationships with May. Or maybe not.

His gaze had moved on to the Turners. John spoke first.

"I'm John Turner," he announced blandly. "I have an import business here in Mostaza. May was our neighbor."

Julie's mouth began to open, but Zack spoke before her.

"I'm Zack Turner," he told the chief. "I liked Mrs. North, so I came over. She was really cool for an old lady." He paused and looked up at his mother.

Julie's beautiful features were haggard. She no longer looked like a model; her round blue eyes merely looked frail, and her high cheekbones could have been the result of famine. She opened her mouth again, and once again, she was too slow.

"This is my mom, Julie Turner," Zack put in. "She's like a full-time mom, you know. She's in the PTA, stuff like that. We live right across the street."

The chief seemed to accept Zack's representation of his mother. Now he looked toward York.

"I'm York Lazar, Cally's brother," he explained. "I have a martial arts studio in Estados called Zartent. I teach a fusion of martial arts that emphasizes intent. May was my student."

With that, his ever straight spine slumped. And I knew that he felt he'd failed May as a martial arts instructor. I wanted to go to him and tell him it wasn't his fault. But not in front of everyone else. Especially the chief.

Chief Upwood looked at Ian and Gerry.

Ian sighed as he stood, his arm still on Gerry's shoulder. Gerry lifted his head, his eyes ravaged but alert now.

"I'm Ian Oxton," Ian declared in a wonderfully Shakespearean voice. "I'm an actor." Then he seemed to remember he was talking to the police. His voice went back to normal. "At least I'm an actor some of the time. Remember that soap opera, *Intrigues and Outtakes*?"

The chief tilted his head, but Francie recognized the name.

"Oh, I remember!" she squealed. "You were that rat, Austin. Oh, I loved that show." She turned to the chief helpfully. "You see, it was all set at a movie studio, and Austin was this absolutely terrible womanizer and trouble-maker." She turned back to Ian. "I thought I recognized you," she said.

"Thank you," Ian murmured, bowing her way. "I was that 'rat' for seven years, then the show was canceled. So I do a commercial here and there, and live off my savings. I board here with May. I—" He cut himself off. Had he just remembered that May was dead? "Phil, Eric, and I are boarders here with Gerry and May."

Ian looked at Gerry much as Zack had looked at his mother. "Gerry Cheng was May's husband," he mumbled. "He's still in shock, I think."

"No," Gerry objected, his voice raspy. "I can speak. I have to speak. May was my wife. She was so sweet, a dear lady through and through, and . . ." He made that choking sound again, and Ian bent over him.

"I'm sorry, Mr. Cheng," Chief Upwood offered. His voice was so sincere that even Gerry looked up. "This is a terrible time for you. We will try to make it less terrible. I can see you have support from your friend Ian. And others, I'll bet. Think about that if you can."

Gerry nodded.

"Mr. Oxton, may I ask you a couple of questions?" the chief went on. Ian looked at him. "You mentioned two other boarders. Where are they tonight?"

"They're upstairs with May," he told the chief.

"Ah," the chief responded. "And the young woman who took the sergeant upstairs?"

"That's Becky Cheng, Gerry's daughter," Ian answered quickly, saving Gerry the trouble.

"I see."

And then the chief was silent for what seemed to be a few lifetimes but was probably only a few minutes in real time.

"Well," he pronounced finally. "This is a terrible situation, but one or more of you may have answers that might ease the pain of those who cared about May North. I would ask now that anyone who saw or heard anything that might be of help, please lift your hand."

No hands went up. Try as I could, there was not one thing that I could offer to help the chief. I just wished there was.

"Now, the hard question," he continued, leaning forward in his chair. "Did any of you kill Mrs. North?"

No one answered. I almost thought someone might. But the chief's charisma only went so far.

I heard the door to the stairway open, and Sergeant Verne was back with Phil, Eric, and Becky.

I wondered how much they'd heard.

"My turn, sir?" Sergeant Verne asked.

"Certainly," he said.

"Right!" she declared and faced us all. "I want to talk to you each separately, do you understand?"

We all nodded.

"And no talking among yourselves," she added. She turned to Ian. "What room can I use?"

But Ian didn't answer, Gerry did. "My study," he told her.

"Fine," she said. Then she clamped her eyes on Ian. "I'll take you first, Mr. Oxton."

I didn't want Sergeant Verne anymore. I wanted the chief back. And how come the sergeant already knew Ian's name. Had Phil or Eric told her?

It was more than three hours later by the time York and

I had both been interviewed exhaustively. After Ian, Sergeant Verne had interviewed Phil, then Eric. The Turners had been next in line, with some discussion of whether Zack was old enough to be interviewed alone. The sergeant decided unilaterally that he was. And once she was through with the Turners, the sergeant took York. And finally, me.

I could tell the interviews were exhaustive because I was exhausted. Sergeant Verne had asked me more questions about my life than a sociology major with a clipboard. She particularly wanted to know about my martial arts training and, of course, my short acquaintance with May. And then, she'd demanded a full report on the party. I did my best. It clearly wasn't good enough.

"I'll be talking to you again," was her parting shot, as I left the olive green of Gerry's study with Officer Affonso.

York was up like a shot when I came back to the living room. The Turners were gone. Becky was sitting with her father, who already looked more peaceful. Phil, Eric, and Ian sat in chairs marking a protective semicircle around Gerry and Becky. Sarah sat a little ways away, staring at Phil. And the Krentzes were on the other side of the room. Francie looked sleepy, but Dutch looked beyond angry.

And Chief Upwood smiled. "You may go now," he told me, and I felt like a prisoner on release day.

Dutch made a clearing sound in his throat. I would have bet that he'd be the last one that Sergeant Verne would interview.

"The forensic specialists are on their way," Officer Daly told Sergeant Verne in an undertone.

Then Officer Affonso looked at the list in his hands. "Sarah Quesada," he announced.

York grabbed my arm and hustled me out the door as fast as I could walk. My mouth was off and running, however, the minute we closed the door of Citrus House behind us.

"Oh, York," I blurted out. "Roy told me not to come to this party."

But York didn't answer me until we were in the Subaru and down the driveway onto the main road.

"Criminy, Cally!" he yelped then. "What does Roy have to do with this?"

I swiveled my head to look at him. York *didn't* yelp. And his sharp, narrow features were stretched way too tightly.

"Well?" he prompted.

"Oh . . . Roy," I tried, bringing my mind back again. "He told me not to go to the party, something about evil."

"Roy is always yammering about evil, Cally. So what?"

"York!" I yelped. I didn't yelp very often either. "What's going on with you? May was killed!"

And then I saw the yellow color of fear emanating from my brother York's body, my brother who was fearless. Even May's murder couldn't account for his fear. Even his own perceived failure as a martial arts instructor.

"It wasn't your fault—" I began.

"Wasn't it?" York asked softly. "I was her teacher, Cally. I teach my students to be aware. You know: front, right, left, back. Someone strangled her from behind—"

"From behind?" I interrupted.

"What?" he asked with a sharp glance. The Subaru swerved ever so slightly.

"York, it really wasn't your fault," I told him. "May was deaf. She wouldn't have been able to hear someone come in from behind."

"But, she never said—"

"She hid it, York. I tested her today without her knowing. I think she must have learned how to lip-read, because she couldn't hear me talk when I was behind her, only when she could see me."

I looked at York again. The color of fear was still surrounding him. I could even smell it.

"York?" I asked.

"Our parents, Cally." He sighed and the fear shifted slightly. "The explosion that killed them. I always thought it wasn't an accident. And seeing May tonight. We never saw our parents' bodies, but I knew. I felt it. So did you. Your leg buckled. I went into martial arts. I wanted to be invulnerable. And I wanted to teach the people I cared for to be invulnerable, too."

"Wait," I objected, suddenly colder than the inside of the car. A mixture of memories swirled through my head: my parents, York's transition from a happy older brother into a sullen warrior, that long-ago funeral. My mouth was dry as I spoke again. "You're saying our parents were killed, killed like May?"

"No," he answered after a pause. "I'm telling you what I was *afraid* of, why I'm afraid now. I didn't protect them. I couldn't protect May. And you—"

"Oh, York." I put my hand on his shoulder. "You can't. No one can protect everyone they love. People die. I . . ." I was crying now, for May, and myself, and that lost, happy, big brother of my childhood. I took off my glasses to wipe my eyes. "I love you. But I can't protect you. It's not my job. You did your best for May. I did my best. Oh, ratsafratz!"

York laughed.

I turned my head again to look at him in disbelief.

"Cally, I try to protect you, and here, you're busy protecting me," He laughed again. "Thanks, little sister."

And the fear evaporated.

We hugged a long time when he dropped me off at my

little house. My goats bleated from down the back hillside, and I unlocked my door and went inside.

All I wanted to do was rest. I didn't want to think. I didn't want to remember anything, May or my parents. I just wanted to lie down and go to sleep. I went to my bedroom, took off my glasses, and began unbuttoning the top of my pantsuit.

And the phone rang.

I picked the receiver up gingerly.

"So, Lazar," a voice brayed on the other end. "Still don't believe in evil?"

"Kapp?" I said cautiously.

"Holy Mary, and you've got that horse's ass, Upwood, investigating. You're going to need some help on this one, kid."

It was Kapp all right: Warren Kapp of civil and criminal litigation fame; Warren Kapp of the balding pate and bulldog face and bulldog nature; Warren Kapp, my octogenarian friend and cane-sparring mate; Warren Kapp, the buttinsky deluxe.

"How do you even know, Kapp?" I asked.

"Hey, remember me, kid?" he challenged, "I see all, know all. May North was murdered, and you were there."

"Fine," I answered wearily. I knew he'd never tell me exactly how he knew. "I gotta get some sleep, Kapp."

"But Cally, we're going to investigate, aren't we?" he asked, and I heard the eagerness in his voice. He would have liked May, I realized. Then I was even more tired.

"Night-night, Kapp," I said, and laid the phone down in its cradle.

I was in my pajamas when the phone rang again. It was my friend, Dee-Dee, clinical hypnotherapist and second only to Kapp in butting-in ability.

"Cally, Kapp called me," she told me. "Are you okay?"

"No, but a good night's sleep will help," I answered truthfully. It was useless to lie to Dee-Dee.

"But another murder, Cally," she bulldozed on. "Whoa, that's too weird."

"I guess," I whispered. I didn't want to think any more tonight. "Dee-Dee, can I just—"

And then I heard the frantic bleating of my goats. I dropped the phone, grabbed my glasses and my cane, and rushed out onto my back deck, just in time to see the goats butting a dark figure, butting that figure until it rolled back down the hillside.

The goats bleated with glee as the figure scrambled away.

FIVE

I held my breath among the silent primroses and poppies and pansies that I'd nurtured so happily. Who was the dark figure scrambling away from the bottom of the hillside, my hillside? And then the figure was gone from my vision. The cold air seemed to slap my face, and I opened the gateway in the latticework fence quickly. I felt my way down the dark stairs with my cane.

Finally, I was on the back hillside. It was slippery on the hillside, the grasses, clovers, and weeds wet in the heavy mist. But I knew my own hill. I stepped carefully and quietly toward the bottom of the hill where the goats were congregated, toward the place where I'd last glimpsed the dark figure, hoping that the figure wasn't watching *me*. But I had my cane . . . and my goats. I told myself I was protected. Then somewhere on the small street that went past the house next door, I heard the sound of running. At least that's what it sounded like, shoes slapping on the wet pavement. I moved faster until I was at the very bottom of the hill. But I couldn't see anything. I could only hear. Was the figure panting, or was that my own heart beating? I couldn't tell.

Ohio bleated a surprised greeting, then Moscow and Persia got in on the act, and the silence of the night was a memory. I reached out a hand to pat each of them in turn, wishing I'd brought them treats. Then I heard it, the sound of a car engine turning over. Dack! I ran to my back fence but could see nothing beyond the house on the next lot. A motor roared, and the sound sped away. Whoever had been on my hillside was gone now.

Ohio bleated again and rolled her upper lip away from her teeth in a smile. I smiled back and threw my arms around her neck. Goats have the right attitude. Everything's funny.

But as I climbed back up the hill, I stopped smiling. Who had made their way up my back hillside? It wasn't an easy thing to do. The intruder had to cross my neighbor's enclosed lot and climb my fence even to get to the steep hill. Why? Clearly, the prowler hadn't wanted to come to my front door. But again, why? May. It must have had something to do with May. Something to do with her murder. Had I seen something I shouldn't have? Or maybe it had nothing to do with May. The prowler might have just been mountain climbing. Or a peeping Tom. Or . . . no, it had to do with May. That dark figure must have been her murderer. I stopped to breathe. I was almost to my back gate. I shook my head as I sucked in the cold night air. A=B=C? I didn't have enough data for the inference that the dark figure was May's murderer. Not yet.

I walked through my back gate and closed it behind me, alone with my flowers and the night sky. I looked up and saw the glistening stars. They were beautiful. I stood, watching the stars until I might have joined them myself. Or maybe I did join them. Because I could breathe the cool night air with enjoyment again. May was dead. And I was alive. It seemed impossible, but it was true.

I walked back into my little house, glad to be alive, and glad it was bedtime. I wanted to sleep. It wasn't until

I returned to my bedroom that I saw the dangling phone.

Keerups! Dee-Dee, I'd been talking to Dee-Dee before I'd rushed onto the hillside! I picked up the phone.

"Hello?" I tried.

But all I heard was a screech. I wondered how long I'd been outside. I hung up my phone and called Dee-Dee. Her voice on the other end was prerecorded. I'd only reached her answering machine.

And then I felt something twining around my legs. The way I jumped told me I'd lost the serenity I'd found under the night sky. Because my own cat didn't usually send me into Olympic-style leaps and twirls.

Leona mewled. The mewl had a sound of concern in it. At least, I thought so. Leona was a split personality: half-Siamese, half-tabby, half–Dalai Lama, and half–Margaret Thatcher. I know that four halves don't add up to one. That was the split personality bit. One day she'd shred my massage table, the next, she'd purr in my arms to comfort me.

I untangled myself, hung up the phone, and crawled onto my bed. Leona pounced up by my side. But I wasn't sleepy anymore. Or maybe I was already asleep. Because the next thing I did was to call Roy.

When Roy answered, he sounded far too awake for the middle of the night.

"Cally?" he asked softly. "Are you okay, darlin'?"

"No," I told him, sudden tears forming. "Roy, a woman was murdered tonight."

"At that party?"

My own anger flared for a moment. He had warned me about the party. Was he happy now? But I didn't hear any happiness in his tone. Not even accusation. Just fatalism.

"Yeah," I said finally. Then, more softly, "Roy, could you come over? I know it's late, but—"

"In two shakes of Ohio's stubby tail," he assured me. "Stay safe, Cally." And he hung up.

I lay next to Leona, cold, even in my flannel pajamas, trying to put together the evening's events in my head. Leona crawled on my chest and purred. My hand touched her silky fur, and beyond cold and fear and analysis, I was asleep, running somewhere, running from something—

In my dream, I registered the knocking on the door, and suddenly there was a door in front of me. Another knock, and I opened my eyes. Leona pushed off my chest and dove for the floor.

I was down the hall and turning the knob on the front door before I gave a thought to how I must look in my flannel pajamas and bedraggled hair. But Roy didn't seem to notice as he came through the doorway.

"Oh, Cally," was all he said, then he reached out to embrace me.

I held on tight and tried to forget why he had ever left me. Sleepy, I just took in the familiar feel of his body— small and lightly muscled, perfectly fitted to my own—and the smell of him. I kept my eyes closed. I wished I could have kept my ears closed, too.

"The darkness is real," he announced. "This is why I kept away so long. I bring it on you, Cally. Oh, darlin', I don't want it to be true. But I just feel that it must be. I can see it now, moving from me and swirling all around you—"

I pushed away from him, opening my eyes.

Roy stood before me, his golden eyes shining in his bony, freckled face. And yes, I glimpsed darkness near him.

"Roy, you weren't even there," I told him, keeping my voice even. "If anyone is making these things happen, it's me."

"No, not you, Cally," he insisted. "This is evil. You've got no evil in you—"

"Nor do you, Roy," I cut him off. "Criminy, Roy! Don't you think I'd see it in you, if you were evil?"

"You don't see evil, Cally," he whispered sadly. "You can't."

I opened my mouth and waited for something to come out. But nothing did.

"Haven't you wondered at this death, just when you and I are seeing each other again?" he asked.

"No," I shot back with certainty. "Because the first murder I encountered was after you'd left me. I hadn't seen you for three months." I couldn't keep the bitterness out of my voice as I spoke. "I can't believe I'm actually arguing with you about this. It's absurd. Do you really think your presence in my life could have anything to do with the murders I've stumbled over?"

"Yes," he answered simply.

I sighed. It was useless. *Was* Roy crazy? Was I crazy?

"Cally, there's a way though. . . ." His words faltered as he looked down at his feet.

"A way?" I prompted.

"Don't get involved any further," he explained, raising his golden eyes. "Stay away from the people who were at that party."

"I wasn't planning on getting involved," I murmured, and even as I did, my mind's eye saw a picture of May, alive and vivacious. Would Chief Upwood find her killer? Could I help? Did I have a duty to help?

"You're already up to your ears in it," Roy stated, his voice hopeless. "Cally, you're not the only one who can read people. I can see it in your eyes."

"Roy," I begged, holding out my hand. "Let's not argue. Help me through this. I need you—"

"Yoo-hoo!" came a voice through the still open door.

Roy stepped away from the doorway, and Dee-Dee came dancing through, her small body buzzing with energy.

"Whoa!" she sang out when she saw Roy. "It's good to see you here. Cally left me talking to air on the phone. I got all frazzled and came to check up—"

"Why'd you leave Dee-Dee on the phone?" Roy questioned. Sometimes, I wished my sweet Kentucky boy was a little slower on the uptake.

"The goats were bleating," I explained slowly. Maybe, just part of the truth would suffice.

"The goats?" Dee-Dee probed.

I gave her the "don't-say-another-word" look, but she missed it.

"Why were the goats making noise at night?" she bull-dozed on.

"Um—" I began. But I couldn't think of a way to finish.

Roy sighed and turned to Dee-Dee. "Take care of Cally, please," he begged. "Don't let her get enmeshed in this thing. I can't protect her. I'll only make things worse."

"That's just not true—" I began.

A cane came through the doorway, propelled in my direction, and with it, the smell of aftershave. I twirled the cane out of Kapp's hand with a new move I'd learned and pressed the tip of my own cane to his abdomen.

"Dammit, Lazar," he objected, and walked the rest of the way in through the still open door. No wonder it was so cold in here. "You ever gonna give me a break?" Then he turned to acknowledge Dee-Dee and Roy. "So, the gang's all here. Even Roy boy. You figured out who killed May North yet?"

I turned to Roy. His face had gone white under his freckles.

"Roy, I didn't invite Kapp—"

"Mr. Kapp," Roy interrupted me. "I'd certainly appreciate it if you'd think of Cally's well-being right now. She isn't going to solve a murder. Even to appear interested in finding the murderer would put her in danger, don't you see?"

"Aw, come on," Kapp argued. He slapped Roy on the shoulder. "Don't you have a sense of adventure? The police chief of Mostaza is a four-star donkey's behind who should be running support groups somewhere, not solving murders. Between the four of us, we can find out more than he ever could—"

"But Cally could be in danger," Roy explained desperately. He turned to Dee-Dee. "You understand, don't you?" he asked.

"Well," Dee-Dee muttered. She ran her hand through her dark hair. Dee-Dee was a dynamo of Irish and Asian ancestry. She didn't run from battles or turn away from the truth. "Cally did it once before. And she's got her cane."

"Hooboy, does she have a cane!" Kapp agreed. "She gets better every week."

"Roy!" I shouted, waving my hand to get his attention. "Don't talk to them. Talk to me. I'm still in the room. And I haven't agreed to investigate May North's murder. Stay with me tonight. We'll talk this thing out—"

Roy stepped forward and threw his arms around me, taking me by surprise. But before I could snuggle in, he had backed away again.

"Cally, darlin', please understand. I love you too much to risk my influence on you. But, please, protect yourself. Avoid this evil—"

"Oh, Holy Mary, is he blabbering about evil again?" Kapp asked the room at large.

I ignored Kapp.

"Stay, Roy," I said, keeping my voice sane with an effort. "We'll talk."

"No darlin'," he answered. "I'm just pulling the dark forces down on you. I'll be leaving now. I love you."

And then he turned and left. At least, he shut the door behind him. But then, Roy was always courteous. Kapp, on the other hand . . .

"How could you?" I asked Kapp.

"Huh?" he said, feigning innocence. It didn't sit well on his bulldog face. He pushed at his glasses and fooled with the thin hair that tried to cover his bald spot.

"You drove him away on purpose," I accused.

"Lazar," he mumbled, his voice more gentle than usual, "you need someone in your life who can commit to you. Roy isn't the guy."

"But he *is* the guy, Kapp," I argued, trying not to cry. "He is."

"Oh Cally, honey," Dee-Dee cooed and put her arms around me. She wasn't Roy, but she was my friend. Even in the worst of times, goodness is present. And right then, Dee-Dee was that goodness. I reminded myself that even Kapp was trying to be a friend. *Very* trying.

"So, whaddaya say we rustle up a cup of tea and talk about murder?" he suggested.

"Cally needs to sleep now, Kapp," Dee-Dee put in, and I mentally blessed her again.

"Tomorrow, then," Kapp pronounced. I didn't have the heart to argue with him.

He left, but not without another lunge with his cane. I was too tired to do more than block it and tap his wrist.

"Mother of God, you're good," he offered, then bowed and left.

A dozen more hugs and sweet words later, Dee-Dee finally left, too. I made my way slowly back to my bedroom, getting under the covers this time. I took off my glasses. A tear dripped from my eyes, and Leona licked it, mewled, and tapped my face gently with her paw. Then she was purring again, my hands were on her fur, and I slept.

Saturday morning, I woke up and wondered why I hadn't called the police the night before about my hillside prowler. I picked some burrs out of the bottoms of my pajamas and socks and answered myself. I'd been in some kind of shock the night before. Today . . . today, I'd take a shower and get dressed. Then I'd figure out what to do.

Over a cup of green peach tea and toasted cranberry-nut bread for myself and Fancy Feast for Leona, I decided I had to call the police. But which police? If my midnight marauder actually did have to do with May's murder, then it would be important to the Mostaza Police Department. But technically, this was within the jurisdiction of the Estados Police Department.

I looked down at Leona. But she wasn't in comfort mode anymore. She stomped down the hallway, and I heard the sound of books falling to the floor. In the past few months, she'd apparently been trying to teach herself to read. She never did her own reshelving though. Margaret Thatcher probably didn't either.

I dialed the Mostaza Police Department. After a few thousand questions and several telephone transfers, I finally found myself on the line with Sergeant Verne.

I told her the whole story, quickly and succinctly. Then I heard nothing from the other end of the line.

"Are you still there, Sergeant?" I asked.

"Yeah, yeah," she answered. "So why do you have goats?"

"They keep the vegetation down," I explained impatiently. "You know, they're lawn mowers, but with hooves."

"Do you think they'd work on flatland?" she asked.

"Huh?" I said.

"'Cause we got some land behind the house that we can't keep under control," she went on. "It costs an arm and a leg to get someone in to do it, you know what I mean?"

I thought about offering her the goats on loan. I did that a lot with friends. But would a goat loan be considered a bribe to a policewoman?

"Sergeant Verne?" I tried. "What do you think about the prowler?"

"Did you see the individual clearly?" she probed.

"No." I took a calming breath. "All I saw was a dark figure."

"The goats don't hurt people, do they?" she asked.

"No, not really. They can butt people, knock them over, but that's about it."

"So where'd you get the goats?" she pushed.

"They came with the land," I told her. "But if you really want to know about goats, I can give you the name of the guy I buy goat chow from."

She wanted his name. But she didn't want to hear any more about my prowler. She told me to call the Estados Police Department.

The officer I got on the phone in Estados was even less interested in my prowler than Sergeant Verne was. But at least he didn't seem interested in my goats.

"If you want, we'll send someone out, ma'am," he told me, the reverse enthusiasm in his voice telling me he hoped I wouldn't take him up on the offer.

I didn't. The officer said they'd log a report of the incident, and I hung up the phone.

I was the only one interested in the hillside prowler, so I put on my jeans and my old gardening coat and went outside to investigate.

It wasn't raining. That was the good news. The weeds and grasses were still wet and slippery. That was the bad news. I made my way slowly down the hillside. Moscow and Persia were delicately nibbling burr-clover, their favorite dish, tasty and nutritious, if you were a goat. Ohio followed me, always the party animal. I was looking for something, but what? A footprint? Something from the intruder's pockets? I saw places where the foliage was mashed. I bent over. Was I looking at my own footprints or someone else's? And then, halfway down, I came to a place where the foliage was really mashed. And I could see where someone had slid to the bottom of the hill.

I hurried down the hill, imagining the place where the dark figure had finally stood up. But once I got there, there was just more mashed foliage. No footprints, no dropped business card, no telltale matchbook, nothing. I bent over farther, and Ohio butted me from behind. I turned, and she rolled up her lip in an engaging smile. Maybe I would lend Sergeant Verne my goats after all.

That was when I remembered I had clients coming for sessions that morning. I made it back up the hill in record time, poured some goat chow into the communal basin tied to the fence, and went back inside.

My first client was a woman whose autoimmune system was eating her alive. I followed the reds and blues and purples of her aura to a well of self-hatred. And then, together, we began to drain the well. This was good. This was what I lived for. My second client was a man whose fears were a bright, flared yellow.

"Did you hear about the murder last night?" he asked as I traced his bladder meridian to his little toes.

"What?" I said, immediately disconnected from what I'd been doing.

"They say some guy killed his wife." His yellow flared again.

And I would have bet mine did, too. They couldn't suspect Gerry Cheng, could they?

It was a hard session to finish. But I did it. I even gave the man an extra half hour for free. It took that long for me to get back into my healing space.

Once he was gone, I just sat. Roy was right. I would be in danger if I pushed myself into an investigation that I really had no right to fault. But what if they actually did suspect Gerry? Did I owe it to May to—

The phone rang before I could search my soul any more fully than I'd searched my hillside.

"Cally?" a voice said when I picked up. It was a high, musical voice, but I couldn't place it.

"Oh, shoot, Cally. It's me, Sarah Quesada," the voice said, and I relaxed. "I just had to call you. I'm talking to Phil here, and we wondered if you could meet with us?"

"Meet with you?" I repeated, Roy's eyes glowing in my mind. Was there really darkness here?

"About May's murder," Sarah explained. "We gotta figure out who did it, ya know. We gotta make it happen—"

"But why do you think I—"

Sarah broke in, her voice even higher with excitement.

"Warren Kapp said you solve these things," she offered. "He said you're the best!"

SIX

"Son of a lizard!" I blurted.

"Cally?" Sarah asked.

"Warren Kapp is not my booking agent," I told her angrily. "And I'm not a detective."

A long silence followed.

"Shoot," Sarah said softly. "I'm sorry, Cally. I must have misunderstood—"

"No, no," I assured her, ashamed of my own outburst. "It's okay."

"Oh." Her voice lightened. "So, you'll come?"

I took a deep breath in, thinking of Roy's warnings, thinking of Kapp's butting in, thinking of May. And, finally, thinking of Gerry.

"In a while," I agreed after a few more deep breaths. "If I can get ahold of my brother York and bring him." I hadn't completely forgotten the figure on my back hill.

"Oh, great!" she enthused. "Together, we can find out who did it. I just know we can! We're gonna do it, Cally."

I stared at the telephone after I hung up. I could still get out of it, I told myself. My commitment was dependent on locating York.

Then I picked up the phone again and dialed York's number.

"Zartent," he answered. York lived in a loft above his Estados martial arts studio. He had one phone line for both floors and both sides of his life.

"Are you teaching now?" I asked.

"No," he answered brusquely.

"Want to accompany me to a meeting at May's . . . Gerry's . . . Citrus House?"

"Why?" he asked.

"About May's murder," I answered.

There was a long silence on York's end of the line.

"Cally," he said finally, "have you ever thought about what Roy really means when he talks about the darkness?"

"Huh?" was all I could say. York had consistently dismissed Roy's theories about darkness as long as I could remember.

"First," York answered himself, "Roy sees a darkness that he associates with himself, but that swirls toward you. He's afraid that his presence brings you into some kind of danger—"

"But—"

"I know, then he leaves you," he interrupted. "But still, a few months later, you're connected to a case of murder. And now the two of you are dating again. And he warns you not to go to a party. You told me that last night. Something about 'evil.' And you go, and . . ." York faltered.

"May dies," I finished for him quietly. My neck felt cold and prickly. "Do you think Roy is really seeing something?"

"There is an internal consistency to his experience," York answered slowly.

"So what are you saying, York?" I asked, my voice rising before I could stop it. "That if Roy and I weren't dating, May wouldn't have died?"

"Of course not," he dismissed my question.

"Well, then, what *are* you saying?"

Another long silence followed.

I hated talking on the phone just then. I couldn't see York's body language, much less his aura. I felt blind. I wanted to put my hand out and touch my brother, to find out what was going on with him. And to remind myself of our enduring link.

Finally, I heard a sigh.

"I guess I'm worried about your becoming any more connected to this than you already are, Cally."

"So you won't come with me to Citrus House?" I guessed.

"No! Criminy, that's not what I'm saying. I'm saying maybe I should go to Citrus House alone, without you."

"Hah!" I snorted in exasperation. I don't know what I sounded like, but I felt like a teenager, an angry teenager. "*You* weren't even the one who was invited. I just extended my invitation to you."

"So, who invited you?" York asked. His tone was reasonable, but suddenly I could feel a link to him. And with that, I could feel his sullen frustration. York was a teenager again, too.

"York," I tried. I straightened my back and reminded myself that I was thirty-six, not sixteen. "Can we start over?"

"What?" he asked, derailed.

"Forget I'm your little sister. Forget about Roy. I'll pick you up at your place, then we'll go to Citrus House together."

"We can meet at your place," he negotiated. He couldn't just take me up on my suggestion. He was older than I was.

"Okay, but I'll drive," I insisted. I don't even know why.

A few minutes later, I hung up the phone and stared at it again. I just hoped York would have aged past adolescence by the time he got to my house: And I guessed I'd have to grow up, too.

I caught up on my weight lifting while I waited for York. I had a small bench in my combination den, library, and everything-else room. I lay on my back and lifted a barbell to my arm's length. I wondered who benefited from May's death financially. I lowered the barbell and wondered how angry someone had to be to murder. I lifted again and thought about Sarah Quesada. What was she doing at Citrus House anyway? By the end of the set, my mind was sorer than my pectorals were.

A set each for biceps, triceps, and shoulders later, York still hadn't arrived. I changed into a nicer pair of jeans and a warm corduroy jacket. Then I danced around with my cane for a while, whirling, slashing, blocking, and jabbing. My mind was going in circles like a hamster on a wheel. May, Roy, York . . .

It was time for the goat treat I'd forgotten to award the night before. I walked out on my back deck, glad of the cool air after my exercise, and grabbed three handfuls of Spanish moss from my stash. The stuff wasn't good for the trees, but Ohio, Moscow, and Persia loved it. I went to the back fence and gave a goat yodel, the one I'd always imagined Heidi giving when I'd read her story as a girl.

All three goats came running, and each accepted her share of moss, snuffling and bleating.

"Thanks for butting in," I told them, remembering the figure rolling down my hillside.

I thought I saw Ohio nod as she munched. I smiled, then heard York's Subaru coming up my driveway.

"Be good, ladies," I lectured the goats as I went out to meet my brother.

When York got out of his car, I could tell he'd made it past the teenage years. His narrow, sharp features wore a look of sheepish regret that I was sure was reflected in the mirror of my own face.

"Sorry, Cally," he murmured. He put out a hand when I walked up. "Shake?"

I shook his hand. We'd always ended our disagreements this way, even when we were kids. Then I gave him a long hug. I couldn't help it. York was my brother. He always would be.

We were in my old Honda Accord and rolling along toward Citrus House when I realized that York didn't know anything about the figure I'd seen on my hill the night before. It felt strange. The previous night's midnight marauder had been such a part of the whole evening of May's death that I found it hard to imagine that he hadn't known. In fact, only the police of two disinterested cities knew. Not Kapp, not Dee-Dee, not Roy.

"The goats butted someone down the back hill last night," I confessed, glancing furtively at York to see how he took the news. Uh-oh, I thought as his face tightened.

"Your hill?" he demanded, his tone cold and angry.

"Yes, my hill," I answered. "I don't suppose you could say 'there, there' or something, could you?"

"There, there," he snapped. Then he went on. "Do you have any idea who it was?"

"Not a clue," I told him. "I even checked out the area."

"Did you call the police?"

"I called Sergeant Verne, but she wasn't all that interested."

"Midgin bureaucrat," he muttered.

"Do you think it has anything to do with May's death?" I asked.

"I think it must," he said slowly. "But what?"

I shrugged my shoulders nonchalantly as my mind whirled with theories. Had I seen something, heard something? Did someone have the same thing against me as they did against May? Had the murderer killed for something they thought I now possessed—

"Do you want to come stay at my place?" York offered.

"No," I replied automatically.

"Then, how about if someone stays with you?"

"I . . . I don't know." I didn't want to get anyone else caught up in this. Oddly, *I* felt protected, but I wasn't so sure about my friends and relatives.

"How about Roy?" York suggested.

It was hard to keep my car on the road while I answered that one.

"Roy thinks his presence harms me, remember?" I kept my tone even. "Internal consistency, I think you called it."

"Right," York tried. "Right."

"I've got my cane," I reminded him.

"Be vigilant," he warned solemnly.

"Thanks, York," I said, and turned my car into the driveway at Citrus House. I knew that was as close to a real "there, there," as I was going to get from him.

May's Citrus House looked even more obnoxious in the misty daylight than it had looked at night. A Citrus Monstrosity was more like it. All that tangerine architecture and all those lime-green gewgaws. And the plaster zoo of animals in front. I smiled for a moment, thinking how May must have loved putting her house up the collective snoot of the natural-earth-tone set of Mostaza.

"Criminy," York muttered as I parked behind a yellow

Saturn in the circular driveway. "How'd she get it past the planning commission?"

"Dutch said Sarah had something to do with it," I remembered. "Maybe I'll ask Sarah—"

"Whoa," York interjected. "Vigilance, remember. And sometimes vigilance means keeping a low profile. I don't think you should ask any questions—"

"But I suppose you will," I accused.

York's head reared back. "But I was her teacher, Cally. I—"

"And I was her healer," I finished up.

York glared at me for a moment, then sighed.

There was no use arguing with a Lazar. We both knew it.

We didn't even bother shaking hands this time. We just got out of the car and marched up to the door of Citrus House together.

I rang the doorbell, expecting Ian Oxton to answer. But the door opened without obvious human assistance, creaking in a satisfying kind of Addams Family tone. I looked more closely and still saw no one. But I could smell aftershave. Kapp!

A cane came snaking around the open door and jabbed my way. I blocked it and twirled the tip of my own cane around it, tangling up the hand that held it. The cane dropped to the floor with an even more satisfying crash than the creak of the door.

"Dammit, Lazar!" Kapp yelped. Then he came out from behind the door, his bulldog features red. "What do you have, psychic radar?"

"Vigilance," I answered with a glance at York. I stepped in the door.

York was busy trying to hide his smile, but I saw it

tugging at the corners of his mouth as he stepped in behind me.

"Why is he here?" Kapp whispered, pointing at my brother.

"He's with me," I answered.

"No, Cally," Kapp kept it up. "We're gonna solve this one together. Remember, like we did before. I've got the connections. You've got the insight—"

"Kapp, we didn't solve the last one," I reminded him. "We got lucky." I thought of Roy, of unexpected death. "Or maybe unlucky—"

"Hooboy, Cally," Kapp plowed on. "We're going to show everyone how it's done—"

"Yeah, how?" I challenged.

"Aw, come on. I can come up with the dirt on anyone. And you can just take a little peek into whatever it is you peek into, and wham-bam-thank-you-ma'am, we'll solve this sucker."

"Kapp, you have to stop this," I told him. I looked around the orange room, hoping no one who had loved May North was hearing this conversation. But it seemed that the three of us were alone in the orange living room.

"Where's everyone else?" I asked.

"They're all in Gerry's study," he answered. "They're waiting for you."

"You haven't told them about the two of us investigating, have you?" I demanded.

"Me?" he came back innocently. Then he grinned. "You betcha."

"Kapp!" I brought up my cane. It didn't seem right to thrash an eighty-year-old man. But at that moment, it didn't seem all that wrong either.

"I just told them what you did before," he defended himself. "Just the truth, and nothing but the truth."

I lowered my cane. I had to talk to Gerry and the others and straighten this out.

"You leave my sister out of this," York threw in before I could even take a step toward the study.

Dack. Kapp and York at each other's throats. That was all the day needed. I closed my eyes and thought of light. White light streaming down—

"You gonna make me, sonny boy?" Kapp challenged.

I opened my eyes again and turned. Under any other circumstances, the confused expression on York's face would have been comical. Because York could probably take just about anyone and dismember them with his bare hands if he felt like it, but he wasn't about to beat up an elderly man. And Kapp knew that. York had taught me cane-fu, but Kapp knew how to argue. He'd spent most of his life doing just that in court.

"Both of you behave," I hissed. I used the voice I'd used to train my cat.

York and Kapp turned my way in a strange synchronicity.

"Shall we meet with the others in Gerry's study?" I suggested.

Each man nodded mutely. Wow, it had taken me a lot more than that to train Leona.

But Kapp always had the last word. Just as we got to the study, he laid a hand on my arm.

"Oh, by the way," he announced, a newborn grin on his face. "I got you an appointment with the mayor of Mostaza."

And then he opened the door to Gerry Cheng's study.

Gerry sat in the arms of a plaid easy chair in the olive-green room. Ian stood across from him, arms outstretched.

"Not if you don't quit riding that bicycle," Ian boomed.

The scattered laughter in the room told me that I'd missed the story leading to his punch line.

But Gerry wasn't really laughing, just smiling wanly. He didn't look well. He seemed shrunken and gray, not just his hair but his skin as well. And he radiated the blue aura of mourning with a yellow backdrop of fear. He glanced up at a picture of May on the wall. The whole study was filled with pictures of May. I tried and couldn't remember if those pictures had been there the night before or were newly placed.

The mop dog saw us and yipped. With that, the Labrador bounded our way, tongue lolling, and the cats turned away in disgust.

"What a laugh!" The parrot squawked.

Gerry looked up at us and nodded in greeting. "May's animals," he explained quietly. "Dang, they loved her."

"Are you sure you're getting enough liquids, Gerry?" Eric asked. He didn't look a lot better than Gerry, his salmon-pink skin blotchy under his beard and moustache. But he *was* the doctor in the house.

Gerry nodded again politely.

Phil walked in with a cup of tea and handed it to Gerry.

"Thank you," Gerry said, and took a long sip.

Eric and Phil exchanged relieved looks. Eric might be the doctor, but Phil's ministry seemed more effective for getting liquids into Gerry.

Phil put his large, dark hand on Gerry's frail shoulder. Gerry looked engulfed by the gesture, but he patted the hand on his shoulder, as if to comfort the comforter.

"Keep on holding on," Phil advised, and slowly removed his hand and walked over to sit on a small rust-colored couch with Sarah.

I stood for a moment, just feeling the amount of love

floating around Gerry Cheng. It wasn't just May's animals, but May's boarders. They all seemed alight with compassion for the widower, each offering what they could to brighten his dark time. Even Ian was there with his endless jokes.

"So, did you hear what the blond said—" he began.

"Cally!" Sarah interrupted. "I'm so glad you came."

"So am I," I answered truthfully. The goodness in the room outweighed any sadness or fear. Kapp was another matter, though.

"And York!" Sarah continued. "May told us all about your martial arts studio. Shoot, she said you were better than Jackie Chan blindfolded."

York's skin pinkened. Compliments always pushed his mute button.

Kapp chortled nearby.

"York taught me cane-fu," I piped in, raising my cane and turning toward Kapp.

Kapp stopped chortling. It was a small victory, but it felt good anyway. For a minute.

"Cally is one helluva detective, too," Kapp announced.

"No, I'm not a detective," I argued. I wanted this settled right away. "I'm an energetic healer. I don't know what Kapp has claimed—"

"Look at the two of them," Kapp interrupted avuncularly. "York embarrassed to be a world-class martial artist, and Cally doesn't want to admit her sleuthing abilities."

He was doing it again. Phil and Eric were nodding. The members of the jury were convinced.

"No, really—" I tried.

"Do you think you could help us find out who killed my dear May?" Gerry asked quietly. Then he shook his head, seeming to shrink a little more. "I know it's not fair to inconvenience you. You have your healing work to do."

"Mr. Cheng," I tried.

"Gerry," he corrected me.

"Gerry," I tried again. "As May's friend, and yours, I would love to help you find whoever was responsible for May's death. But I'm really not a detective. I'm—"

He dropped his gaze to the floor. Criminy, his wife was dead.

I changed tack, reminding myself to maim Kapp later. "But I can talk to people I suppose, if that might help."

Gerry's head came up again.

"Would you?" he asked. "I could always pay you—"

"No, no," I insisted. "May's friendship was worth more than money."

"Isn't she great?" Kapp threw in.

I ignored him. So did York.

"So what have the police done so far?" York asked.

"Diddly-squat," Kapp answered.

"Very little that I can see," Gerry confirmed. "I called Chief Upwood this morning, and he told me that they were looking into it. Then he recommended a grief group for me to attend."

"Man's a horse's ass," Kapp muttered.

"And Cally," Sarah threw in. "They haven't even called in the county to help."

"Their evidence technician is their computer expert and makes coffee," Ian added.

"So, did any of you see anything last night—" I started.

Phil cleared his throat loudly. He was good at it. My goats could probably hear him in Estados.

"Ms. Lazar, I do believe that you might want to talk to us each separately," he pronounced. "After all, with the exception of Mr. Kapp, we are all murder suspects." He paused for a moment. "Even you," he finished.

SEVEN

My mouth was still hanging open. But I couldn't think of a thing to say. Lulled by the goodness surrounding Gerry Cheng, I'd forgotten the gruesome reality of May's death. And worse, I'd forgotten the reality of murder, of a person who had truly done this awful thing. My mouth felt dry. We *were* all suspects, and I didn't want to acknowledge it. I closed my mouth and swallowed, closing my eyes for a second, too.

"Phil is right," York agreed from my side. I opened my eyes again. "Any of us could be the murderer. Cally should talk to everyone separately. Still . . ." He paused. "I'd like to be with her. She's my sister."

Phil turned and looked at me, a question in his eyes.

"I'd just tell him what everyone said anyway," I answered that question. "Remember, I'm not a real detective. I'm not even an attorney. So, I'm not in any role of confidentiality. And, more important, I'd trust York with my life."

"Of course," Gerry Cheng chimed in. "You two belong together."

"And I, on the other hand, *am* a real live attorney, so my presence—" Kapp started in.

"Won't be necessary," York finished for him.

"Hey, I'm the one who got you two in here in the first place," Kapp argued. "Holy Mother, you two are probably too naive to recognize real butter, much less a murderer."

"Good point, Counselor," I told him. "I just wish you'd made it earlier."

Kapp laughed. "Touché," he allowed, bowing my way. "Just keep in touch."

He raised his cane. I blocked it with a simple movement.

"Fine," he finished up. "I'll see you tomorrow. And don't forget the mayor."

"What do you mean—" I began.

But it was too late.

"Ta-ta," he cooed, and slipped out the study door.

"Shoot," Sarah said. "Was that really *the* Warren Kapp? I heard he was a some big shot attorney, but he acts really goofy."

"That was him," York confirmed.

Sarah just shook her head.

"So, how do you want to do this, Ms. Marple?" Ian asked. "Tea and interrogation in the library? Old lace and probing questions in the conservatory?"

"I suppose we could use the living room," I suggested tentatively.

"Is that private enough?" Phil questioned.

"Unless the parrot squawks," Ian answered, laughing. He immediately sobered though.

"How about my study?" Gerry offered.

"Oh, I don't want to inconvenience you—" I began.

"There's no inconvenience for me," Gerry insisted. "The rest of us can go to the living room or the kitchen. It's practically lunchtime anyway. You just do what you can to find out about my sweet May, okay?"

"I'll do what I can, but—"

"I know, I know." Gerry waved his hands in the air. "You're not a real detective. But I think May would like you helping. Talk to us today, maybe to some of the others who were here some other time. Don't do anything more than you want to, okay?"

"Sounds good," I told him gratefully.

"Thank you, Cally," he murmured, and left the study. His dogs trailed out after him, along with one cat. I wasn't sure if it was Tomato or Catsup.

Phil, Ian, Sarah, and Eric were the next to leave, and then York and I were alone. Well, almost alone.

"Hey, where's the party?" the parrot asked.

He had a point. Now that everyone was gone, it seemed cold in Gerry's study. I walked around the room slowly. I wondered if Gerry or May had chosen the olive green for the walls. And the plaid for the easy chair and rust, mustard, and pumpkin shades for the rest of the furniture. Dack. But the pictures of May were beautiful. *She* was beautiful. As a young woman her hair had been dark and her face radiant. She had a face that reminded me of someone. A movie star? With those lush lips, high cheekbones, and saucer-sized eyes, she certainly could have been an actress. I wondered how she'd ended up a madam.

"Cally?" York said.

"What?" I asked slowly, brought back to the present reality by his voice. I sniffed. Somewhere in the house, someone was cooking. I could smell onions for a moment, then the sweet fragrance of baking.

"What are we going to ask them?" York whispered.

It took a little while to come up with a list, but we did it. The list wasn't very long. We would ask each person about their background and their relationship with May. Then we'd move on to their feelings about May, and find out if they'd noticed anyone who seemed to be her enemy or anything else suspicious.

"Have we missed anything?" I asked finally.

"I guess it depends if we're asking the person if they killed May or if they know anything about who did," York answered.

The room felt cold again.

"Who do we take first?" York asked.

It didn't take me long to answer that one.

"Go get Phil," I ordered. "This one-on-one bit was his idea in the first place."

Even as I said it, I knew by all rights Kapp should have been our first victim. But Kapp was gone, and we didn't have any instruments of torture anyway. *And* he wasn't a suspect. I sighed and plopped myself down in the pumpkin-colored chair.

York was in the door a minute later, with Phil trailing behind him. Phil sat across from me in the mustard-colored chair. York crossed his arms and stood in front of the study door like a prison guard.

I looked at Phil's face for a minute. Dark and round, his face would have been unremarkable except for the intensity of his raisin-black irises. And his aura would have been unremarkable, too, except for the silver-and-gold threads sparkling here and there, threads that for some meant spiritual connections.

"I expect you'll want to know a bit about my background," he suggested.

I jerked my head up at York. Had Phil been studying our mental notes? Meanwhile, Phil plodded on, his voice deep and soothing.

"I'm the pastor of the Mostaza Church of Divine Love,"

he told me. "We're a young church. It is our belief that spirit is more important than ritual, and compassion more important than what is written only on paper. We're concerned with what is written upon our souls."

"Do you believe in evil?" I asked him. Somehow, I was already deviating from the list.

"Evil?" He returned the word, cocking his head and gazing toward the ceiling.

At first I thought he didn't understand my question, but then I realized he was only considering it.

"I don't believe in evil people," he answered after a few breaths. "Perhaps there are acts that appear evil." He closed his eyes for a moment. "Once you say the word *evil,* you have labeled and dismissed a person. I imagine we all have degrees of anger and pain. Some of us aren't blessed with the circumstances to nourish our spirits as much as others. But we all have the potential for goodness."

"Yeah," I agreed eagerly. Maybe I could get him to talk to Roy. "There's always light, goodness. It's a matter of looking for it. See, I think—"

"Do you think the murderer has the potential for goodness?" York asked from the door.

Phil flinched. York's question had jolted the minister.

"Yes," he answered after another moment. "I do believe even a murderer has the potential for goodness. It's in all of us. It is difficult to embrace the notion when thinking of May's death, but it doesn't make it any the less true, just harder to accept emotionally."

"How did you meet May?" I asked, scrambling to remember the outline of our list of questions.

"May visited our church the first day I gave a sermon." He smiled gently in memory. "I don't expect it was a very good sermon. People tell me I'm too earnest, not entertaining enough. I've asked Ian to help me out, but I don't think I have it in me to tell jokes. Still, that day, May gave me a standing ovation. And later, she asked me where I was living. You see, the living quarters provided by the church for the minister are still occupied by the last minister, the Reverend Perry. Everyone loves him. He's a good and fair man. But he has no place to live now that he's so ill. So I was staying at the YMCA in Peyzer until we could figure out what to do. Well, May just bundled me up in that way she had and told me I could come stay here as a tenant. The church only makes as much money as people donate, and I'm afraid that's not much, now that *I'm* preaching. But May lets me stay here for so little that I can make it. At least, she did." He frowned. "I hope Gerry will keep the three of us on who live here. But it may be too painful for him to continue to live here himself." He closed his eyes. "Divine grace will show us the way."

"Tell me more about May," I led him on.

"Ah, May," he murmured, smiling gently again. "May North was a true innocent. I know many unkind words have been said about her, especially about her past, but the May I knew was a true child of God. She loved animals and nature . . . and people. She did a lot of good for a lot of people. Yes, indeedy. And she didn't expect a gold medal for her actions. She was just good and kind."

"Did she have any enemies?" York asked from his position at the door.

Phil sighed and looked down. "There were many in this community who couldn't accept her. She didn't hide the fact that she had been a madam in Alaska. But they couldn't seem to see who she was now. A kind woman who—"

"Who exposed herself nude to a teenage boy?" York interrupted.

Phil's head jerked.

"May didn't 'expose' herself." His voice wasn't gentle. "She was sunbathing in the nude. She thought no more of it than a child. And then she saw the boy across the street and waved. She was sorry for the interpretations people put on her actions later, but there was no malice in it." Phil paused. "I must admit that I, myself, was taken aback the first time I saw May sunbathing. But in time, I realized that her intentions were innocent. She just liked the feel of the sun. It was her way of being with nature. Who are we to judge her?"

"I'm sorry, Phil," York said. "I didn't intend to judge May. I just wanted to see how you felt about the incident."

"Ah," Phil assented. "I supposed I asked for it when I said we should all be treated as suspects. Well, I've made peace with May's eccentricities. It wasn't difficult. She was too good a woman to hold at fault. Yes, indeedy. I'll miss her."

I glanced up at York. I couldn't think of another question for Phil. Or maybe I'd lost the heart for it. York nodded at me.

"Thanks, Phil," I offered. "You did a good job of filling us in about May."

He stood up from his chair.

"Thanks to you two," he offered back. "I know you're not really detectives. I expect this is difficult for you. But, if nothing else, it will make Gerry feel better. Bless you for the kindness."

And then Phil left the study, shutting the door behind him with his accustomed gentleness.

"Phew," was all I could say.

"He really cared for her," York added.

"Unless he's an awfully good actor," I agreed.

"Actor," York repeated. "We've got one of those in the house."

"Time to interview Mr. Ian Oxton?" I asked, rubbing my hands together in mock anticipation. Or maybe it was real anticipation. "He is the butler, after all."

"Har-har," York muttered. Then he grabbed the knob to the study door. "I'll get him."

York was gone for a good ten minutes. I was ready to get up and search for him when Tomato, or maybe it was Catsup, landed in my lap with all the grace of a bowling ball. I smoothed his charcoal gray fur, and he blinked his coppery eyes at me.

I was at the "ookums, snookums" stage when York opened the door, and Ian Oxton entered. The cat jumped off my lap, leaving me tottering in my chair, and wound himself around Ian's legs.

I couldn't blame the cat. Ian held a silver tray with all sorts of interesting things balanced on top. My nostrils began working without being asked.

"I've got herbal tea, vegetable frittata, pumpkin bread, and whipped honey-butter," Ian announced. "Oh, and stuffed avocados."

"Did you make all that?" I asked in awe.

"No." He shook his head. "Gerry made the avocados and tea. The rest is reheated from last night."

"Oh," I said, instantly somber.

"I brought it in so I could butter you up," Ian quipped. I didn't think Phil should learn to tell jokes from this man.

But then again, Ian didn't look up to par. His perfectly sculpted actor's face was pale. There were deep circles under his reddened eyes. And his eyes weren't alive with mischief. They were barely comatose. Even his aura had a murky, sluggish quality.

Still, he was efficient enough as he dropped a foldout contraption under the tray, creating an instant table, and drew up two more chairs around the food. He handed me a plate, and I filled it happily with a little of everything. York did the same, but not as happily. My brother only ate dairy products when socially necessary. And finally, Ian made a plate for himself.

"Yum," I mumbled, shoving pumpkin bread with honey-butter into my mouth. Questions could wait. I was busy. I discovered that the avocados were stuffed with blue cheese and a tangy dressing, and the frittata tasted of potatoes, onions, and cheddar.

"So," Ian put in after a few minutes of eating. "You're going to want to know how I felt about May. Well, she was a kick in the pants, and it stinks to high heaven that she was killed. She was one fun lady."

Food and self-interrogation. The combination was perfect. I took another bite and a sip of tea as Ian went on.

"I keep asking myself who could have wanted to kill her. May made everyone mad once in a while, but then she could charm everyone right back. She liked to pull tigers' tails, but never too hard, if you know what I mean. I can't imagine anyone actually hating her that much. Gawd, why couldn't some old bore like Dutch Krentz or someone have been killed? Not May. May was never boring."

"So how did you come to live with May?" I finally asked.

"Hah!" Ian exploded into a bark of laughter. Then his face went passive again. "I was at a bar in my motel. I say 'my motel' because that's where I lived after *Intrigues and Outtakes* was canceled. And May North flounced into the bar and sat down next to me. Then she proceeded to do a perfect imitation of my nemesis in the show, this goofy space cadet who always foiled my evil schemes. She made me laugh so hard, I fell off my barstool. Literally. Jeez, she was funny. I saw her a couple more times. I guess I complained about my money situation. So she offered me a reasonable rent if I wanted to come stay here. Pathetically low, really. And I took it. I really wasn't paying her enough, so I did a little butler-and-cook stuff when I could."

"Was this before she and Gerry were married?"

"Uh-huh." Ian took a bite of his own lunch. "But Gerry was really cool about her tenants. He's a cool guy generally."

"Why would people say you were a virtual prisoner here?" York asked.

"Oh, gawd," Ian replied, raising his brows so high they almost disappeared into his wavy hair. "I don't know who started that rumor, but everyone was always asking me. It got to be so boring. I ask you, is it virtual imprisonment to pay reasonable rent and live with fun people? But, nooo, these fools were always asking if May made us sign papers or something. Which, for your information, she never did."

"May fought with Gerry's daughter last night," York put in.

"And that neighbor, Julie or something," I added.

Ian rolled his eyes. "You see, that's what I meant about May pulling people's tails. She couldn't help getting in people's faces who were uptight. Gerry's daughter, Becky, has always been jealous of May, and Julie Turner has been on May's case ever since the famous nude-sunbathing scene. So May gave back as good as she got. She was pulling Sarah's chain, too, about the planning commission, and she got into it with Dutch earlier, but that was just May. She was only teasing. And I think everyone knew that. If they didn't, they should have." Ian sighed. "I don't know. Some people have no sense of fun. Maybe May just teased someone a little too hard."

Tears were glinting in his eyes by then.

"But she had fun," I put in gently.

"Oh, man, did she have fun," he replied, his voice sub-dued now. "And I guess that's as good as it gets. May was the best."

Ian cleared the tray and table and left after that, promising to send Eric our way next.

York and I looked at each other after he closed the door behind himself.

"He cared for her, too," I said.

"He *is* an actor," York argued halfheartedly.

"But—" I began, and the door opened again.

Eric came in. He didn't take a seat, but stood waiting, flickering in shades of uncertainty and mourning.

"Have a seat," York offered in the tone he'd use for a frightened child.

Eric sat down. Then he looked up in the air above him. He didn't look guilty to me. He looked terminally shy. His grooming wouldn't have helped him in front of any jury either. Longish, unruly hair, and a beard and moustache to match hid most of his face. His crinkly, brown eyes were his redeeming feature, but they were the most effective when he actually looked at you. And he wasn't making eye contact.

"So, Eric," I started, "tell us about yourself."

"Um, I'm an eye doctor," he murmured, lowering his gaze to a point somewhere between York's chair and mine. "Not a very successful one though."

That's right, I remembered. Eric was the bankrupt doctor York had told me about.

"I was part of an IPA—"

"A what?"

"I'm sorry," he mumbled. "An individual practice asso-ciation. See, they were supposed to take the insurance risks collectively for those of us who took HMO referrals, only they went bankrupt, and so did I."

"Oh, I see," I told him. But I didn't really. He'd lost me somewhere in the first sentence. "So how'd you meet May?" I tried instead.

"Oh, she knew a friend of mine," he answered.

"And—" I prodded.

"Oh, and my friend introduced me and told May about my financial problems, and she offered to let me live here while I restarted my practice."

I waited for more. There wasn't any.

"So, did you like May?" I probed.

"Oh," he said, a blush mottling his pink skin. "I adored May. She was my role model. She helped me restart my business. I'm sharing an office three times a week with another eye doctor and some alternative healers. She helped me put together the deal."

"You like living here?" I asked.

"I love it here," he said. Then his eyes clouded over. "May always said we were her harem. But Gerry understood. May and Gerry were true soul mates. I'm so sorry she died. Poor Gerry."

"Can you think of any enemies May might have had," York cut to the chase.

"Small-minded people," Eric pronounced, and now his voice held strength in its anger. "May was tolerance personified. There are always small-minded people, and they always hate the Mays of this world."

"Who do you think killed her?" I asked. It was worth a try.

Eric's shoulders slumped. "I don't know," he whispered. "I just wish I did."

After Eric left, York went looking for Sarah Quesada. But Sarah had eaten lunch and gone back to selling real estate. York and I stared at each other. Because now we only had one more person to talk to, Gerry Cheng. What do you ask a widower of less than twenty-four hours?

As it was, we didn't ask Gerry very much after York escorted him back into his own study, just how he met May.

"There she was, talking to the zookeeper," he told us. "Dang, she was angry. He wasn't treating the bears right. May always loved animals. She was a real lady, my May."

That was enough for me. And it was enough for York, too.

We invited all the boarders back into the study.

After a few dog maneuvers, Gerry was seated in his plaid chair again. Only this time he was fidgeting. Phil and Eric sat. Ian stood. York paced and glowered.

It was time to end everyone's agony.

"Can anyone think of anything to help us find our murderer?" I asked.

No one answered. But Gerry continued to fidget.

Secrets, I thought. And it was as if someone had spoken the word. This murder was about secrets. For a moment, I felt sure of it. And then, I wished I'd asked Gerry about secrets when we'd been alone. But it wasn't too late.

"Was there a secret?" I demanded, turning to the grieving widower.

Gerry jerked his head back around toward Phil, ignoring my question. "I want a memorial service tomorrow," he said to the minister. "Can you do it?"

EIGHT

"Tomorrow?" Phil asked, visibly taken aback.

"Yes, tomorrow," Gerry repeated. "May needs to know that she was loved. She was a real lady. Folks need to know that. It's not right, all the things some people are saying about her. I, I . . ." Gerry faltered and dropped his head into his hands. The Labrador retriever snuffled up next to him, licking his ears. The mop dog sat on his foot and whined. The dachshund just trotted behind his chair.

Eric and Ian weren't far behind the dogs, rushing to each side of Gerry's plaid chair with hands extended.

Had I caused this crisis by asking about secrets?

"Well, let me see, tomorrow is a Sunday, so I have morning service and the church group afterward . . . but maybe in midafternoon." Phil spoke slowly as he thought. He rose from his chair. "We won't be able to have a newspaper notice, but—"

"We can call May's friends," Ian offered, one hand on Gerry's shoulder.

"Cally and I will come," York put in quickly. He wasn't pacing anymore. "And I'll call the other students from May's class." He paused. "Gerry, I wondered about what Cally asked—"

"May's friends," Gerry said wistfully. "She didn't have many, but they loved her."

"I expect I can make an announcement to my parishioners," Phil thought out loud.

"And I could go through May's phone list and call people," Eric piped in.

"Thank you," Gerry whispered through his hands. "My May was a sweet woman. I want everyone to know that."

"I'll give the memorial eulogy," Phil proposed, his eyes wide. He stared into the air. Was he already writing it in his head?

"Did May have any other relatives?" I asked.

We all turned to Gerry. "Well, I'm not sure," he murmured. He looked up at the ceiling. "I got the feeling her people had mostly written her off."

"If she was still in touch with any of her relatives, they ought to be on her phone list," Eric said.

Gerry nodded solemnly. "She was good and kind, my May," he reminded us all once more.

"Yes indeedy," Phil agreed. "And I plan to tell everyone that tomorrow afternoon."

By the time York and I finally left the study, the plans for the memorial service were being made, and Ian had already started a phone tree to get the news out. And, of course, Gerry still hadn't answered my question about secrets. I wondered if more than one actor lived within the tangerine-and-lime walls of Citrus House as York and I let ourselves out of the house through the living room's front door and walked to my Honda in silence.

Once I'd turned the key in the ignition, York looked over his shoulder, to both sides, then spoke. His voice was a whisper.

"What did you mean by 'secrets'?" he demanded.

"Criminy, I don't know," I answered. "It just popped into my mind. Shouldn't I have asked?"

"Of course you should have," York said impatiently. "The real question is why it set Gerry off like that."

I let go of the parking brake and began my way around the circular driveway and out.

"He never answered me," I muttered, mostly to myself, as I reached the main road.

"I know," York shot back. "That's what worries me. Did he put on that whole grieving widower act to avoid the question?"

"Or was he truly upset because of the question?" I added. "Or maybe his sudden upset had nothing to do with my question."

"Unlikely," York replied. "You ask a question, and he's suddenly demanding a memorial service. Cause and effect."

"Do you think he knew some secret that he was afraid would put May into a bad light?" I suggested tentatively. It didn't feel quite right.

"Maybe," York murmured. "Or maybe he was protecting someone."

"Who?" I asked quickly.

I drove for a while as York thought.

"He'd protect his daughter, Becky," he suggested finally. "Or maybe even one of the tenants. He obviously feels affection for them."

"Yeah . . ." I chewed on the idea for a few more blocks.

"But we're not asking the important question," York put in then. "If Gerry is withholding information, does it have anything to do with the murder?"

"I can think of an even more important question," I upped him without satisfaction.

"What?"

"Is Gerry withholding information because he murdered his own wife?"

I expected York to object, but he didn't. That got me really worried. I kept my eyes on the road and tried to imagine Gerry as the actual murderer. I just couldn't. His love for May had been palpable at the party. It couldn't have been faked. But as Kapp had said, I was probably too naive to recognize real butter.

"Cally," York ordered as I crossed over into Estados, "stop at my place. We have to talk."

I opened my mouth to say that we could talk just as well at my house, but then remembered that he was my older brother. We'd talk at his place. At least Kapp probably couldn't track us down there.

York leased a building from the estate of a deceased artist, Fay Stiller. From the outside, it was an impressive piece of architecture, almost frightening on first sight. After the long drive up a narrow road in a forest of evergreens, it suddenly came into view, a raw unfinished-looking structure of concrete and glass on the steep hill. When Fay had been alive, she'd used the downstairs as an art studio and the upstairs as living quarters. And she'd studied with York, practicing martial arts appropriate to her failing body. That was York's specialty, martial arts for the elderly and the disabled. I was in a special class for people whose legs were unreliable, whether weak or painful or even missing. Wheelchair sparring was a sight to behold. And I blessed my brother for the physical security that my "cane-fu" had brought me. York had earned black belts in aikido, karate, judo, and jujitsu. He'd studied tai chi, chi gung, sword form, and archery. But he didn't compete anymore. He worked with those who were the least likely to defend themselves and empowered them. I respected my brother for that decision, and so had Fay.

When Fay Stiller died, she willed York a perpetual right to lease the building at an incredible two hundred dollars a month. And even more amazing, none of the relatives had argued. So York lived and worked in the two-story studio. The bottom story was one immense room with three whitewashed concrete walls and wooden flooring lit by a fourth wall of floor-to-ceiling windows. These windows continued up to the second story, where York had his living quarters: a kitchen, two bathrooms (one for students), a bedroom, an office, and a large living room. Three of the four walls upstairs were whitewashed concrete, too. York had spartan tastes: a futon for a bed and sparse, thrift-shop living room furniture. I didn't blame him for the dearth of wall hangings. He had to drill concrete to hang a picture. Only the kitchen seemed comfortable. A skylight lent a soft warmth to the cherrywood table and chairs, and to the elderly, rounded white gas stove and refrigerator. Open shelves with brightly colored, handmade pottery added to the cheer.

We let ourselves in the building the easy way that day, entering the studio at the bottom and riding the gated, open air elevator to the top floor. It was easier than the long outdoor trek to the upstairs door or the crumbling indoor stairway, which had been boarded up for safety's sake last year. The elevator had been necessary for Fay and was essential for any of the disabled students who wanted to use the bathroom. Before we got off the elevator, York bent over the gate and stretched his arm to pick up something from the floor.

"Keerups!" he hissed urgently as he opened the gate.

"What?" I asked.

He pressed a finger to his lips and looked around, his back straightening, his eyes moving. I could almost smell the sudden focus of his mind. And I could feel the threat of danger.

Then all the tension seemed to flow out of his body.

"No one's here," he assured me.

"Of course, no one's here, York," I griped. "Why would you even think—"

He held out his hand. A matchstick lay cradled in his palm.

"Okay," I told him. "You've got me. Are you trying to tell me you've taken up smoking?"

"No." His skin flushed. "It's the old matchstick trick. I left a matchstick propped up against the elevator gate before I left. I always do. Lots of times, I leave the studio open."

"So, someone came up to use the bathroom," I guessed.

"I locked the studio today, Cally. Too much weird stuff was going on to leave the place open."

"Couldn't the matchstick have fallen down from the vibration of the elevator?" I tried, not wanting to hear what he was saying.

"It never has before," he insisted. "I wedge it in too tightly." He looked around him once more. My skin tingled into goose bumps. "Someone came in through my locked door."

We went to the kitchen after York did a quick scan of all the rooms. No one was there except us. But even the watery sun shining through the skylight didn't make the kitchen feel cheery that day. And York's place was cold as always. It was too hard to heat the immense space. He didn't even try.

"Who?" I asked finally.

"The same person who was on your hillside last night?"

Neither of us said "May's murderer," but we were both thinking it.

"At least it couldn't be anyone from Citrus House," I rallied. "We were there the whole time—"

"While the suspects came in one by one," York finished my sentence, way ahead of me. "Anybody we weren't talking to could have gone to my house, knowing I wouldn't be there, and gotten back in time to be interviewed."

"But wouldn't someone have told us?" I insisted.

"The rest might not have even known if one of them took off for a little while. And it only takes five or ten minutes to get here. Say, five minutes to get here, five to . . ." York faltered.

"To?" I prodded.

"That's the question, isn't it?" He sighed. "What is this intruder looking for? What do they want?"

"What if they think you're investigating?" I tried. "What if they were looking for your notes or something?"

"Criminy!" York hissed and stood up. "I can't believe it. We're sitting in here talking, and I haven't even checked to see if anything's missing. I'm losing my vigilance, Cally."

"No, you're not," I assured him. "As long as there's no one here, there's no reason to search right away."

But we searched anyway. Nothing was out of place in the living room or in either of the bathrooms. The bedroom looked the same to me, with its futon neatly made up as a bed on the floor. But when York got to the closet, he wasn't happy.

"Someone's been in here," he announced.

"How do you know?"

"See that gap between the clothes?" he said, pointing at his neatly hung wardrobe. "It wasn't there before."

"Is there anything missing?" I whispered.

York didn't answer right away. He pushed the hangers around carefully, peeked behind the clothes, and got down on all fours to look at the floor.

"No," he told me finally. "I think whoever was here just shoved the clothes apart to look into the closet."

It was the same story when we got to York's office. Nothing was missing, but he was sure someone had been through his drawers.

"If I hadn't seen the matchstick, I never would have noticed," York confessed once we were back in the kitchen.

I put on the kettle for tea, lighting the old stove with a match. Maybe tea could warm my cold hands. And York's. York was pale, the scent of his acrid sweat filling the air. Even with my back to him, I could feel his unaccustomed fear. I wondered if that fear had always been there and if I just hadn't wanted to see it in the brother I'd always perceived as fearless.

"There's one thing worse than paranoia," York announced. "Finding out that you're not paranoid. Finding out someone really is spying on you."

I turned to him then.

"York, can I help you?" I asked. "Would you like a session—"

"Cally," he cut in, his voice a mixture of frustration and affection, "I know you'd like to help ease the fear in me. I can imagine the aura you're seeing now. But the fear is good. It helps my vigilance. If I mellow out, I won't be alert."

I shook my head silently. In my experience, overwhelming emotions were as likely to make a person careless as careful. But I wasn't about to lecture my older brother. And I wasn't going to force a healing on him. I turned back to the stove and the shelves that held the tea and the cups.

I picked a cup with a thick, blue ceramic glaze for York and a chunky purple one for myself.

"Remember what I told you last night?" he began. "About how I was afraid when our parents died?"

I nodded as I opened a box of chamomile tea.

"I've always been convinced they were killed—"

"But—"

"I know, I know," he stopped me before I could start. "It's a crazy idea. I'm not saying it's true. I just always believed it. I've never told anyone because I was afraid I'd sound paranoid. But now with May dead, it doesn't feel like such a crazy notion anymore. It actually seems possible."

I wanted to weep, because it seemed possible to me, too, right then. I remembered my musician mother laughing as she danced with me, and my brilliant father's good-natured attempt to explain simple math to a ten-year-old girl. I remembered a long walk when my parents had looked with such love into each other's eyes. I remembered—

"Cally?" York's voice cut into my memories. "Cally, are you all right? Dack, I didn't mean to upset you."

"I'm fine," I muttered, but I wasn't. I felt like I was trapped under a wall of water. The shelves seemed to shimmer. And York's voice echoed in the cold room. My leg was buckling. I leaned on my cane and gritted my teeth.

"Cally, sit down," York ordered.

"No, I—"

"Now," he insisted, pulling out a chair and all but shoving me into it.

"Hey, who's the healer here?" I demanded, after a series of deep breaths. I forced a smile.

"You are, little sister," York answered softly. "You are for me."

I looked up and saw that he was telling the truth. The fear in him was gone. But I couldn't credit my healing powers. York wasn't afraid anymore because he was too busy taking care of me.

"York," I told him, "just for the record, I never felt right about their deaths either. In fact, I can't even think about them without flipping out."

"I just realized that," he admitted. "I always thought it was only me. Thank you, Cally."

"It's not every day you get thanked for breaking down," I pronounced solemnly. "And thank you, too."

York smiled. "You might do well to let yourself break down more often," he advised. Then he threw up an arm as if to shield his face. "Not that I'm a healer or anything."

"And you might do well to be careful what you say," I growled back, shaking my cane at him. "Not that I'm a martial artist or anything."

He laughed then. And, finally, we could talk about May.

"The intruder on your hillside was probably the one who broke into my house," he summed up after a few minutes. "And probably the one who killed May."

"So we're in this thing, whether we want to be or not," I added.

"Let's put our heads together and figure it out," York said . . . as if it was that easy.

"Over dinner," I suggested.

"What?"

"I'm hungry," I told him. And I was. However short a time we'd been at York's place, the emotions that had played out in my body had burned up all my energy. I needed some calories.

"Actually, I'm hungry, too," York conceded. He sounded surprised.

"Rainbow Harvest?" I proposed.

I ate fish and fowl, but York was a true vegetarian. And for a vegetarian, Rainbow Harvest was the best choice in Estados.

"Okay," he agreed. "Come with me while I check my answering machine, and then we'll go."

I followed York to his office, where he pushed the button on his machine. For an instant, I wondered if a threat from the murderer would come through the speaker. But all I heard was a series of people verifying class times, and a seductive male voice verifying another kind of date. I blushed. Then a voice I recognized spoke.

"It's Geneva," the machine said.

"And Melinda," another voice added, and giggled.

"We're here with Arnot," Geneva went on. "We got together as soon as we heard that you and Cally were there at May North's murder—"

"Kapp told her," Melinda put in.

"Butt out," Geneva ordered her, and spoke into York's machine again. "We want to help. Call us at Arnot's tonight, or call me tomorrow at the shop."

And then the answering machine was finished.

"Criminy!" York and I both yelped together.

It was just like when we were kids. Our three older siblings were never far behind us. There was no escaping Geneva, Melinda, and Arnot Lazar.

"Don't touch that phone," I warned.

"No way," York agreed. "They don't know we're here."

So we left our well-meaning family on hold and went to the Rainbow Harvest. At least it was warmer at the restaurant than it had been at York's.

We discussed suspects over a meal of corn bread, cashew chili, and coleslaw. There were Gerry, Phil, Eric, and Ian to consider. And Sarah, who had left before we had a chance to interview her. And then there was Gerry's daughter. And we couldn't forget the angry neighbors: the Turners and the Krentzes. By the time we'd finished our carrot cake, we were no further forward than we had been before we'd started. Everyone was suspect. But no one was really credible.

"This wasn't as easy as I thought it would be," York commented.

"Should we quit?" I asked.

York didn't answer. After we split the bill, we got into my car to go to my house. York's Subaru was still parked there. On the way, he suddenly hit the dashboard with his fist. I just hoped he didn't dent it. Martial artists shouldn't hit things, animate or inanimate.

"Don't hurt the car, okay?" I requested.

York didn't make any promises about my car. "It's Eric," he explained. "I just remembered where I've seen him before."

"Where?" I asked eagerly, imagining an assassin's convention or better.

"At the Queen's Night," he answered. "It's a . . ."

"A gay bar," I finished for him.

There was a silence in the car. York was not about to discuss gay bars with his little sister.

"There's always Sarah's position on the planning commission to follow up on," I offered, changing the subject. "I'll call her."

York pulled a cell phone from his pocket and tapped out the number Ian had given him for Sarah.

"Answering machine," he reported. "She's out."

Then we were at my house. There was a car I didn't recognize at the bottom of my driveway.

York looked at the car and went still.

"York—" I began.

"Shhh," he hushed me. "It might be the intruder."

I parked my car there, behind the other car, and we hiked up my own hill stealthily, ready for the intruder.

Or were we?

NINE

Two figures stood on the doorstep of my front door, their backs to us. One was tall and clearly male. He was peering in my window. The other was medium height and female. She had her hand on the door.

"I'll take the guy on the left," York whispered in my ear, as we came to the top of the little flight of stairs from the driveway. "Do you think you can handle the one on the right?"

I had my cane. I nodded silently. But as we moved a few steps closer, I wondered what he meant by "handle." What if these guys were solicitors? What if—

The familiarity of the pair struck me as we moved forward another step. Where had I seen—

"Now!" York hissed. He drew himself into a fighting stance in less than a blink, his left arm a shield and his right arm cocked to jab, or punch, or chop.

"No!" I shouted back as the tall figure turned and smiled benignly.

York lifted up his arms in a circular motion above his head and then dropped them, resuming a normal stance as if he'd only been stretching. Cat-fu at its best. He must have been taking lessons from Leona.

"Ah," Chief Upwood commented. "What an interesting exercise. Is it martial?"

"Yeah," York muttered.

"Zartent," I offered helpfully. "York invented it."

York turned and gave me an, "I'll get you later," look I recognized from earliest childhood.

"Well, you must be a very busy man, Mr. Lazar," the chief commented. He smiled like a kind teacher with an unruly pupil. "I understand you teach martial arts exclusively for a living."

"Yeah." York answered again. He sounded a little confused.

I didn't blame him. I was confused, too. What did Chief Upwood want from York? And it was cold out here.

"You said you taught Ms. North some form of martial art," the chief continued. "Did any of the others at the party happen to be your students?"

"No, no," York said, shaking his head.

There was a silence. Chief Upwood stared at York, his expression mild, but his intent strong. I stared back at the man, still wondering where he was headed. I felt the moisture in the air increase.

"Except for Cally," York quickly amended his statement. "Cally's my sister. I don't think of her as a student."

"Ah," the chief murmured. "I can imagine you might not."

A drop of rain hit my nose. Standing outside any longer was ridiculous.

"Chief, Sergeant," I suggested, "would you like to come in and sit down?"

"Thank you so much, Ms. Lazar," Chief Upwood answered. "Let me say good-bye to your brother first."

"Good-bye?" York repeated suspiciously.

"It's been good talking to you, Mr. Lazar," the chief

explained. "But it was really your sister who we've come to see."

"Wait a minute—" York began.

"Listen, Bub," Sergeant Verne threw in. "It's friggin' cold out here, and the chief wants to talk to Ms. Lazar, okay? Is that clear enough for you?"

"But why?" York asked. Now, he sounded really confused.

"Does your sister tell you everything?" the sergeant demanded. "Huh? Maybe she'd like to talk to us alone, okay?"

"But . . ." York faltered. "Cally, do you want to talk to them alone?"

"No," I answered without thinking. Then I saw York come into martial focus. I didn't want him angry with the police. "But I'm fine. They just want to talk." I hoped I was telling the truth.

"Cally, I'll stay if you want me to," my brother offered.

"Jeez, what are you, her shadow?" Sergeant Verne taunted.

"Hey!" I snapped. "He's my brother, that's all. There's been a murder, and someone tried to get in my house. He's just protecting me."

"Sheesh," Sergeant Verne shot back. "Aren't you a little old to have your brother around all the time?"

"What are you trying to do, start a fight?" I demanded. I really didn't understand her. I looked at her more closely and saw frustration in her haggard features. And she was clearly having a bad aura day, full of fear. I wondered who else they'd tried to interview that day. Or maybe it'd been York's aborted attack that had scared her.

"Ms. Lazar," the chief cut in gently, "we would like to come in if that's okay with you. It would be simpler to speak to you privately, but if you wish your brother to stay, it's up to you."

That was enough reassurance for me. The chief might bore me to death, but he wasn't going to use a rubber hose. As long as he didn't leave me alone with Sergeant Verne.

"It's okay, York," I told my brother. "I'll be fine. Let me find out what they want. I'll call you later."

I watched as York struggled with himself, then finally heard what I'd said.

He gave me a quick hug good-bye, whispering, "Remember your cane," in my ear. And then he left.

I brought the chief and the sergeant into my client room, the three of us sitting in overstuffed chairs around my massage table. Generally, I fold up the massage table for guests ahead of time, but then I hadn't actually known I was going to have guests.

"Your bookshelves are lovely, Ms. Lazar," the chief observed. "Did you build them yourself?"

"No, the former owners built them," I said, letting my gaze linger a while on the patterning of the wood. Then I got to the point. "Why were you guys picking on York?" I asked.

"Your brother is a pain in—"

"Your brother can be a bit intimidating," Chief Upwood broke in. "We were rather startled by his . . ."

"His martial arts exercise," I finished for him.

"Yes, thank you," he replied, smiling.

Sergeant Verne looked down at her feet, embarrassment exuding from her pores.

"You never know when some gonzo is gonna take you down," she commented. "We try to be on guard, you know, but he snuck up on us."

Sergeant Verne was human. The jury was still out on the otherworldly Chief Upwood as far as I was concerned, though.

"So, did you come about the intruder?" I finally asked.

"What intruder?" the chief answered mildly.

"Oh, some guy tried to climb her hill last night," the sergeant belatedly informed him. "Her goats butted him down the hill, though." Verne smiled. "She's got three goats."

But Upwood wasn't as interested in the goats as he was in my midnight marauder.

"Did you actually see the intruder, Ms. Lazar?" he asked.

"Call me Cally," I suggested, and went on. "No, I never saw more than a figure. Though I know someone was here. I went and looked. The grasses are all mashed where I saw the person."

Chief Upwood was quiet, his hands folded in his lap. He might have been meditating, but I was pretty sure he was considering whether the person who had climbed my hill had anything to do with May's death.

"Do you want to look at the places where everything is mashed down?" I offered.

The chief brought his gaze up to mine. I was pretty sure he was thinking how lousy the weather was outside. But he rose anyway.

"What a good idea," he agreed graciously.

So I led the two of them down the hall and through my kitchen to my back deck. It was still wet and cold out there. I opened the gateway door in the latticework fence and pointed down the slippery hillside. Ohio bleated. Moscow and Persia continued to nibble.

"Those goats are so cool!" Sergeant Verne enthused, and for once, she didn't look so tired. "Can I pet them?"

"Ohio butts," I warned, smiling. The sergeant's enthusiasm was infectious. "Still if you want—"

"Perhaps later—" Chief Upwood suggested.

"Aw, Chief," Verne tried, clearly disappointed.

But Chief Upwood was just as clearly the indoor type. Still, he seemed to be the kind type. "I'll stay on the deck," he said. "Sergeant, search for evidence of the intruder."

So I stuffed my pockets with Spanish moss, and Sergeant Verne and I made our way down the slippery hillside together. I wasn't sure how much evidence she found, but she did get to pet all three goats, and Ohio did butt her while she was petting Persia. All in all, police/community relations were well served.

"Well, Sergeant," Chief Upwood prodded once we were back in the kitchen, seated at my table. "Was there evidence of an intruder?"

"Yes, sir," she answered. "Looks like whoever it was made it about halfway up the hill before the goats got to 'em and butted 'em back down. Marks of someone sliding. Can't really tell much, though."

"Do you think we should call in forensics?"

"Heh-heh," she chortled. "I wouldn't mind seeing ole Max getting butted down a hill. I'd—"

"Sergeant," Chief Upwood interrupted, his tone mild but reproving.

"Sorry, sir," Verne apologized, sitting up straight at attention. "I don't think forensics would find much . . . sir."

So much for the hillside investigation. My mind went back to the arrival of the Mostaza Police Department in the first place.

"What did you guys want to talk to me about anyway?" I demanded.

"I believe you have a friend, Warren Kapp?" Upwood hazarded.

I nodded as a flare went off in my mind.

"Well, Mr. Kapp had quite a bit to say about your experiences in the town of Fiebre," he went on. My skin tightened.

"So we called the local chief of police in Fiebre, one Deborah Dahl—"

"It wasn't my fault!" I blurted out. "Kapp always exaggerates, and—"

"Please, Ms. Lazar," Chief Upwood murmured. "Let me finish."

I shut my mouth. If I went to jail because of Kapp, he'd better get me back out.

"Deborah Dahl told us you'd been most helpful in solving their little mystery in Fiebre," the chief finished. "She said you were in fact, most cooperative. She suggested we call upon you for your opinion concerning May North's death."

Then the chief finally quit talking.

"Huh?" I said.

"He wants to know if you can tell us who the perp was," Sergeant Verne translated. "You know, who killed May North?"

"Me?" I yelped. "I'm just an energy worker. I don't have a clue—"

The doorbell rang then. It was just as well.

Chief Upwood and Sergeant Verne followed me back down the hall and through my client room as I went to open the front door. I hoped it was the intruder. I was certainly well protected.

But the person on my doorstep was no intruder. It was Joan Hussein. Joan Hussein is my good friend, a lushly big and beautiful woman of Arab ancestry with full lips, doe brown eyes, and a strong nose under a no-nonsense pageboy haircut. And she is an attorney. She hadn't turned her back on the law like I had. But somehow she forgave me, even for my twelve-step Attorneys Anonymous group.

"Are you okay, Cally?" she asked before I even got a chance to say hello.

"Sure, I'm fine," I told her. I turned to introduce my guests to Joan, and Joan to my guests.

After I'd finished, she took my arm, smiled politely at Chief Upwood and Sergeant Verne, and announced, "I'd like to speak with my client alone."

So much for police/community relations.

"Joan," I objected. "It's really okay. We're just talking and petting the goats and—"

"You are such an innocent," she stopped me short. "These two are the police, and they are 'talking' to you. And you have no legal representation."

"But—" I began.

"That'll be fine, Ms. Hussein," Chief Upwood put in. "We have no wish to subject Ms. Lazar to any undue pressure. She has been kind enough to cooperate—"

"That's exactly what I mean," Joan objected. "She shouldn't be cooperating without representation."

And they were off and running.

As the two discussed my legal status, Sergeant Verne whispered in my ear, "Hey, you really don't know who killed the old lady?"

"Nope," I whispered back.

"Chief," Verne cut in, "it's time to go now."

"Oh, my," the chief murmured. He widened his child-like eyes. "Is it?"

"Absolutely," Sergeant Verne assured him.

And the two representatives of the Mostaza Police Department left.

After I closed the door, I turned to Joan.

"Who sent you here?" I asked.

"York," she answered, and suddenly everything was clear. "He called me a while ago. He said the police were on your case, and he didn't know why. He was superworried. As soon as I could get free of Kapp, I came right over. I was fairly sure you wouldn't want Kapp involved."

"Kapp?"

"Kapp was at my place," she explained. "He said you and I were having lunch with him sometime soon."

"He also said I was supposed to meet the mayor of Mostaza tomorrow, but I don't know whether to believe him," I put in. "And he was the one that sicced the police on me in the first place. He keeps telling people that I've figured out who killed May North, or at least that I can figure it out."

"That could be very dangerous, Cally," Joan said solemnly.

"I know!" I shouted.

And then I spent a couple more hours talking to my friend Joan and trying to undo any harm to our friendship that my shout might have done. I called York and assured him somewhere between Joan's second and my third cup of tea that the police hadn't hurt me. I did not call Kapp.

When Joan finally left, I considered phoning Roy, but gave up the thought. If he wanted to talk to me, he would. I asked my cat, Leona, what I should do next. She lay on her back and put her legs up in the air.

So I went to bed and slept, with my cat beside me.

Sunday morning I woke to a damp, drizzly day. I showered and dressed and prepared for my morning clients. Energy workers don't take weekends off. Not if they want to remain solvent. My first client was hurting mentally. My second client was hurting physically. I hoped my work brought them each some relief.

By the time I'd eaten lunch, York had called with the hour and place of May's memorial service. I threw on a black jumpsuit for the occasion. And then I thought of May and her love of color. I changed into a flowered turtleneck and purple blazer and finally, I sat in meditation until I could think of May without crying.

Phil's Church of Divine Love was a small building, but its pews were filled to overflowing. I took a seat in one of the folding chairs that had been added in the back and wondered who all of these people were. Their voices buzzed around me.

"Quite a character . . ." I heard.

York touched my shoulder and sat down next to me in silence as the buzzing continued.

"Never knew her well . . ."

My eyes sought out Gerry Cheng and found him in the front row with his daughter, Becky. Ian and Eric were on his other side.

"Helped out my nephew when he was broke . . ." someone put in behind me.

Was that Sarah Quesada in the second row?

"She could really dance. . . ."

I saw Francie and Dutch Krentz near the front on the same aisle as Julie and John Turner.

"Did you ever see her topiary? . . ."

And Sergeant Verne and Chief Upwood were there, too, a few rows in front of us.

"Of course, that house . . ."

Then an organ played something that sounded like a Willy Nelson tune, and the voices quieted.

When the room was almost completely silent, Phil Morton stepped up to the podium. I barely recognized him in his ministerial garb. He wore a multicolored robe over a white clerical collar and stood straight as a yardstick. But his raisin-black eyes were still as intense as ever.

"May North is a child of God," he began, his deep quiet voice moving earnestly and slowly. "I expect there are some who might ask why I am certain of this. But I am certain. Lord, I am certain. Many of us have been led to believe that God wants us to suffer, but I truly believe God wants us to rejoice. Why else are we blessed by flowers in the field, oceans shimmering in the light, sun and rain, animals, the love of God, the love of friendship, the creativity of the mind, laughter, and the moon and stars at night? We are given these things, and God asks only that we accept them unconditionally. May North was one who accepted divine grace and joy unconditionally. Lord, she felt the sun on her skin and smiled, she saw an animal and reached out to touch it, she laughed heartily, and she loved greatly. In her, Lord, heaven and earth truly sang."

I heard sobs as Phil paused, and not just from Gerry Cheng. York placed his hand on one of mine gently as I removed my glasses with my other one.

"May is a child of God," Phil repeated. "And she knew this, deep in her soul. Unlike those of us who doubt, she received God's blessings unconditionally. And Lord, she gave back, without strings, to those in need. She loved her husband, Gerry, deeply and passionately, without artifice or self-consciousness. She loved many, and she loved us well. And now she is gone from our presence. But you need not worry; May is still accepting joy, perhaps the greatest joy of all. It is those of us who are left behind who grieve, Lord. But might we rejoice, too, in having had a woman like May North in our midst? Might we accept joy as unconditionally as this woman did?"

"Amen," a few scattered voices replied. A few others simply said, "Yes."

"I ask you to join me in prayer and thanks for the woman who was May North," Phil moved on. "And I ask you to rejoice as you do so."

And so we prayed, unfamiliar prayers for me and York from our freethinking household, but ones that were able to move us nonetheless. And then we sang. And, finally, Phil spoke again.

"We thank you, Lord, for the blessing of May North's presence in our lives," Phil pronounced. "Amen."

Phil bowed his head and stepped away from the podium.

A woman I didn't recognize was up next. "We have food and music," she announced. "You're all welcome to stay and join us."

York and I stayed to mingle.

An impromptu receiving line for Gerry Cheng was set up. He graciously shook hands and thanked people for their condolences and memories. When York and I got to him, he smiled wanly.

"I know May would appreciate your coming," he told us.

As we moved out of line, I thought, No, this man can't be a murderer. York stopped to talk to Eric as I made my way toward the food table.

Sarah snagged me before I could grab a cookie though. "Shoot, Cally, wasn't Phil great?" she demanded.

I nodded. But her radiant eyes told me hers wasn't an unbiased opinion.

"The donations are really coming in" she said, pointing at a large box with a slot at the top.

I took the hint and dropped a twenty-dollar bill in. Phil had done a good job for May. I just hoped his earnest words would help his own financial cause as well.

"I think May would have loved Phil's sermon," I agreed. "It was beautiful."

"Especially the bit about 'the sun on her skin,' huh?" a voice beside me put in. I knew whose voice it was before I turned. Dutch Krentz's. "That loser sounds like he had a thing for May."

Criminy, this man was mean. I looked around for Sergeant Verne. Maybe she could arrest him for pure nastiness.

Instead, I saw Julie Turner headed our way. I hoped it wasn't going to be the party all over again, and searched the room with my eyes for York.

Meanwhile, Sarah had shut her gaping mouth and reopened it.

"How dare you?" she challenged Dutch. "Just because May had a good heart, and Phil noticed. You wouldn't notice if your heart was on fire—"

"Dutch?" Julie's uncertain voice cut in.

"Yum, the lovely Ms. Turner," Dutch said. "I'd like to see the sun on *your* skin."

And then he put his hand on Julie's shoulder and moved it slowly up to her cheek.

Julie reared back. But it was Sarah who slapped him.

TEN

The sound of Sarah's slap was loud in my ears. Still, the buzz of the rest of the voices in the little church must have muted it. No one came rushing our way. No one even seemed to have noticed the altercation. Except, of course, for Dutch Krentz and Julie Turner.

Dutch had not only heard the slap, he had clearly felt it. A red blotch shaped like a hand stained one side of his angry face.

He raised his own hand and cocked it into a fist, ready to return Sarah's blow.

"You're going to be sorry you ever—" he began.

My cane flew up, blocking his hand. I didn't even feel my own body moving, it happened so fast.

Instead he turned on me. He dropped his head and thrust his face forward, his blue eyes glinting. I could feel his anger right down to my bone marrow.

"You think I have no right to hit her," he hissed. He twisted his mouth into a smile. "Fine. I'll just ruin her career in real estate. It shouldn't be hard. It isn't much of a career to start with."

Sarah paled. "I . . . I . . ." she tried. "You can't do that."

."I can do anything I want," Dutch responded. "You'd best remember that, girlie."

"Oh gosh!" Julie gasped. "I'm sorry, Sarah. I didn't mean—"

Dutch turned his blue eyes on Julie, and she stopped talking, cold. Then she turned and made her way across the room to her husband, John, her gait somewhere between a walk and a run. She pressed her face against her husband's chest. He looked over at the three of us still standing there, frowned, and put his arm around his wife's trembling shoulders.

"See you later, ladies," Dutch said, his tone almost merry. But I didn't buy the tone. His aura was orange with fury as he walked away, grabbing his wife, Francie, by the arm and exiting the church.

I turned back to Sarah, my pulse easing back down into the double digits. Sarah's clear skin was still pale with shock under her black hair.

"Shoot, Cally," she murmured. "I hope I'm not in trouble. It was just the way he was going on with Ms. Turner. That's sexual harassment. I couldn't just stand there, could I?"

"No," I agreed, smiling at Sarah Quesada. Ill considered as her slap might have been, she'd been trying to protect Julie Turner. Sarah was a true gentleman in a female's body.

She smiled back at me tentatively. "Hey, thanks for stopping him from hitting me," she whispered. "That was really something, huh? I mean, sometimes I don't think things through, but jeez, he was scary."

"Can he really make trouble for you?" I asked.

She frowned. "I'm not sure. But I gotta go for it, you know. I mean, I can't let him scare me. I gotta keep on keeping on."

I reached out and patted her arm. "You will," I assured her, hoping I was right. "Dutch will make more trouble for himself than you if he tries anything."

Julie Turner came walking back up to us, dignity back in her step.

"I wanted to thank you both," she offered, her high-pitched voice roughened by tears. "I get overwhelmed sometimes. It's hard to know what to do. I don't know what's the matter with Mr. Krentz. I'm just sorry to get you two involved."

"Hey, it's okay," Sarah told her. "I would have been weirded out, too. He's a nasty old man. Gotta realize that after the things he said about May."

"I thought maybe you two could come over to my house," Julie suggested diffidently. "We could talk. I could make some tea."

"Oh, shoot, Ms. Turner—"

"Julie, call me Julie."

"Can I visit another day?" Sarah suggested. She bent forward and whispered. "See, I have this kinda date with Phil this afternoon. At least, I hope so." Her skin pinkened with pleasure. "He's so cool."

Julie nodded. She even smiled a little. It looked good on her face.

"And *I'd* love to come over, but I still haven't had lunch," I told Julie. Her smile faded. "But I could see you in an hour or so," I added quickly. I wanted to see that smile again. And I did.

"Oh, sure, Cally," she trilled. "Anytime. I have some neat herbal teas. John travels all over and brings all kinds of teas home."

I nodded. There was something that felt wounded about Julie Turner. I looked at her more closely, seeing self-consciousness, self-pity, and fear. For a PTA mom, she was awfully insecure. I hoped she wasn't really looking forward to a career in politics. Her skin wasn't thick enough.

Julie nodded across the room, where Gerry Cheng stood with his daughter, Becky. "The poor man," she murmured. "I don't know what to say to him. It usually seems like I talk too much, but I can't think of a single word to say about his loss."

"Want to go talk to him together?" I offered.

"Oh, that'd be nice," she answered gratefully.

"I'm gonna try to catch Phil," Sarah whispered. Her skin pinkened again. "Gotta try, right?"

"Go get him," I urged.

Julie and I watched as Sarah trotted over to Phil at the door of the church and tugged on the sleeve of his robe. He turned to her, and a sweet expression of happy surprise softened his features. I wished it was that easy with Roy. But I still had to help Julie pay her respects to Gerry Cheng, so I shook off the thought of Roy and walked with her to the grieving widower.

"Julie," Gerry greeted her. "I'm so glad you came. May cared about you more than—"

"Oh gosh," Julie interrupted, blushing. "I know May loved *you*. You were all she talked about. You made her life so happy."

"Aw, I'm just an old dog," Gerry demurred, but he looked as pleased as seemed possible for someone in his stunned state. Julie had done pretty well for all her fears about finding the right words to say.

"May adored Daddy," Becky Cheng put in. "I can't say I blame her. I just wish I'd gotten to know her better without judging."

"Me, too," Julie told her sadly. "Me, too."

Ian and Eric stood like bodyguards behind Gerry. I nodded at each of them. Eric nodded back, and Ian winked.

"I was just telling Becky how May got into topiary," Gerry began. "We went up to these big ole gardens on some island in Canada, and May saw a bush shaped like an elephant and went crazy. She wanted a whole zoo. So she took this class and, dang, if she wasn't whacking away at the bushes herself. Goofiest thing you ever saw, but she could make them look just like animals."

"Except for the porcupine," Ian put in.

Gerry's snort of laughter rang out. "Yep, she couldn't keep the quills on the porcupine."

Ian sniffled in appreciation. His nose was red, as if he were coming down with a cold.

"May was quite a woman," I put in. "I didn't realize she sculpted those bushes herself."

"May could do just about anything she put her mind to," Gerry pronounced, and began to tell stories to prove it. Phil had been eloquent, but Gerry spoke with the animation of love. It didn't matter what he was saying, as much as the way he said it. There was no doubt in my mind that he'd truly adored his wife as much as she'd adored him.

I don't know how much later it was when York tapped me on the shoulder.

"Cally," my brother whispered in my ear, "I saw Roy outside."

"Roy?" I repeated, my mind slowly shifting gears.

"Yeah, he's across the street. I think he's keeping his eye on you."

I said my good-byes abruptly, shaking Gerry's hand and promising Julie I'd see her in a little while before I hurried toward the church door, where Phil was deep in earnest

conversation with Sarah. I passed them without their noticing and burst out into the cold light of the winter's day.

Unfortunately, I wasn't the only one on the sidewalk. A
camera flashed in my face.

"Were you a friend of May North's?" a voice asked. The
voice was attached to a handheld microphone and a
woman with tall blond hair. The media, such as it was in
Mostaza, had arrived.

"How do you feel about Ms. North's death?" another
voice asked. "Is it true that the police are treating this as a
case of murder?"

I looked over the bobbing heads and across the street, hoping for a glimpse of Roy's reddish brown hair. And then I saw
him, turning his back and walking away down a side street.

I stuck out my cane to clear the way and sprinted across
the street to the sound of shouts behind me. But Roy was
gone when I got there. I turned the corner where I'd seen
him disappear, but I still couldn't find him. If York was
right, and Roy was keeping his eye out for me, his vision
was better than mine. Dack.

I was panting with exertion when I smelled aftershave
behind me. I turned, raising my cane as I did.

"Hey, Lazar," Kapp greeted me, lowering his own cane.
"Good job with the press. Mother of God, they're obnoxious. Good thing they haven't heard that you're a psychic
detective yet."

"You wouldn't!" I hissed, raising my cane again.

"Heh-heh," Kapp chortled. He put his hand over his
heart. "Would I do something like that?"

"Over your dead body," I told him.

He was still laughing when my friend Joan walked up
behind him.

"I'm hungry," she announced, patting Kapp's arm as

she passed him to give me a hug. "Are you through pulling Cally's chain? Can we go to lunch now?"

I looked at my watch. It was still before five. Maybe I'd get my lunch before dinner after all. Or maybe I'd just have a two-for-one meal.

"Let me say good-bye to York, then we can eat," I offered.

York wasn't hard to find. He'd made his own way past the media and was almost to me when I looked up.

"Did you catch him?" he shouted.

I shook my head.

"Catch who?" Kapp asked, frowning. He hated to be left out of anything.

York opened his mouth. I turned quickly to Kapp. "Why weren't you at the memorial?" I demanded.

York shut his mouth on cue. Lazars are smart that way.

"People to see; sources to pump," Kapp answered me. He was smiling again. "Hooboy, people are talking about this death. Let's eat and share information."

There was a café across from the church that looked worth trying. We peeked in the windows and saw comfortable leatherette booths and a bakery case stacked high with cakes and pies. That was enough for Kapp.

"This is the place," he announced, and headed toward the glass doors.

A handsome young man with rhinestone studs in *both* ears showed us to our booth and read off the specials of the day: soups, salads, and sandwiches. Then he handed us our menus and left us on our own.

"So who do you think did it?" Kapp whispered the minute the waiter was gone.

Joan just shook her head and rolled her eyes.

"I don't have a clue," I whispered back.

"Huh!" Kapp snorted. "Well, at least I have clues, lots of them."

"But do you know what you want to eat?" Joan pressed him.

Kapp made harrumphing noises, but he opened his menu. I opened mine, too, peering over the top at my two remaining attorney friends: Kapp, the elder statesman and wiseacre, and Joan, truly wise and peaceful as a sunny day in the country. I smiled, thinking that May would have liked them both. And then I really looked at my menu.

When the waiter came back, Joan ordered the soup and salad special, Kapp got the cheesesteak and fries, and I asked for the "as you like it" salad with cheddar and Swiss cheeses, avocado slices, hard-boiled eggs, and marinated green beans.

"So, who do you think has a previous drug conviction?" Kapp quizzed me the moment the waiter was gone.

I thought. Dutch Krentz flashed through my mind, but he wasn't really the right age group. Then it came to me.

"Ian," I said.

"Damn," Kapp complained. "You really are psychic. It isn't fair."

"If she's psychic, how come she doesn't know who did it?" Joan threw in.

Kapp turned and glared at her.

"Do you think Ian still has a drug problem?" I asked, remembering his red nose. Cold or cocaine?

"Hell, the kid could do drugs every hour on the hour, for all I know. All my guy got was that Ian was convicted a few years back for drug possession. Just for his own use, he claimed. He pled out, got community service. Why? You think his drug use could be a reason to kill his landlady?"

I thought about May. She never would have turned in Ian, even if he was using drugs. So how did that make a motive?

"Come on, Cally," Kapp prodded. "I can't ever tell what you're thinking. Do you know something I don't know?"

Joan cleared her throat. Our waiter had returned with our drinks.

Once he'd left, I sipped my herbal tea thoughtfully. "I can't think of anything more about Ian than you can," I finally admitted.

"Well, there're still two boarders to go," Kapp tossed out, leaning forward in the booth.

"Eric Ford?" I prompted.

"Man's broke, and he's a doctor," Kapp declared, shaking his head. "I know enough about broke lawyers, but doctors. Hell, that's downright strange."

"It's 'cause of some sort of insurance thing—" I began.

"Oh, I know all about that IPA crap," Kapp cut back in. "But the malpractice suit. Betcha didn't know about that."

"No, tell me," I agreed eagerly.

"That guy is a real idiot when it comes to insurance. Got screwed by his insurance deal when he was in it, then he kept practicing after he was *uninsured.* Someone sued over a minor operation, and he had to settle. It broke him."

"Poor man," Joan said gently.

"Huh!" Kapp snorted. "It's damn stupid, that's what."

And our meals came. I wondered if the waiter was listening to Kapp. There was hardly anyone else in the place at that time of day. He probably couldn't help it.

I poured a ginger-sesame vinaigrette over my salad and dug in hungrily. All anyone was going to hear from me for a while was crunching.

But Kapp couldn't resist the possibility of sharing more

information after a few bites of his cheesesteak. First, he asked me what I knew about Gerry Cheng.

It was a good question. All I really knew was that he was May's husband. And that he was wealthy in his own right. At least that was the impression I'd gotten from his daughter. I took another bite. The salad was tasty, the dressing not too vinegary and well matched with the cheese and avocado and eggs.

"Gerry had his own software company," Kapp told me between bites of cheesesteak and french fries. "Only some people thought he stole some of his software. It was a big scandal a few years back."

"Racism," Joan pronounced, her soup spoon still in the air.

Kapp nodded. "That's the way it looked to me. Racism and jealousy." He dipped a fry in catsup. "Everyone hates it when someone else scores big-time, and Gerry Cheng hit the top. Sold his company for a bundle. But there're still people in Silicon Valley who don't trust the guy."

I swallowed. "How about Becky?" I asked.

"Clean as far as I can tell," Kapp muttered, frowning.

"You don't have to look so disappointed," Joan told him. Her soulful brown eyes hinted at laughter.

"All right, all right," Kapp grumbled. "She teaches biology at Glasse State University. And she's political, people say. That's about it."

"Where do you get all this information?" Joan asked.

Kapp grinned and smoothed the sparse hair over his bald spot. "Connections," he answered. "Nothing like connections for building a case. I got 'em in law enforcement, legal fraternities, the media, you name it—"

"The old boys' club," Joan summed up.

"Hey, when you get as old as I am, even *you* can be in

the old boys' club," Kapp told her, and wiped his mouth with his napkin.

I laughed. I couldn't help it. Kapp was some old boy, all right.

"I'll join as long as they have a swimming pool," Joan commented placidly, spearing a piece of carrot from her salad.

"Speaking of pools," Kapp went on, after popping the last of his cheesesteak into his mouth. "Julie Turner is a medium-sized frog in a tiny pool called the Mostaza PTA. She wants to run for school board. But she has a prior conviction for drunk driving. It was a long time ago, but it might turn the voters off if it became public."

"Do you think May knew?" I mused.

"A better question might be whether May would have *told* if she had known," Joan put in.

"Right," I agreed. "I don't think she would have. As far as I can tell, May put a lot of people's backs up, but she wasn't an informer. She had enough trouble defending her own past. Not everyone can relate to the concept of madamhood. I have to admit, it bothered me when I first found out. It's so midgin easy to be judgmental."

"Damn shame she was killed," Kapp muttered, shaking his head. "I would have liked to meet her."

"Yeah, you would have," I assented.

"Anyway," Kapp went on, "John Turner looks as clean as Becky Cheng. And, yes, I am disappointed. One parking ticket was all I could find. He has some kind of import business." He paused, then smiled. "Still there's always Phil Morton, our saintly minister."

"Don't tell me you found dirt on Phil," I said, my pulse jumping as I thought of Sarah Quesada's pinkened face.

•

"Guess where he found God?" Kapp asked.

I thought of Phil in prison, or in a prisoner of war camp, or . . . in a mental hospital.

"Was he institutionalized?" I tried. "A mental breakdown?"

"Dammit!" Kapp shouted, hitting the table with his fist. "You are psychic. Phil found God in the loony bin!"

ELEVEN

"It's called deduction, Kapp," Joan murmured. She calmly took another bite of lettuce. "Cally knows that Phil's too young for a prisoner of war camp and too ethical for prison. But she's not so sure about his mental stability. There aren't that many possible places to be institutionalized."

I glared at Joan. Dack. I wasn't the psychic one. She was. I searched my mind. There had to be other places to be institutionalized. Orphanages, maybe—

"All right," Kapp grumbled. "Fine."

Then I remembered just what we were talking about. Poor Phil. Poor Sarah.

"What kind of breakdown did Phil have?" I asked quietly.

"Aw, figure it out yourself," Kapp replied ungraciously. But something must have shown on my face because he relented. "Morton was a severe manic-depressive, according to my sources. He tried to commit suicide when he was just out of high school. They put him in the loony bin. Then he told everyone he'd found his calling about a year later. He got out and went back to school: four years undergrad, four years in the seminary. He was in a branch of his weirdo church back East somewhere, and they sent him out here."

"What do you mean, 'weirdo church'?" I demanded.

"It's called the 'Church of Divine Love' for God's sake," Kapp snapped. "You ever hear of it before, huh?" He put up his hand and began counting his fingers. "Catholic, Lutheran, Episcopalian, Baptist, Methodist. Those are churches—"

"Christian churches," Joan reminded him. "Christianity isn't the only religion on this planet."

"Yeah, okay. But I still don't think it's a real church."

Somehow, the question of Phil Morton's viability as a suspect was becoming lost in a religious debate.

I took a breath and broke back into the conversation, loudly. "Has Phil had any mental problems since he . . . he found his calling?" I asked.

"Nah," Kapp admitted. "At least as far as I know, nobody's popped him back in the loony bin."

That was a relief. But I didn't have long to enjoy it. Just as I was reassuring myself that Sarah wasn't courting a psycho, Kapp leaned forward and threw out another tidbit of information.

"Now, Dutch Krentz was charged with assault twice. But neither of the charges ended up in convictions because both of the victims were prostitutes. Prostitutes don't make credible witnesses."

My stomach lurched. I thought of the way Dutch had cocked his fist at Sarah. Dack. Would he hurt her in some way? Would he hunt her down and hurt her physically?

"Sarah—" I began.

"Sarah's clean, too," Kapp interrupted me, misinterpreting my use of her name. I'd wanted to tell him about the incident at the memorial. "She's got a couple of speeding tickets. She's on the Mostaza Planning Commission."

"Any hint of corruption there?" I asked, distracted from Sarah's plight by her possible suspectability.

"No, why?" Kapp shot back, sudden alertness in his tone.

"It's just that she liked May," I said defensively. "And May's house doesn't look like it belongs in Mostaza. Someone at the party said Sarah helped May get approval for the place."

Kapp laughed. "Holy Mary, that house doesn't belong in this *country*. Maybe May North greased a few palms, but no big deal." He looked thoughtful for a moment. "Dutch Krentz is on that commission, too."

"And—" I prodded.

"I don't know," he admitted. "Just a coincidence, I guess. It's a helluva small town."

"What else?" I demanded, looking at my watch. It was getting close to six, and I'd promised to visit Julie.

"Francie's clean, too," Kapp obliged. "Married a rich older man some years ago. He died. She married Dutch. End of story." He sighed. "Nobody in this town has any good secrets."

I smiled at Kapp for a moment. Then I got up from my chair and threw a ten-dollar bill on the table, reaching over to give Joan a shoulder hug at the same time.

"I gotta get going," I told them. "I'll try to find you some better secrets."

"Whoa." Kapp stopped me, holding up his hand. "What about your appointment with the mayor?"

"Aw, cut it out, Kapp," I objected.

"Hey, would I kid you?" he asked. "You've got an appointment to talk to the Honorable Natalie Gleason at seven o'clock."

"Seven o'clock!" I yelped. "She wants to meet with me on a Sunday evening?"

"Hell, she thinks you're interesting, Lazar," Kapp filled me in. He shrugged. "What can I say?"

"But—"

"City hall, seven o'clock," he insisted. "You can't miss it."

I pretty much ran to my car. I passed city hall on the way to Julie Turner's house. Luckily, they were minutes apart. But even in those few minutes, I saw a car that looked like Roy's Saab behind me. Or at least, I thought I did; then it disappeared from my rearview mirror.

Julie's home was at the address I'd looked up in the phone book that sat in the backseat of my car, on the other side of the street that May North's house presided over. *Her* home looked like it belonged on the street, a large, tasteful, mission-style adobe building in a yard of ecologically correct shrubbery. The door I knocked on looked like a recent addition, made of intricately carved wood with an Asian flavor.

Julie was at the door within seconds of my knocking.

"Oh, Cally, you came!" she exclaimed as if surprised, her blue eyes large in her model's face.

"Of course I did," I answered. "But," I warned her, "I have an appointment at seven. You have to help me remember to leave a little before the hour so I can make it."

"Oh, I will," she promised, and crossed her heart with her hand like a child would.

A Persian cat wandered out to join us as Julie ushered me into a living room filled with designer treasures. Thick carpets, a brass gong, a carved Buddha, and painted ceremonial masks gave the room a character oddly different than Julie Turner's classic beauty would bring to mind. It even smelled exotic, of cedar and incense and more.

"John's down at the store for a little while, working on the books," Julie told me as her son, Zack, entered the room. "So, it's just us three."

Then she stared at me. I wondered if she wanted to tell

me something. I could see the wisps of fear in her aura again.

"Hey, Mom," Zack broke into the awkward silence. "Do you want me to make tea or something?"

"That would be great, sweetie," she told him.

Zack stood up and ambled into the kitchen. Julie and I sat across from each other on chairs as intricately carved as her front door. I was glad for the cushions of brightly woven colors that padded the seats. Without them, the chairs could have been used as medieval torture instruments. Even with the cushions, they weren't really comfortable.

"It's so nice to see you," Julie tried once we were seated. "I wanted to connect, you know, to someone else who knew May."

I nodded, though I didn't really quite understand because I didn't really know May that well. The Persian cat slid behind a cabinet with more than a dozen little drawers with brass pulls.

"I have a lot of friends from the PTA and stuff, but May was, I guess, special, you'd say," Julie went on. Her eyes filled with tears. Criminy, she was truly grieving over May North's death. Of course, she wanted to talk.

"She *was* special," I agreed quickly, my mind racing to add something. "She made me laugh," I offered finally.

"Me, too," Julie murmured. "All those silly stories. She could really tell a story."

"Did you know her long?" I asked.

Julie blinked. "I—" she began.

"Oh, Mrs. North," Zack answered for her, back from the kitchen. "I kinda liked her. She was pretty cool for an old lady—"

"Say 'a senior citizen,' " Julie corrected her son. "Or 'an

elder.' It might hurt someone's feelings if you called her an 'old lady,' honey."

"Nah," her son disagreed. "Mrs. North was cool that way. She called herself an old lady lots of times."

I heard the teakettle singing from the next room.

Zack made his way back to the kitchen before his mother could start another round of corrections.

"Your son's a good kid," I told her. "Not many teenagers offer to make tea."

Julie smiled. "He *is* a good kid. I probably push him too hard." She shook her head. "Being a mother isn't as easy as I thought it would be. I always thought that when it came my turn, I'd be perfect. Even after fourteen years, I still get delusions like that." Then she laughed, a bright startled sound.

I tried to laugh with her. But I wasn't relaxed enough for a real laugh. Something made me want to help Julie out of her morass of insecurity. Maybe because I could feel true wit and sweetness hiding inside of her. But I wasn't there in my healing capacity.

"Is Zack your only child?" I asked.

"Oh gosh, yes," she murmured fervently. Maybe her difficulty as a mother wasn't just a joke.

"How about you, Cally?" she returned. "Do you have kids?"

"Nope."

"Well, don't worry, there's plenty of time yet," she assured me.

It seemed like people were always saying that to me. It was as if I had a sign on my forehead that read Woman Seeks Child, only the sign wasn't mine. As far as I could tell, all I wanted at the moment was Roy. And, of course, my goats and cat. I was still trying to frame a reply when

Zack came back in the room with a steaming teapot, three cups, teaspoons, and a jar of honey on a tray.

"Get another cup, will you, Zack?" his mother requested. "Your father's coming home soon."

"He's not my real father, okay?" Zack snapped. Yep, motherhood was not perfect for Julie. "My real father's dead."

"Now, Zack—" she began.

"Well, he isn't," he insisted. "He's just my stepdad. And he won't let me do anything really cool. Like my hair." I looked at his medium-length brown hair. It looked fine to me. "My best friend has this really cool cut with purple spikes and everything. But Dad would kill me if I did that. We have to be like the perfect American family or something."

"Zack." This time Julie's voice held a real warning.

"I know, I know," he said. "I shouldn't complain. Like everything's cool when it isn't. I should be glad I have nice clothes—"

"Stop it, right now," Julie ordered. I was surprised she could even say the words.

Zack looked surprised for a moment, too. He looked into his mother's eyes. "I'm sorry," he mumbled.

"It's okay," I put in automatically. "No one makes it through adolescence without being angry—"

"John's been a very good second father to Zack," Julie pronounced. "He takes good care of us both."

Zack sighed and took a seat, placing the tray on a table in front of him.

"He has some kind of import business, doesn't he?" I asked, trying to smooth the conversational waters.

"Oh yes," Julie answered, brightening. She pointed around the room. "He imports beautiful stuff from all over the world. Carvings, weavings, paintings, rugs, all kinds of things. Mostly from African and Asian countries. He served in Vietnam. That's when he got interested in collecting."

"Your décor is beautiful," I told her honestly. Even if it wasn't exactly comfortable. "Did John find these things?"

"Oh, yes," she breathed, looking around her living room happily. "He has wonderful taste. Did you see the door?"

I nodded.

"He brought that door home from one of his trips. He knew it would be perfect. It had been on a Buddhist monastery that was torn down. When he got it here, it was too big for the doorway. We had to pull down the entire structure around the door to get the doorway big enough. But it was worth it."

I nodded again and snuck a look at my watch. It wasn't anywhere near time to leave yet.

"John has a real eye for beauty," Julie gushed on. At least she seemed relaxed now, even if I wasn't. "He even chooses my clothing, sometimes."

And probably Zack's, too, I thought, but kept my mouth shut.

"Anyone want some tea?" Zack asked now.

"Yes, please," I told him.

Zack did the pouring ritual for me, then for his mother. He still hadn't brought out a fourth cup for his stepfather.

"Clothing can be an important factor in the way people perceive you," Julie went on, as Zack handed us our cups. I eyed her conservative cream-colored cashmere sweater and wool pants and decided that she and my sister Geneva would never be on the same design team. And I would have bet that Zack would have preferred some kind of rocker T-shirt over his blameless, golf knit.

"You see," Julie recited. "Nonthreatening clothes encourage community and meaningful dialogue. I've learned a lot in the PTA. And now that I'm running for school board, it seems like I'm finding my true self. Oh gosh, I'm jabbering away again, aren't I?" she finished.

I looked back at her, caught off guard for a moment of silence. "Oh no," I answered finally. "Wonderful tea."

I took a sip. It was sweet with honey and tasted of cloves and licorice. Actually, it was good. I would have bet John had chosen it—and I would have won my bet, too.

"John found this tea in Holland of all places. It was imported from someplace else, I can't remember where, but he found the source and gets it shipped directly to us."

I took another sip.

"Unique," I offered.

"Oh, gosh, yes," Julie agreed, smiling. "Everything John finds is unique. Have you ever visited his store?"

"No, is it in Mostaza?"

"Uh-huh," she murmured, sipping her own tea. "It's right downtown. He carries really nice things."

"No Grateful Dead T-shirts?" I asked, smiling to show I was joking.

Zack let out a snort of laughter, but Julie wasn't cued by my smile or his snort.

"Oh, no, Cally," she replied solemnly. "John carries all quality things. All imports."

"Mom," Zack said gently, "she was joking."

"Oh!" Julie looked at me. I kept my smile in place. "I get it! Grateful Dead, right." Then she giggled.

My body began to relax again. I reminded myself that I had felt real sweetness and wit in this woman.

"Oh, Cally, you're so funny," she told me. Then her face clouded. I just knew she was thinking of May.

"Julie," I murmured. "May was unique, too. She's probably loving whatever journey she's on now. And I'm sure she wouldn't want us to grieve for too long."

"Do you really think so?" Julie whispered, her eyes filled with tears again.

"I really think so," I pronounced, as if I knew. "And there's nothing wrong with crying either."

"Oh, Cally!" she keened.

Zack got up and put his arms around his mother while she cried. He *was* a good kid.

I heard the front door open, and Julie and Zack looked up over my head.

I swiveled around and saw John Turner walking into the room, handsome, well dressed, and well coifed, of course.

Julie wiped her tears. Zack stood up and stepped away from us.

"Hi, Dad," he greeted his stepfather.

John nodded and patted the boy's shoulder, looking with concern at his wife.

"Hello, Ms. Lazar," he said. "I hope I'm not interrupting." I would have thought he was teasing if his voice hadn't been so quiet.

"Call me Cally," I suggested. "No, you're not interrupting. Julie and I were just talking about May."

John walked behind his wife and put his hands on her shoulders.

"Honey, are you still feeling bad?" he asked.

"A little," she answered. I didn't want to see her feel a lot of bad if what I'd just witnessed was "a little."

"My wife's delicate," he explained. "But she's got me and Zack to take care of her."

"Oh, John," Julie objected mildly. She blushed and smiled shyly, reaching back to pat the hand on her shoulder. For a moment, I could see her attraction to this quiet man with all the answers. At least he didn't see dark forces when she needed him.

John sat down in the chair that Zack had vacated and slowly poured himself a cup of tea, mixing in a teaspoon of honey. He took a long sip and looked at me. His brown eyes were remote. I snuck a peek at his aura . . . and saw nothing.

There are a myriad of reasons that an aura can be invisible. Sometimes issues are so deeply buried that the aura is buried with them. Sometimes a person can be so overwhelmed that their aura shrinks away into invisibility. Drugs can do strange things to an aura. And sometimes a person's core value of privacy is so great that they put up unconscious shields. I was figuring John for one of the private ones.

"So you're a psychic," he threw out.

"An energetic healer," I corrected him. "I can't read people's minds. I just sense their needs and blockages and help their bodies heal themselves."

"And that's what you were doing with May?" he asked.

I nodded. His face didn't change, but I could feel his sneer. People sneered at my work all the time. But most of them did it with their faces.

"My wife was very attached to May," John commented. "May was just a neighbor, but she wasn't a bad old broad."

I waited for Julie to correct him on his language. But she just nodded and looked at her lap.

John took another sip of tea and then pronounced, "Those boarders of hers were trouble though."

My mind took in what he was saying slowly.

"What do you mean?" I asked finally.

"May told me that one of her boarders was giving her some trouble," he clarified, shrugging as if it weren't that important to him. "She never said which one though."

My brain flipped through the cards. Ian? Eric? Phil?

The phone rang, and Julie leaped out of her chair and ran through a side door, snagging the phone before a second ring. It was impossible not to overhear her.

"Dutch," Julie said after a few moments. "No." It wasn't clear whether she was talking about Dutch or to him.

John got up from his chair and followed in Julie's footsteps. Then I heard *his* voice, but his voice was too muted for me to understand his words.

I tried though. But as I concentrated on eavesdropping, a new voice entered my consciousness.

"Mrs. North was really cool," Zack whispered in my ear. So much for my eavesdropping. "All that stuff that people said about her being weird, waving from her balcony, you know . . ."

"Nude," I prompted gently, turning his way.

"Yeah, that," he agreed. "She didn't mean anything weird. She was just being, like, friendly, you know?"

"I know," I told him sincerely. "She didn't think any more about clothes than a cat or a dog would."

"Yeah!" Zack exclaimed, his young face brightening. "That's it. See, it was cool."

But before we could talk any more, Julie and John were back in the living room.

"Was that Dutch?" I began. "Did he apologize—"

"Oh, my gosh, Cally," Julie interrupted excitedly. "It's almost seven. You have to go!"

I looked at my watch. Actually, less than half an hour had passed. But Julie was right. It was time to go. I could tell by the way John was looking at me, his hands on his wife's shoulders. The Turners needed their privacy.

TWELVE

After a quick round of good-byes, I got in my Honda, with more than a half hour to kill before I met the mayor. As I pulled away from the curb, I wondered why Julie had wanted me to leave so soon. Was she having some kind of nervous breakdown? Maybe that was why John was so protective of her. Then I remembered what Kapp had said about her drunk-driving conviction. Was Julie a secret drinker? Or maybe she was just naturally more emotional than most people. Her grief over May's death had seemed sincere enough.

I drove slowly down the road, searching my rearview mirror for Roy. I had to drive slowly since I was thinking about the Turners and wondering if Roy was following me at the same time. Somehow, I imagined he was. I just wished I could see him. But he was as invisible as John Turner's aura.

Still, there was someone visible in *front* of me. Francie Krentz was walking down the sidewalk. There was no way I could miss her round, smiling face and dripping curls. She'd changed into what looked something like an abbreviated ministerial robe, tie-dyed and beaded over pale yellow leggings. She wouldn't fit on the same design team as my sister Geneva any more than Julie Turner would, though for far different reasons. Francie raised her arm and waved my way.

I pulled my car over without hesitation. I wanted to know what was going on with Dutch Krentz, mayor or no mayor. And where Francie was, Dutch would hopefully be nearby.

"Hi, Francie!" I greeted her once I'd parked the Honda and leaped from the driver's seat with a cane assist. I didn't have much time, and I wanted to make the most of it. "Are you on your way home?"

She bobbed her head up and down. "I always take a little stroll this time in the evening," she told me. "The twilight is so magical, you know. So freeing."

She was right. I looked up. The sky was the blue of a Maxfield Parrish poster, shimmering onto the gardens of this Mostaza street. And I hadn't even noticed until Francie had pointed it out.

"It's lovely," I muttered. I felt ashamed that I'd considered this woman shallow. She saw the magic of light.

"Would you like to come in?" Francie offered, pointing to a nearby grayed redwood house, surrounded by a sea of ice plants with early purple blooms.

"Why, thank you," I said sincerely. "Though I have to leave for an appointment before seven."

"Oh, do come in for a moment," she insisted. "It's cold out. And I just know that Dutch will want to see you, too."

Francie saw the light, but I wasn't so sure about the quality of her perception of her husband. Still, I agreed readily, and we finished her stroll home together in the cool evening air.

Two little dachshunds greeted us in a fervor of excitement when Francie opened the door. I thought I could hear

Dutch in the background, speaking to someone in what sounded like German. And then all I could hear was the yipping of the dachshunds.

"Oh, my little Lammfleisch," Francie murmured bending over to pat the squiggling dogs. "And my little Zwiebeln. Have you been good boys?"

The dachshunds yipped their reassurances and turned, prancing into the Krentzs' warm living room.

Francie and I followed. It was clear that two different people with different designer preferences lived in the Krentz household. The walls were a soft mauve, and the rug the same mauve, just a shade deeper. Plush furnishings in several pastel shades were interspersed with crystals of various sizes mounted on brass pedestals. And then there was the nautical theme. Paintings of boats in dark wood frames hung on the walls next to multicolored collages. A ship's clock dominated the mantelpiece. I was fairly certain that the crystals and collages and pastels belonged to Francie and that the ships belonged to Dutch. But I could have been wrong.

"Is it all right if I call you Cally?" Francie asked me.

"Of course," I agreed.

"Then you can call me Francie," she offered with a giggle as if she had said something very witty.

I smiled back as I frantically searched my brain for small talk. I'd been working on people with serious issues for too long.

"You have a healing practice, don't you, Cally?" she said.

I nodded energetically. "Are the collages yours?" I guessed.

"Oh, they are!" Francie exclaimed. "You're so clever."

She took me by the hand and led me to the wall where a canvas that had to be at least a couple of yards wide hung. It was festooned with swatches of cloth, newspaper clippings, and recipes. The recipes were sweet: cookies and cake. The clippings weren't. BRUTAL SLAYINGS, BLOODBATH, TERRORISM, RAPE jutted out from the canvas. I kept my eyes on the collage while I tried to find the right words to comment.

"Wonderful juxtaposition," I pronounced finally.

Francie clapped her hands together. "Oh, yay! Most people don't understand—"

"Francie, what the hell—" Dutch interrupted.

We turned as he walked into the living room, a frown on his face. His frown deepened when he saw me, but he changed it into a smile in less than a breath.

"To what do we owe the pleasure, Ms. Lazar?" Dutch asked.

"Oh, Dutch, call her Cally," Francie instructed him in a teasing tone. "I do. Cally stopped by because I asked her to. She likes my work."

"I see," Dutch answered.

"Come, have a seat, Cally," Francie offered, gesturing to a pale blue armchair. "I know you can't stay for long, but I wanted to ask you more about your healing practice."

I lowered myself into the soft embrace of the chair, and Francie and Dutch sat across from me on a lavender sofa. The two dachshunds settled in, bracketing their owners' feet.

"So, Cally—" Francie began.

"She's here to ask about May," Dutch interrupted her. "She wants to know who killed May."

I thought about arguing but conceded instead with a short, "Yes, I do."

"Well." Dutch leaned forward. "I'd look at those boarders, myself. They're all such losers. I don't know what hold

May had over them. But why else would they live like that, one to a room, sharing the same bathroom? They all live on the top floor, you know."

"Dutch thinks she got them drunk and made them sign a contract or something," Francie added.

Dutch nodded smugly, settling back into the plush cushions of the sofa. When he wasn't angry, he was a good-looking man, with his lush moustache and intense eyes. And his story about the boarders sounded plausible. Maybe he truly believed it.

"You know, if I were you," Dutch went on. "I'd especially check into Ian Oxton. I'd bet he's on some kind of drug."

"Oh, Ian is an artist, honey," Francie objected. "And artists have their own way of looking at the world."

"Francie thinks everyone is an artist," Dutch explained. "Including herself." Then he laughed.

The smile left Francie's round face. I wanted to slap Dutch like Sarah had.

"I think it's that weird minister," Francie finally put in. She shuddered and rubbed her arms. "He's so, so—"

"Black?" Dutch asked innocently.

At that, I wanted to slap them both. I took a couple of long breaths, reminding myself that there was good in everyone. It just wasn't very obvious at that moment. Then I remembered that John Turner had said something about the boarders.

"Was one of May's boarders giving her trouble?" I asked.

Dutch rubbed his chin. "I don't know," he replied after a few seconds. "May was pretty tough. She wouldn't put up with any trouble that I can think of. She was more likely to give it. Why, what did you hear?"

"Just some gossip," I said quickly. I didn't want to give

information. I just wanted to extract it. What if Dutch was the murderer?

"People always gossiped about May," Dutch told me, his voice less abrasive now. "They were just jealous. She was a smart woman. Worked hard. She was a winner, made her own money and invested it well—"

"But Dutch," Francie objected. "Just look how she made her money." Was Francie one of the jealous ones, jealous of her husband's attention to May?

"She made her money honestly," Dutch shot back. "She wasn't lucky enough to have a husband die on her."

Francie's face fell again, and I realized that shot had been aimed at her.

"People are always jealous of people who accomplish their goals," Dutch lectured, having finally silenced his wife. "I did well in business early on, made my money and invested it the smart way. Now, I do a little real estate. And there are always going to be people who are jealous of my success. But I'm on the planning commission. I do my civic duty."

"Did you help May's house get past the planning commission?" I asked.

"Sure," he shot back. "Nothing wrong with that. That's what's the commission's for. Just ask your friend Sarah."

"Sarah Quesada?" I prompted.

"Yeah, her," he confirmed. "She's a smart girl. Just needs to learn to control her temper." He smiled, and I squirmed in my chair. His smile didn't *feel* like a smile.

"Did May have any enemies?" I tried.

"May rubbed a lot of people wrong, that's for sure," Dutch mused. Now, his smile felt real again. "She liked to pull people's legs. If they were snotty to her, she made fun of them. You want to find her enemies, just get the local phone book out. Like that balcony scene."

"How come everyone in Mostaza seems to know about May's 'balcony scene'?" I demanded.

Dutch laughed. "It was that dumb Turner kid. He told his little friends, and they told their parents, and their parents told everyone, and pretty soon it got back to his mother. What a mess. Like it really mattered."

"But, honey—" Francie started to object.

"What do you know about it?" Dutch challenged his wife angrily. He swiveled his head toward her. "Maybe May was just expressing herself *artistically*."

Francie tightened her lips and looked away to the side. Criminy, I was glad I wasn't her. But maybe she was just as glad she wasn't me. Couples have their own dynamics.

"Listen, Dutch," I said, after a glance at my watch. It really was time to get in my car and go to city hall. But I had one last question. "Did you call Julie Turner a little while ago?"

Dutch reared his head back, and for a moment I was physically afraid of him. I felt the reassurance of the cane in my hand.

"You women!" he hissed. "You're always sticking together. Why would I call Julie Turner? You and her and Sarah are all too damn nosy for your own good—"

I stood up. It *really* was time to go.

"Thank you, both," I said formally, "for inviting me to your house and sharing information."

"Thank you for coming, Cally," Francie answered, but the earlier animation was gone from her voice.

"Anytime," Dutch added jovially. It was as if he hadn't been angry at all.

I left their house carefully, gently shaking hands, and kept myself from running to my car once I was outside.

I didn't have much time to think about the Krentzes

while I drove the last few miles to city hall. And a part of me didn't want to think about them. Because Dutch seemed to me to have the anger necessary for murder, and yet he had spoken of May fondly. I was sure his affection wasn't feigned. But still, I could imagine him killing in anger all too easily. And Francie? Just how jealous had she been of May? I wondered if Dutch always treated his wife so badly, or if his behavior was a reaction to Francie's low opinion of May.

I reached city hall before I could reach any conclusions. And Kapp had been wrong when he'd said I couldn't miss the place. If I hadn't been there once before with a friend, I would have driven right by. Mostaza's city hall was in a small, two-story, whitewashed building that looked as if it might have been a church sometime in its existence. Only the brass plaque in front proclaiming its function gave the modest structure any distinction.

At least there was plenty of free parking out front on a Sunday evening. And I'd made it there before seven. I took a breath, straightened my collar, and strode to the front door.

Once inside, I smelled something that might have been mothballs. And then I saw a woman close to my sister Geneva's age of fifty sitting behind the reception desk. She had sparkling green eyes, thin lips, and long dark hair pulled into a ponytail. I was impressed that the mayor could afford a receptionist on a Sunday evening. I smiled and opened my mouth. Then I shut it again. What was the mayor's name? I'd forgotten.

"I'm here to see the mayor," I announced after a moment. "I'm Cally Lazar."

The woman behind the desk smiled back at me.

"That would be me," she said. She rose from her seat

and stuck out her hand. Something about her shantung Burma shirt seemed familiar. "Natalie Gleason."

The name rang a bell. The mayor! This woman was the mayor.

"Oh," I remarked, and shook the proffered hand. It was rougher than I expected. It didn't feel like a mayor's hand.

Mayor Gleason laughed.

"I don't get an office, you see," she said finally.

"You don't?"

"No, being mayor is purely voluntary. They don't even have to pay me."

"But you're in charge of the city," I objected.

The mayor laughed again. She was enjoying this.

"They tell me that the city council and I are in charge of policy," she explained. "But the city manager carries out the actual work of it. We aren't a very big city."

"So what do you do?"

"I speechify and talk to irate citizens occasionally. I have a restaurant nearby, but it's fun to actually be in city hall sometimes."

"Did Warren Kapp tell you I was coming by?" I prodded. I was beginning to think this whole thing might be Kapp's idea of a joke.

"Yes, he did." Her face lost her smile. So, this wasn't a joke. "He said you might be able to help out on this May North thing."

"Kapp exaggerates my abilities," I told her.

"Kapp exaggerates everything," she agreed, smiling again for a moment. "Still, the city manager is upset. We're all upset. There hasn't been a murder in Mostaza in seven years, and certainly never one like this. People don't visit cities with unsolved murders. They certainly don't eat in our restaurants. Do you understand what I'm saying?"

"Either you're saying May wasn't murdered," I guessed. "Or else you're asking me to help investigate May's death."

"Oh, May was murdered," she fired back. Did that mean she was asking me to help investigate? "Even Chief Upwood is clear on that fact, as much as it offends his sensibilities."

"Did you know May North?" I asked.

"Yes, I knew May. I actually liked her personally. But let me tell you, half of the irate citizens I talked to were complaining about May North. They accused her of everything under the sun. She had a harem. Her house was a crime against nature. She was a drug runner. She was a nudist. She was a Satanist. She was a child molester. I spoke to her a few times. She would just laugh."

"I don't know who killed her," I put in. "Still, it sounds like she had enough enemies."

"Yeah, but only a few of them were in the house that night from what the chief tells me."

"Like me," I ventured.

"Like you," she agreed.

I was silent then. Did the mayor of Mostaza think I killed May North?

"You've seen Gerry Cheng since the night of the murder, haven't you?" she asked then.

"Gerry?" I repeated. Then I answered. "I've seen him a couple of times. He's in pretty bad shape. He really loved May."

"It's the worst when a husband and wife fall out," the mayor said. The words seemed to hang in the air for a minute. Then I understood what she was saying.

"You think Gerry Cheng did it."

"I don't think anything," she answered. "Still, statistically, odds are that the husband did it."

"No," I muttered, shaking my head. But now I wondered. Gerry might have done it. How would I know? People who loved could kill the people they loved. "No," I said again. "Not Gerry. You should have seen them that night. They were in love. He loves her now—"

"You doth protest a lot, Ms. Lazar," Mayor Gleason cut me off. "Are you absolutely sure it wasn't him?"

"Not absolutely," I admitted. By then I was cold. Didn't they even heat city hall for the mayor? "But I don't believe it—"

"Try," she suggested. "Try and believe it. You liked May. When you talk to Mr. Cheng, notice things. That's what Kapp says you're good at, noticing."

"But—"

"If it was May's husband who killed her, would you want him to go unpunished?"

I shook my head. All of a sudden, I knew what Mayor Natalie Gleason was asking of me. She wasn't asking me to solve a murder. She was asking me to spy on Gerry Cheng. If the city of Mostaza found that one of its citizens had merely been killed by her spouse, would people eat in their restaurants again? Was it that simple? Now I knew why Natalie Gleason had taken the job of mayor. It was a springboard to a higher position. This woman was a real politician. I could see the love of power emanating from her.

"I'm just asking you to observe," she pushed, as if she'd heard my thoughts. "We don't want to railroad an innocent man."

"I'll observe," I told her. "I'll observe everyone."

"Good," she said, as if we'd struck a deal. She put out her hand again.

I shook it tentatively.

"It was good to meet you, Ms. Lazar," she finished up formally. "I'm glad Kapp sent you."

She wouldn't be glad for long, I thought. Because I would do everything in my power to make sure that Gerry Cheng wasn't wrongly suspected of a crime he didn't commit. But was it even in my power to know *if* Gerry had committed a crime?

"Good to meet you too, Mayor," I said in what I hoped sounded like a sincere voice. And then, I turned and left city hall.

I drove home, my body feeling as numb as a zombie's, my thoughts buzzing. How could I find out the truth? Because I was truly frightened now. Could a city pin a murder on a vulnerable man like Gerry Cheng? He wouldn't be good on the witness stand. He probably couldn't even pick out his own clothing. I knew that Kapp would say that in itself was enough for an indictment. Then I remembered that Chief Upwood was in charge of the case. Would the chief's sensibilities allow him to charge an innocent man? I certainly hoped not. I began to calm down. Even the mayor probably wasn't that ruthless.

By the time I'd reached the haven of my home, I'd convinced myself that Gerry Cheng wasn't in real danger. I heard my goats bleat as I unlocked the front door. I stepped into my house happily, sniffing its mixed smells of cat, and onions, and tea. Then Leona yowled. All was well.

When I got to my kitchen, I sat down and pondered. Who could help me think this out, York? No, York was probably way too worried about me already. Sarah, I decided after discarding a number of other ideas. I found Sarah's phone number and called.

"Hey, Cally," she greeted me after her phone message had run. "What's up?"

"I want to throw some ideas around with you," I told her as Leona leaped onto my lap. I didn't tell her about the mayor's suspicions. I just started asking her for her impressions of the players.

Sarah had plenty of good words about May and even better words about Phil. Gerry was "a real sweetheart." Then we got to Dutch.

"I gotta say I don't like that guy at all," she admitted. "I just hope he doesn't make trouble for me. Ya know, I'm really going for it in real estate."

"Did you help push May's house design through the planning commission?" I asked.

"Kinda," she murmured. She didn't sound happy about it. "Listen, Cally. I gotta run. Can we talk more about this tomorrow? I'll be showing a house on the corner of Santana and Pine. A couple of people might be interested in it. We could talk then."

It sounded like a good idea. We made plans, and I hung up.

I was just turning on the flame under my teakettle when the doorbell rang. I approached my front door cautiously, cane first.

But I didn't know the young man on my doorstep. And he was holding a bouquet of flowers.

"You Cally Lazar?" he asked.

I told him I was.

"Someone must really like you," he informed me, handing me the flowers: hothouse roses, sweet peas, and poppies in a sunrise of colors. "Sunday evening costs double."

I closed the door, buried my nose in a lush apricot-colored rose, then ripped open the tiny envelope that held the note. It wasn't from Roy. It read simply, "Thank you for taking care of May, Gerry Cheng."

Gerry Cheng?

The doorbell rang again. I wasn't as careful opening the door that time, thinking it must be the flower man again. But it wasn't. Sergeant Verne stood on my doorstep. And her haggard face was grim when she looked at me.

THIRTEEN

I heard a scream from my kitchen, and for a moment I thought it was a human one. Sergeant Verne did, too. She straightened her spine and sniffed like a bloodhound. Then her hand went under her blazer and came out with a gun.

"It's only a teapot," I told her quickly. "I forgot to turn off my teapot."

The sergeant shouted over the sound of shrieking steam as she tailed me back to the kitchen.

"So, you've been to see the mayor!" she accused.

I turned in my tracks, teapot forgotten once more.

"How do you know?" I asked.

"I'm a friggin' policewoman," she answered, her hands on her hips, her gun magically gone again. "Not that anyone seems to notice anymore."

The sound of the teapot was still piercing the air. I circled back toward the stove and finished my quest, turning it off thankfully. The air was humid in the kitchen.

"What do you mean about no one noticing you're a policeman?" I demanded in the quiet.

"The police solve crimes, not the mayor. Not psychic amateurs. You got it?"

"That sounds right to me," I conceded. "I'm just worried about Gerry Cheng—"

"Because it's statistically most likely to be the husband, huh?" Verne interrupted. "Well, statistics are a pile of bull when you're dealing with human beings!"

"But—"

"And now, you with the mayor and the chief—"

"Is the chief going along with the mayor's theory about Gerry Cheng?" I stopped her.

"The chief isn't sure," she said in a mocking falsetto. "He has to think about it. What a pile! And then you siding with the mayor—"

"I'm not siding with the mayor," I put in.

But Sergeant Verne didn't seem to hear me. "I could just as well arrest you, ya know that, *you!*" she yelled. "How'd you like to be accused of something you didn't do?"

Keerups! Where were Joan and Kapp when I really needed them?

"I'm a cop, but does anyone listen to my opinion, huh?" she asked rhetorically. "Noooo—"

I held out my palm in the international position for "chill out."

"I do not think Gerry Cheng murdered his wife!" I shouted.

The sergeant stared at me for a moment, her haggard face red. Then she said, "You don't?"

"No, I don't," I tried more softly. "That's what I told the mayor. I don't think she's sure of it either. She just wants it to be that simple."

"Yeah!" Sergeant Verne cried enthusiastically. "That's exactly what she wants. She wants a simple case that can go away and leave Mostaza looking squeaky clean again."

"But it isn't simple," I offered.

"Yeah!" Verne cried again. I was preaching to the choir. "It's not simple at all. There's no evidence that points to Gerry Cheng any more than to anyone else. Just motivation, since he was her husband and all."

"Anything else?" I asked.

"It looks like he inherits. Cheng says she set up trusts years ago to take care of the rest of her relatives. So he's the only one who benefits financially. At least, that's what it looks like now."

"Does he need the money?" I pushed. The sergeant was in an answering mood, and I was taking full advantage.

"No!" she shouted, punching the air with her fist. "That's the point. He's already wealthy, really wealthy. He doesn't care about the money. Sheesh, he's thinking of giving it to charity. So why would he kill her, huh?"

"He wouldn't," I concluded. "Unless he was angry with her, but I don't think he was."

I tried to remember the night of the party. There had been a lot of people angry at May, but her husband hadn't been among them, as far as I could tell. Of course, Becky Cheng was a different story. The hair went up on the back of my neck. Would he have killed his wife to protect his daughter?

"What?" asked Sergeant Verne. She was acting pretty psychic herself.

I edited the theory from my mind. May hadn't been any threat to Becky. Gerry just didn't make sense as May's killer.

"Tea," I suggested instead. "Would you like some tea?"

Sergeant Verne hesitated. Was she suddenly remembering that she was a policewoman, fraternizing with the enemy?

"Well, I guess so," she agreed finally.

A little while later, we were sitting across the table, drinking raspberry tea and talking about goats and about suspects and about her troubled relationship with her boss. Leona sat in the sergeant's lap, purring.

"The chief, see," she was saying, "he always wants to do the absolutely right thing. No, not exactly the *right* thing, but the thing that'll please the most people. He hates to disappoint people. So when the mayor comes up with her big theory, that it's *always* the husband, like that's some kinda rule or something, he wants to agree with her. But he isn't sure, so then he leans on me to find some evidence. Not to find out who did it, ya know, but to find something that could put Mr. Cheng away for this. I like the chief, but he's so easy to manipulate. And I'm afraid he'll cave if I don't find out who really did it soon. Once they decide someone did it, they can make it happen—"

Sergeant Verne stopped midsentence. She looked across the table at me.

"You won't tell anyone I talked about this, will you?" she asked. "I shouldn't talk to civilians. It could get me in a lot of trouble."

"Of course I won't tell," I promised. "I work with clients all the time. I know how to keep secrets."

She stared at me for a moment, her face tense. Then she seemed to soften.

"I tried to talk to my husband, but he just said, 'Annie, do your job and keep your mouth shut.' He calls me Annie. And I can't talk to the officers. We're all supposed to support the chief. And really, I do support him. He's a good guy. It's just the mayor that's got him going. Jeez, what a mess."

I nodded and took a sip of tea.

"You know, I met May North a couple of times," she

murmured. "There were a lot of complaints about her. I liked her. Half the people in town wouldn't give her the time of day, and now that she's dead, everyone just wants it to go away. It's not right."

"Do you have any idea who really killed her?" I tried.

"No, do you?" Sergeant Annie Verne asked back.

I hesitated, thinking of Dutch.

"What?" she demanded, leaning forward.

"You went to May's memorial service today, right?" I asked.

"Yeah, with the chief. Why? Did I miss something"

"Well, a weird thing happened at the church. . . ."

I realized that *my* mouth was running. I told her about Dutch's odd remarks, and how he'd touched Julie, and how Sarah had slapped him. Then I talked about visiting the Turners, and Dutch and Francie. By the time I was finished, I figured that the sergeant and I were even in the confidentiality game.

"Damn," Verne murmured. "I knew there was a reason I didn't like that guy. We don't have much on him yet. It's only been a couple of days, and over the weekend at that. *And* we need some major computer help. But still, well, let's just say that Mr. Krentz is nobody's sweetheart."

"I heard about the assault charges on the prostitutes," I put in.

"Jeez, how'd you find out about that?"

"Warren Kapp," I told her.

"Oh, man," she muttered. "That's all we need, the Melvin Belli of Glasse County mixed up in this. What's his connection anyway?"

"Um," I began, blushing. "He's my friend, so he wants to figure out who did it. Or he wants me to figure it out. Something like that."

Sergeant Verne just shook her head, in what I was pretty sure was sympathy.

"And I think he's a friend of the mayor's," I added. I didn't want to hold out on her. "He set up my meeting with Mayor Gleason this evening."

The sergeant blinked and got back to business.

"So, do you think Dutch is our guy?" she demanded.

"I don't know." I sighed. "That would be simple, too. Just because he's a nasty man with a nasty temper. But I got the feeling he actually liked May."

"Do you think they were lovers maybe?"

"No . . ." I shrugged. "More like good friends. He seemed to respect her. He acted like he wanted to know who killed her, too." I paused. "I get the feeling that he and John Turner suspect one of the boarders."

"Which one?"

Now I was remembering John Turner's words. "No one in particular. Something about one of the boarders giving May trouble."

"Yeah, maybe—" the sergeant began, then stopped herself.

"I know about Ian Oxton's drug conviction," I told her.

"Warren Kapp?" she asked.

"Yeah."

"Man's a menace," she offered.

"Dack, he drives me crazy sometimes," I agreed. "But he means well in his own weird way."

"Him and the chief." She shook her head. "Men."

We contemplated the species in silence for a while. I don't know if Sergeant Verne was thinking of Kapp or the chief or her husband or someone else entirely. I was thinking about Roy, myself. The sergeant was the first to break the silence.

"So, do you think there was some funny business with

the planning commission?" she asked finally. "Mr. Krentz and Ms. Quesada both were members, and look at that mess of a house they let Mrs. North build." She took a sip of tea, and added, "Wouldn't that just make the mayor happy, if her precious planning commission had something to do with this?"

Somehow, I felt guilty repeating what Sarah had told me in confidence. "Kapp said a little palm-greasing was normal with these things," I threw out instead.

"Is there anything your friend Mr. Kapp doesn't know?"

"Who the murderer is," I answered, and we both laughed, but not for long. My body was tired. My leg was sore. And I was hungry.

But apparently, Sergeant Verne wasn't as tired as I was, since she just kept on ticking.

"That Julie Turner sounds nuttier than a fruitcake," she remarked. "Whaddaya think the deal is with her?"

"I think she's sad and afraid," I answered slowly. "But she doesn't seem angry. I can't imagine her killing anyone."

"Me neither," the sergeant agreed unhappily. "She's more the *Princess and the Pea* type."

I searched my mind for the reference.

"You know, the fairy tale about the princess who could still feel the pea under a hundred mattresses or so." The sergeant widened her eyes and raised her voice. "I am so, so sensitive. Boo-hoo."

"Well . . . yeah," I finally agreed uncomfortably.

"How about her husband?" Verne persisted.

"All he seems to be doing is protecting his wife," I said, feeling even more tired. But the sergeant seemed to be gaining energy as I lost it.

"Okay, the tenants," she proposed. "Ian Oxton's got a drug record. Know anything about that minister?"

I shook my head innocently and told myself that I really didn't know anything about Phil that could help the investigation. If the Mostaza Police Department didn't know about his earlier mental problems, I wasn't going to tell them.

"Eric Ford is gay," Verne told me.

"No big deal," I argued. "So's my brother." I was sorry the moment I said it. That was York's business, not mine. Sometimes I thought I needed a time machine to undo the things I said before I said them.

Verne leaned forward eagerly.

"That's right," she breathed. "And he's some kind of martial arts nut, too."

Now she thought it was York!

"He's not a martial arts *nut*," I corrected her, infusing my voice with calm. "He's a martial arts instructor. And true martial artists don't strangle people from behind. They don't need to."

"But he attacked us from behind, remember?" Now, she was really excited.

"No," I told her. "He stopped once he saw who you were. He was just freaked because someone had been in his house, and he thought you two were trying to break into mine—"

"If we had been, what would he have done to us?" she asked eagerly.

"Grabbed you, maybe," I guessed. "Just stopped you. He has this code of never acting offensively, only defensively—"

"Like Jackie Chan?"

Again, my tired mind searched for the reference.

"You know, the martial arts guy in the movies," she reminded me. She darted her hand above the table. "Pow, kapow!"

"Right," I said. "Just like Jackie Chan."

"I can't remember if Jackie Chan ever snuck up on anyone from behind," she thought aloud. "Wait, I think he did."

I waited.

"Is your brother honorable like Jackie Chan?"

"Absolutely," I assured her.

The sergeant seemed to deflate.

"Sergeant Verne, I want to thank you," I announced, rising from my chair.

"For what?" she asked, rising with me. It worked!

"For being as honorable as Jackie Chan," I told her. "I know you won't let anyone railroad Gerry Cheng."

"Damn straight, I won't," she agreed. "And thanks for your help. Maybe . . . maybe you could keep on checking people out?"

"Sure," I promised. Then I saw Roy's concerned face in my mind.

I walked the sergeant to the front door.

She turned and shook my hand before she left. I liked the feel of her hand better than the feel of the mayor's.

Once the door closed, I thought of my hungry stomach. And I thought of Roy.

I went back to the kitchen and dialed his number.

He answered the phone on the first ring as if he'd known I was calling. Maybe he had.

"Roy," I tried. "I'm hungry. You got anything good for dinner?"

"Oh, Cally," he answered, sighing. "You're attemptin' to figure out this death, aren't you?"

"You should know," I accused. "You've been following me."

There was a short silence, then he asked, "How'd you know about my following you?"

"York saw you."

"Oh," he said quietly in a voice that made me want to cry. "Cally, darlin', please stay away from these folks. I'm so truly afraid for you."

"Roy," I answered honestly, "I just wish I could. But they want to pin it on poor Mr. Cheng. His wife was just killed—"

"Don't you see the darkness?" he asked. "You're so good-hearted, Cally. You only see the light. But where there's a murder, there's darkness, too."

"So come over here and protect me," I ordered. Only my voice was shaking.

"No, can't you see that I'm causing this in some manner? I've tried to get clear on it in my mind, and I just know that I'm causing it—"

"How, Roy?" I challenged. "*How* are you causing it?"

"I can't say that I know. But why else are you in the middle of this, Cally?"

Dinner seemed to be postponed on account of darkness. I hung up the phone after a few murmured pleas from both ends of the line. And Leona was nowhere to be found.

The doorbell rang just as I began the cat search. I needed comfort. For a moment, I imagined that Roy had relented. Then I realized that he couldn't have gotten to my front door within minutes even if he'd wanted to.

So, once again, I approached the front door cautiously, cane first. It was late now, after nine o'clock.

"Who's there?" I shouted through the door.

"Acuto from Pluto!" a high-pitched, nasal whine replied.

I groaned. Only one person could be ringing my doorbell, my sister Melinda, creator of the Acuto from Pluto comic strip. But I was wrong.

"They're all here!" shouted another voice. That was

York. And by everyone, I guessed he meant all of the Lazar siblings.

I opened the door slowly and saw that my guess was right. Melinda was there, grinning her goofy grin. My oldest brother, Arnot, was behind her. He bowed deeply and dramatically. York was next, eyebrows raised hopelessly as if asking for my forgiveness. And then, of course, the eldest, my sister Geneva, who had raised me from the age of fifteen and still considered me a child, her child.

"Well, Cally," Geneva announced with slow authority, "I understand you're in trouble again."

"I'm not exactly in trouble—"

"You are," Geneva cut off my objection, her finger pointed in reprimand. Dack, I was fifteen again.

And then my siblings filed in my front door, one by one. The good news was they'd brought snacks.

Once we were all stuffed in my kitchen, after dragging in an extra chair, the goodies came out of a bag that Arnot was carrying.

"Avocado-almond salad," he announced with a flourish. "Chinese spring rolls with hot mustard, tofu balls in sweet-and-sour sauce, and apple tarts." Then he kissed his fingers and tossed me the kiss. Arnot was the romantic of the family, an artist who built designer cabinetry and was safely married, for all of his flirtatious mannerisms.

"Criminy, did you rob a gourmet chef?" I asked, my salivary glands revving up.

"No, we just hit a yuppie deli," Melinda answered. She mimed whipping out a gun and blowing on its tip.

I grabbed a spring roll, dipped it in the mustard, and stuffed it into my mouth. Heaven.

After I'd eaten enough to be able to think again, I looked around at my sisters and brothers.

"We came to help," Geneva said solemnly.

Even with York rolling his eyes behind her, I felt a familiar warm glow. My family was there.

"I met with the mayor," I began, hoping to impress.

"Natalie Gleason," Geneva put in. "She's ambitious. I design clothes for her."

No wonder the mayor's Burma shirt had looked familiar. It was one of Geneva's creations.

"So tell us everything," Melinda commanded.

And I did. Actually, York and I did.

At the end of our recitation, Melinda hummed a little, Arnot smiled a "there-there" smile, and Geneva steepled her fingers.

"Cally, we're here for you," Geneva pronounced finally. "It would be groovy if we could investigate, but I'm not sure how. Still, if you want to stay with me—"

"Or me—"

"Or me—"

"Or me—"

"That would be cool," Geneva finished. "We love you."

I cried a little after they left. But they were good tears. I climbed into bed warmed by the light of my family's affection. I saw Roy's face in my mind, then one of Francie's collages, and I was asleep.

Monday morning, I woke up late. I didn't have any early clients scheduled, so I took my time with breakfast and drove into Mostaza to talk to Sarah Quesada.

I found the house on the corner of Santana and Pine easily enough. It was a white elephant of a place, literally. The two stories were huge and gleamed like alabaster in the sunlight. A Realtor's sign was at the front door. The door was unlocked when I tried it, so I made my way in, feeling like a burglar.

"Yoo-hoo!" I called. The living room was white, too, and empty. My call echoed off the walls. But Sarah didn't answer. I wandered into another empty white room. Maybe it had been a dining room before it'd been empty.

"Sarah!" I tried again, crossing the bleached rug and stepping into the next room. The next room was different.

Something that wasn't white lay crumpled on the rug in a pool of color. A workman's tarp? No, a human, I realized with a start.

I moved closer, my cane out instinctively. The person on the floor had wide, staring blue eyes, a lush moustache, and a rust-colored crater where his chest had been. It was Dutch Krentz, and he was . . . *no,* my mind cried out, but it didn't change the vision before me. Dutch Krentz was irretrievably and horribly dead.

FOURTEEN

And then the smell hit me. How could I have missed it? Denial? Shock? As I reached up to cover my face with my hand, the room brightened unnaturally. The air seemed to shimmer. Some part of my mind reached out and told me I was going to pass out. I didn't want to pass out; not there, not then. I closed my eyes and grasped my cane with both hands. When I opened my eyes again, I saw something else I'd missed. A gun. It lay on the stained, white rug about a foot from Dutch Krentz's body. I took one step toward the gun, intending to pick it up. Then I stopped and deliberately turned around and walked out of the room as steadily as I could. I wouldn't touch the body or the gun. I'd get help.

I looked around the empty room for a phone, but saw only a jack where a phone had once been plugged in. All the time, my mind was whirling. Had Dutch been shot? Did attorneys ever lie? Of course he'd been shot. But—I told my mind to quiet down. The important thing was to find a phone. But not one room in that house had a phone. I found out the hard way, searching chamber after chamber. There was no phone in the kitchen, none in the spa, none in the living room or the bedrooms or the bathrooms.

This is why everyone else carried cell phones. I'd have to leave the house to make a call.

I left the way I'd come in, out the front door. Once outside, I felt a drip on my face and then another and another. It was raining and I had to find a phone soon. It might not be such a bad thing to pass out once I'd called the police. It might not be such a bad thing to lie down and rest.

I took a deep breath and walked up the stony driveway to the next house and rang the doorbell, my glasses wet and blurry. No one answered. Monday, I reminded myself. It was Monday, and most people were at work.

The next house had a large brass knocker. I picked it up and let it fall. A voice shouted out, "No solicitors! Can't you see the sign?"

"But, I'm not a solicitor!" I shouted back. "I need—"

"You need money," the voice cut me off. "You all need money. Leave me alone!"

I left the house and struggled up to the next one. I couldn't see a bell or a knocker here. I reached up and banged my fist on the bare wood, my eyes closed.

"Can I help you?" a small voice asked after a few knocks.

I opened my eyes. Through the blur of my glasses, I saw a tall, brown-haired woman with a newborn baby at her shoulder standing in the doorway. She had a look of concern on her kind face. Goodness was there in front of me, wearing a pink, fuzzy sweater and blue jeans. And just as important, she probably had a phone.

"Something terrible has happened in the house at the end of the block," I told her. I couldn't say murder, not in the face of such goodness. "I need to call the Mostaza police."

"Oh, man," she murmured. "Come on in. The closest phone's in the kitchen. That okay?"

"That's more than okay," I told her. It was all I could do to keep from hugging her.

I cleaned my glasses with the corner of my shirt, breathed in though my nostrils, then dialed 911 to report a dead body in the house at the corner of Santana and Pine. I whispered, "I think he was shot."

"Shot?" the dispatcher asked. "As in 'shot with a gun'?"

"That's it," I agreed more loudly. "Get Chief Upwood and Sergeant Verne," I ordered. "It's their case."

The dispatcher told me the police were on their way and started a round of questions that seemed endless. I answered each one dutifully. I was still answering when I heard the sirens at the end of the block.

"Gotta go," I cut in, and hung up the phone.

I turned to the tall woman, who was hovering behind me.

"Thank you for being such a wonderful person," I said quietly. "You're a true hero."

"Me?" she questioned, tilting her head.

"Yes, you. No one else would open their door for me." I looked at the baby and smiled. "She is a hero, isn't she?"

The baby gurgled in confirmation.

I went back out in the rain, still smiling, and walked to the house on the corner of Santana and Pine.

My glasses were a mess again by the time I got there. But even through the drops and smears, I could see Sergeant Verne as she walked toward me. And I could see the anger in the motion of her body.

I took my glasses off and tried to clean them again.

"You!" she accused as she finally reached me. "You called it in."

I put on my glasses and nodded. I saw not just anger, but betrayal. Who did the sergeant feel had betrayed her?

"I talked to you!" Sergeant Verne hissed. "I talked to you

as a friend. And now . . ." Her voice stopped. She pointed over her shoulder at the house where I'd found Dutch.

Suddenly, I understood. "You don't think I killed Dutch, do you?" I demanded.

"Well?" She put her hands on her hips. "Did you?"

"No!" I shouted in the rain. "I didn't kill Dutch. Why would I call it in if I killed him?"

"I don't know," she answered. "Why?"

I was getting truly cold. And it wasn't just the rain. Last night, the sergeant had made it clear that the police could build a case against a person they suspected. And now *I* was suspected.

"Do you want to substitute me for Gerry Cheng?" I asked, keeping my voice steady. "Because I didn't kill anyone. I couldn't kill anyone. I found Dutch's body, and I went to get to a phone as fast as I could. Isn't that what I'm supposed to do?"

Sergeant Verne eyed me silently. She stared at my clothing. Was she looking for bloodstains?

"What were you doing here?" she asked finally.

"I came to talk to Sarah."

"Sarah Quesada?"

I nodded.

"What does Sarah Quesada have to do with this?" she demanded.

"She was supposed to be showing the house," I told her. "That's what she said last night. I was supposed to meet her here so we could talk. But when I got here, I couldn't find Sarah. I looked through the house, and I found Dutch."

"Was the door open?"

"Well." I hesitated. "It wasn't open, but it was unlocked, so I just opened it and walked in."

"Where's Ms. Quesada?" the sergeant asked then.

"I don't know," I answered. Then I panicked. Had someone killed Sarah, too? I thought of all the rooms I'd searched, looking for a phone. Sarah hadn't been in any of them. "Is Sarah okay?"

"Sheesh, how should I know?" Sergeant Verne answered. Her hands flew into the air as if seeking answers. "All I know is that we've got another dead body in there, and you're the only one who knows anything about it."

"I'm sorry," I murmured. And I was sorry. Sergeant Verne wasn't as angry as she had been before, but she was frustrated and afraid.

She looked at me sharply. "Damn if I don't believe you. You really didn't kill Mr. Krentz?"

I shook my head.

"Well, then, I'm sorry, too," she muttered. "I shouldn't have yelled at you like that. I guess I'm all freaked out."

I nodded. I wished I had her on my table. She needed some work. Dack, I wished I had *me* on my table.

The sergeant led me under the eaves. It wasn't exactly cozy under there, but at least it wasn't raining on me, and some of the warmth of the day seemed to reflect off the white side of the house.

"Will you be okay here for a little while?" Sergeant Verne asked me.

"Sure," I answered. But I was shivering.

"Take off your jacket," she ordered.

"Am I under arrest?" I asked, frightened all over again.

"No, you're cold!" she snapped back.

So I took off my soggy jacket, and she handed me her own blue parka. It was warm and dry when I put it on, a good exchange.

"Now, I gotta go get the chief, but I want you to stay here, okay?"

"Yes, ma'am," I rattled off, saluting. It seemed the right way to speak now that I was in her parka.

The sergeant almost smiled then, saluted back, walked to the front door, and disappeared.

I was craning my head around, looking at the cars parked in front of the house when Sarah Quesada pulled up in her yellow Saturn. She popped out the door, unfurling an umbrella, and came walking up the sidewalk. But I could still see her face under her umbrella. Her brown eyes were frowning.

She started toward the front door, but looked from side to side before entering. That's when she saw me.

"Cally!" she shouted. She jogged over to where I stood under the eaves. "What are you doing here?"

"I came to see you—" I started. Then I stopped. Should I tell her I'd found a dead body? I pictured Sergeant Verne's face. Even in my imagination, the sergeant wasn't smiling.

"Were you the one who called me?" Sarah demanded.

"What?" I asked.

"Someone called me on my cell phone," she explained. "Said Phil had an emergency, that he was waiting down at the church for me. But he wasn't there, Cally. Shoot, it's really weird. I tried May's number, you know, and that goofy Ian guy answered. He didn't know where Phil was. What's going on?"

I didn't answer her. "Did you leave the house open?" I asked her instead.

"Of course not," she retorted. "I put the key in the little lockbox by the For Sale sign." She turned and pointed. Her eyes widened. She jogged over to the lockbox and yanked on its cover. It came off in her hand.

"Holy cow, someone pried it open!" she yelped.

"Calm down—" I tried.

"Oh, Cally, someone got the key. I'm tying to make it here, and someone's trying to mess with me. I could get fired." She stopped for a moment, thinking. "Do you suppose it was Dutch? Do you think he's trying to get me in trouble?"

"Um, Sarah," I put in. "Maybe you ought to go inside. The police are here—"

"The police! What are the police doing here?"

"I don't think I'm supposed to say," I told her as gently as possible. "Maybe you could just go in and talk to them. I promised to stay out here."

"But why, Cally?" she pushed. "What's going on here?"

"Sarah—" I began, then I saw Sergeant Verne and Chief Upwood heading our way. Yes, there always was a little light when you needed it.

Sergeant Verne put on a burst of speed when she saw Sarah there.

"Did you tell her, Cally?" she barked.

"No, ma'am," I barked back. "Sarah just got here. Someone called her and got her to leave. And they broke into her lockbox—"

"That's enough," the sergeant stopped me. She turned to Sarah.

"What's going on?" Sarah asked, a plea in her voice. "I didn't mean to leave. Someone called me and said there was an emergency—"

"Ms. Quesada, you have the right to remain silent—"

"But—"

"You have the right to an attorney. . . ." I stared at Sarah's face as the sergeant's voice droned on. I didn't think her mind was receiving Sergeant Verne's words any better then mine was.

"But—" she tried again.

"Do you understand your rights?" the sergeant demanded.

"Sure, I guess so," Sarah answered weakly.

The sergeant shook her head and put up an admonishing hand. "Do you understand your rights?" she asked again, more loudly this time.

"Sure, fine," Sarah said, her voice angry. "Yes, I understand my rights." She paused and narrowed her eyes. "What's happened? You've got to tell me what's going on."

Verne turned to me. "You heard her. She understands her rights."

"Well," I muttered. "Maybe she—"

But the sergeant turned back to Sarah. "Did you know a man named Dutch Krentz?" she asked.

"Yeah," Sarah admitted, her eyes widening. "Why? Is he here? What did he say about me?"

But Sergeant Verne wasn't giving Sarah anything. "Did you slap Mr. Krentz at May North's memorial service yesterday?" she asked instead.

I flushed. I'd told the sergeant that. And now I was sorry I had.

"Yeah, but I had a good reason," Sarah claimed. "Just ask Cally. She'll tell you the truth. Don't believe Mr. Krentz. He's a liar. He's just trying to get me in trouble."

"I don't think so," the sergeant said quietly.

"Why?" Sarah yelped. "What's he saying about me?"

Sergeant Verne looked closely into Sarah Quesada's face as she delivered her line. "Mr. Krentz isn't saying anything about anyone. He's dead."

Sarah's skin turned the color of the white building that held Dutch Krentz's lifeless body. And then her eyes rolled up in their sockets.

I stepped up and caught her as she swayed. But she didn't pass out.

"Dead?" she murmured, a few loud breathes later. "He's dead?"

"Ms. Quesada, did you kill Mr. Krentz?" Sergeant Verne asked formally.

"No!" Sarah protested. "Shoot, I just wanted to stay out of his way. He was really weird, you know. No way I woulda gotten in his way." She shook her head. "No way."

"Then why was he at the house you were showing?" the sergeant asked.

Sarah's skin turned even whiter.

"No," she tried again. But her voice was small now. "He wasn't killed . . . here. No, it can't be. Why would he be here? Jeez, now I'll lose my job for sure." A shudder went through her body. "You don't think I killed him, do you?" When no one answered she said, "I wouldn't kill him, honest."

"Time to get the young lady an attorney, I believe," Chief Upwood intervened. I'd forgotten he was there. I'd have bet the sergeant had forgotten, too.

"But I don't need an attorney," Sarah insisted. "I didn't do anything."

"Well, as long as you feel comfortable," Chief Upwood conceded. He smiled at Sarah. She smiled back tentatively. Then Upwood turned to his sergeant.

"Perhaps you and Ms. Quesada could ride to headquarters together while I finish questioning Ms. Lazar," he suggested amiably.

Sarah's smile disappeared. "Listen, it wasn't my fault I was gone," she told us, her voice gathering speed. "Someone called and got me to leave. Anyone could have found out I was showing this house by calling my office. I must have been set up."

"We'll have plenty of time to talk about it downtown," Upwood assured her. "We'll clear the air."

But Sarah didn't look reassured.

I took off Sergeant Verne's parka and handed it to her. She took it back hesitantly. I stepped up to her and whispered in her ear, "I don't think she did it."

The sergeant looked at me thoughtfully. She opened her mouth and closed it again.

"Officer Affonso," she yelled out. "You got this lady's jacket?"

The dark-haired officer who had been at May's came from the direction of the front door, holding out my sodden jacket in front of him. Once he'd delivered it, he and Sergeant Verne led Sarah Quesada to a police car with the Mostaza Police Department insignia on it. Sarah and the sergeant got in the back. Officer Affonso got in the front and drove the two off. And I was left with Chief Upwood.

"Perhaps you could give me a brief rundown of today's events from your perspective?" he suggested.

My mouth opened and words poured out like the morning rain. I told him everything I could remember, everything I surmised, everything I believed.

"And you don't believe Ms. Quesada killed Mr. Krentz?" he finally asked.

"No," I told him.

"How about Mr. Cheng?" he proposed.

"Nope," I said.

"And how about you, Ms. Lazar?" he asked, searching my face.

"No!" I yelped.

At least they didn't take me away in a police car.

Once I was dismissed, I got in my Honda, turned on the heat, and drove slowly away, my mind outpacing the car.

Sarah couldn't have done it, could she? Or Gerry? But who? Dutch had been my best bet for May's murder, and now he was dead, too.

By the time I got home, I was no further along than I'd been before I started, and I wanted to lie down.

But Dee-Dee and York were waiting for me when I got to my own front door.

"Hey, Cally," Dee-Dee cried out. "Don't you know when to come in out of the rain? You're sopping. And we've been here forever—"

"Dutch Krentz is dead," I announced.

York reached out and touched my shoulder while Dee-Dee cooed. It felt good. But I still needed something neither of them could give me. A warm shower for one thing.

So the three of us walked into my little house, and Dee-Dee fixed tea while I showered. As I dressed in warm, dry clothes, I breathed in from above and below until I could see a kind of light, a light that reminded me of the peace inherent in chaotic transitions. And then I was actually able to think about Dutch Krentz's death. And to think of a newborn gurgling happily at the same time.

I went to the kitchen where Dee-Dee and York sat and told them everything I'd told Chief Upwood. Dee-Dee handed me crackers and some kind of avocado dip she'd made from the none-too-plentiful ingredients my kitchen had offered up.

I ate thankfully and quietly. And my brother and my friend respected my quiet. At least until I'd finished eating. Then York spoke up.

"Cally, you've got to make sure no one thinks you're investigating," he warned me.

"Too late," I answered. What else could I say?

"You know, Geneva and Arnot and Melinda are into it

now, too," he told me. "They want to find the murderer and protect you."

"Oh, criminy!" I objected.

"Well, I can't stop them," he complained. "You know that."

"But they'll get in trouble," I said, as if he didn't know.

"And we won't?" he asked.

Dee-Dee giggled. Lazars were funny if you weren't one.

"York!" I shouted. "What about your martial arts?"

"I can't stop a gun," he reminded me practically.

"Well, I can," I said. "With my cane."

"Oh, Cally," he murmured, shaking his head. "Come stay with me for a while."

"I don't need protecting," I argued.

"Maybe I do," he came back.

It was my turn to sigh.

Then I saw York smiling.

"York," I began, shaking my finger, then I looked at the clock over his head.

I had a client in five minutes.

Dee-Dee and York vamoosed without argument.

Five minutes later, I had Virginia McFadden on my table. She was a longtime client, and more than that, a friend.

I was clearing out an old well of anger that had seeped into her liver when she asked me if it was true that I was a psychic detective as well as a healer.

I shook my head and kept on working.

"But you're going to help Gerry Cheng," she insisted.

"Where'd you hear that?" I demanded.

Of course, she'd heard it from Warren Kapp. It made sense. They were both old-time Glasse County residents and cronies. And she'd heard a lot more things. By the time I'd finished working on her, Virginia had offered me as many theories about May's death as I'd heard from all the rest of my friends combined. I was just glad she hadn't found out about Dutch yet. Finally, I did the finishing touches on her healing session, and Virginia sat up straight on my massage table and looked me in the eye.

"What you need, my dear, is to know May better," she calmly told me. "Then you'll know why she was killed."

FIFTEEN

I stepped back for a moment, startled by Virginia's pronouncement. Know May better?

"But how?" I asked aloud.

Virginia frowned. "I don't suppose you can just channel her up or something?" she returned my question finally.

"No," I said, shivering. Because it was possible that I might be able to do just that. And I didn't want to.

"Well, then, I suppose you must get to know her nearest and dearest," Virginia proclaimed. "I knew May ever so slightly. We took an art class together some years ago. She was really quite good. But once she got going with her topiary, mere paints and pencils weren't enough for her anymore."

"Did you find out anything else about her?" I demanded eagerly.

"No." Virginia shook her head. "She was a hard woman to know for all her friendliness. She seemed to have secrets. That's why I suggested blackmail as a motive. That and too many murder mysteries on my part," she admitted ruefully. "But still . . ."

"May wouldn't blackmail anyone," I stated. I was sure of it, well, almost sure. "She had everything she needed financially—"

"How about emotionally?" Virginia put in. "A little subtle pressure to get her emotional needs met?"

"But . . ." I stopped and thought about it. I hadn't really been listening to Virginia's theories when I'd been working on her, but now I was.

"She *was* a madam, Cally. Who knows what secrets she knew about those who worked for her or used her services."

"But she kept things confidential," I objected.

"What if you were someone who wasn't so sure she'd keep things confidential, hmmm?" She paused. "Or what if May did someone some unforgivable harm in those days? I mean, dammit all, I liked May pretty well myself. But let's face it, she was no saint. Prostitution is an intrinsically nasty business no matter how you gussy it up. She pretty well had to háve hurt some people along the way. What if she hurt someone in a way they couldn't forget? Or even someone else's nearest and dearest? The possibilities are endless. Someone's true love becomes a prostitute. Someone's home is wrecked when papa falls in love with May. Someone squanders the family fortune on girls of the night. Some brutish client is injured by the bouncer. Daddy meets his own daughter when he comes a-visitin'—"

"You have an imagination that won't quit," I told Virginia, smiling a little in spite of the subject matter. "You could be writing for soap operas."

"But people are like that, Cally," she insisted, her eyebrows scrunching up. "Always longing for what they can't have, resenting those who do, making the wrong decisions. Actually, that's what makes people so interesting."

"How about loving the right people and admiring success and making the right decisions and—"

"Oh, Cally, you are such a sweetheart," Virginia told me, and laughed. Then she frowned again. "What I don't understand is how you get in the middle of these terrible muddles."

"Me neither," I admitted. "When I saw that body this morning—"

"Whoa!" Virginia stopped me. "This morning? You saw a body this morning? I thought May was killed on Friday night."

"Um," I mumbled.

"Don't ever play poker," Virginia warned me. Then she demanded, "What happened this morning?"

I thought for all of two heartbeats before telling her everything. At least Virginia wasn't a suspect.

"Hmmm, Dutch Krentz," she murmured after I'd finished. "I knew him ever so slightly—"

"Keerups!" I exploded. "You and Kapp. Is there anyone either of you don't know?"

Virginia just laughed. Then she got up off the massage table and gave me a hug.

"Cally, I'll think on it," she promised me seriously. Then she put on her coat and shoes and left.

Once Virginia was gone, I sat in one of my stuffed chairs and thought. I *did* need to know May better. I hoped I didn't need to know Dutch better, too. So why was I in the middle of this "muddle" as Virginia would say?

I put the thought aside. There was no good answer. Instead, I considered May's nearest and dearest. The top of the list had to be her husband, Gerry. I went to my phone and dialed the number for Citrus House.

"Cheng, Morton, Ford, and Oxton," a deep baritone answered, as if I'd dialed a law office. "Ian Oxton speaking."

"Why don't you just say Citrus House?" I asked, then added, "Cally Lazar speaking."

"Is that you, Cally?" Ian asked, his voice eager. "I'm just

trying to have a little fun. Things are absolutely grim here."

"Have the, um, police—" I began tentatively.

"Oh, they've been here all right," he replied. "They hassled all of us, especially Gerry. Gawd, what a mess. Dutch Krentz was killed this morning. And for some reason, we're all suspects. This isn't any fun. And Gerry is really whacked. Damn, I wish May was here."

"Do you think I should come over?" I asked, half-hoping that Ian would veto the idea.

"That'd be great," he answered. "We're all just getting on each other's nerves. And I don't know where Phil is. The police seemed to find that terribly suspicious." He snorted. "And I thought reruns were bad."

I laughed. I couldn't help it. Ian was funny even if the situation wasn't.

"Shall I come by in a little while?" I asked.

"All the members of the zoo are jumping up and down for you," he sang in answer.

I took that as an affirmative.

"See you soon," I told him, and hung up.

I walked out on my back deck, breathing in the cool, wet air. It wasn't raining anymore, and I could see my goats grazing down below. It was good to just be for a moment. Then the doorbell rang.

I walked back through the house, wondering who my visitor was. I was betting on Sergeant Verne.

I would have lost my bet. My friend Dee-Dee was at the door, back again, her Irish-Asian face looking more elfish than anything.

"What?" I demanded.

"You think these deaths are your fault," she stated. Then she tilted her head and looked up at me for a reaction.

"Have you been peeking into my subconscious?" I protested, halfway seriously.

"No!" She did a fiery little dance in place, looking even more like an elf, a deranged elf. "I just know you, Cally. I know how your mind works. That's why you're trying so hard to figure out who did it. You blame yourself."

I considered her words. It *was* weird that I'd been there each time. It was as if Roy's darkness was real, following me and seeping into the lives of others—

"See?" she put in. "I knew you thought it was your fault. But it isn't, Cally. You know how we get the clients who are really sick and think that they must have done something really uncool to be so sick?"

"Well, yeah—"

"You're like them. Only you think that something about you must have caused these deaths. It's the old question of why bad things happen to good people—"

"The question that there's no answer to?" I reminded her.

"Yeah, that one." Dee-Dee grinned. "But what do you tell your clients?"

I shrugged. I didn't actually talk a lot when I worked. But Dee-Dee obviously did.

"You tell them that there are always reasons for suffering, cool reasons, but sometimes we just can't see the reasons," she prompted impatiently.

"I'm not so sure—"

"Of course you are," she assured me. "Maybe you're the light to balance the darkness of these deaths. Had you thought of that?"

"No," I said slowly. "I hadn't actually thought about my relationship to these—"

"Not consciously," she corrected me. "Unconsciously,

you're seething with questions. You're in pain from worrying. You're—"

"So you *were* peeking," I accused. But I couldn't help smiling. Real friends care enough to intrude psychically, I told myself.

"Oh, Cally," she lilted. "You know your true nature is good—"

"*Everyone's* true nature is good," I answered seriously. "But we don't all *act* on our true natures—"

"You try to," she proclaimed. "That's what matters. Do you want a session?"

"No," I answered. "I think I just had one."

Dee-Dee giggled, then hugged me so tightly she almost pulled me over.

I felt a little dizzy when I shut the door behind her. Still, it was always good to have friends who made you feel completely mainstream in comparison.

I talked to my cat, Leona, after that. She didn't hold a very high opinion of Dee-Dee's views, but she certainly enjoyed her treat of tuna fish.

Once Leona had stalked from the room, I knew it was time to visit Citrus House. A few minutes later, I was in my Honda and driving.

May's former home hadn't changed since I'd been there last. At least not on the outside. It was still three stories of tangerine-and-lime–trimmed eccentricity. I looked at the plaster animals in the yard and the columns and turrets and balconies on the house, and I shook my head. This house was May. I couldn't imagine anyone else ever buying it unless they were blindfolded.

I pulled up in the circular driveway and parked behind May's gold Mercedes, a high-end Honda, a tired looking Toyota Corolla, and a vintage Volkswagen Bug.

I took a deep breath and shut my eyes for a few moments. Then I got out of my car.

By the time I got to the front door, it was already open. Ian Oxton's head popped out like a puppet's.

"Bonjour, bonjour," he greeted me, grinning. The grin looked labored on his long, lean face. He bowed and swept me through the door into the orange living room with an elegant hand gesture. "We await," he said, and I realized he was as high as the highest turret of Citrus House. Not drunk, I decided, sniffing unsuccessfully for the sour smell of alcohol, but high. I wondered what the police had made of his drug use.

Eric Ford didn't look high though. He sat in a chartreuse wing chair, looking about as low as a man could, his shoulders slumped and his bearded face hidden by his hands. A charcoal gray cat huddled in his lap.

Then I saw Gerry Cheng. Gerry's grayed features and frail body made Eric look good in comparison. I wondered how long it had been since Gerry had eaten. I opened my mouth to ask him, but Gerry spoke first.

"Did you hear that Dutch Krentz was killed?" he asked me from the orange easy chair that he sat in so stiffly.

I nodded. Maybe sometime I'd tell the Citrus House inhabitants that I'd found the body and how, but it wasn't the right time.

"The police think I killed him," he added simply. He lowered his eyes, looking at a spot of light on the carpet. "They think I killed my May, too." Fear and confusion seeped from his body in swirls of citrus colors.

Dack. I didn't know what to say. "I'm terribly sorry, Mr. Cheng," I tried.

"I would never have hurt my May," Gerry went on. I wasn't sure he'd even heard me. Maybe he didn't even know I was in the room. "I loved May. But Dutch . . ." He shrugged.

"How well did you know Dutch?" I asked.

"Dang," he swore softly. "Dutch? Oh, I knew Dutch. He was May's brother—"

"May's brother?!" Ian and I demanded in concert.

"Did you say he was her brother?" Eric added belatedly, pulling his head from his hands. The gray cat leaped from his lap and flounced away.

"Oh, yes," Gerry replied calmly. "He was May's younger brother. He worked at her . . . her establishment. He was her right-hand man there. He wasn't a very nice man, but May couldn't see that. I never pushed her on it. He was her brother, you see."

"She never told us," Eric muttered.

"Why the secret?" Ian asked at the same time.

"Dutch wanted it kept secret," Gerry explained. "He wanted people to think he made his money as a self-made entrepreneur, not as his sister's employee, as if that was something to be ashamed of. She settled a lot of money on him years ago."

"But he cared for her," I guessed.

Gerry sighed, then confirmed my guess. "He did. He had a lot of affection for May. And May cared for him, too. Family." Gerry sighed again. "There's nothing harder to explain. He really loved May. He wasn't expecting any more money. He knew he'd gotten what she was going to give him, but he liked to live nearby, to be a part of her life." Gerry shrugged. "He was quite a bit younger than she was, you know. She partly raised him. He always treated her like a sister . . . and a mother."

"Dutch was younger than May?" Ian repeated unbelievingly, as if this were the most bizarre part of Gerry's story.

"Dutch was always May's little brother, you see. And May treated him like a boy who could do no wrong." Gerry stood suddenly and walked toward the door that led to the kitchen. "And Dutch admired May for her money sense. She was the brains of the family. Once in a while he'd resent it, but mostly he just thought she was great. Well, she *was* great!"

"Does his wife know?" I asked.

"I don't think so," Gerry answered slowly. Then he opened the kitchen door, and the joyful sounds of dogs yipped and barked and yapped into the room: Labrador retriever, dachshund, and mop dog all accounted for. "Dutch was good at keeping secrets," Gerry went on. "I think he wanted to impress Francie, too. She liked his self-made-man act."

"Gawd," Ian muttered.

"Gawd," the parrot above him repeated. Had the parrot just woken up? It sounded sleepy.

The Labrador jumped on my chest, his tongue lolling out toward my face.

"Down," I ordered after one lick, and he obeyed. I gave him a pat for May. He must have missed her.

I sat down on a yellow ottoman. I understood Eric's and Ian's surprise. I felt it myself. Virginia McFadden's words about "nearest and dearest" returned to me. In knowing May, I was knowing Dutch. And in knowing their secret connection, I knew something about both of them. They both kept secrets well. Suddenly, some of Virginia's theories didn't seem so far-fetched. Secrets could be dangerous.

"May spoke German to Dutch," I blurted out, remembering just then.

Gerry nodded. "Their parents were German immigrants. They spoke German at home. It was easy for Dutch and

May to speak that way. I think they enjoyed another little secret that way. They could talk, and no one would know what they were saying. It was a game for them."

"May was German?" Ian asked, his voice dazed.

"Of German ancestry," Gerry corrected him. "Just like I'm of Chinese ancestry. We had that in common, my May and I, feeling like outsiders. Germans weren't very popular after World War II." Gerry sat back down again. I could see the tears forming in his eyes. "My May was different. She never quite understood why she offended people. She was proud of her body, proud of her taste, it was all the same as nature to her. She loved nature, May did. She loved animals and plants. She . . . she . . ." He faltered and put his head into his hand to cry in earnest.

Criminy, I thought. I can't let them railroad this man.

The doorbell rang. But Ian didn't even make it to the front door before it came swinging open on its own.

"Daddy!" Becky Cheng yelped and ran to her father. "Oh, Daddy, don't cry. We all miss May. She was a good woman."

The two of them held each other, and I was glad Gerry wasn't alone. And glad that his daughter finally seemed to value May.

"I'm confused," Eric muttered into the relative silence of the living room. "Was Dutch—"

But the door swung open again before he could finish his question.

Phil Morton entered the room and closed the door gently behind him.

"The police have spoken to me," he announced quietly. "They were waiting at my office. I was out at the hospital ministering to Mr. Duval; the poor soul's got cancer." He paused as Gerry looked up at him. "They asked about you,

Gerry. I told them how much love you and May had for each other." He closed his eyes and seemed to sway. "I would do anything for you, for her, you see," he murmured. Then his voice broke into a cry of pain. "I'm so sorry," he keened. He wrapped his arms around himself and began to rock in place. "I'm so sorry, so sorry, so sorry."

SIXTEEN

"Phil?" I said.

But Phil couldn't hear me. He continued to rock himself, chanting, "so sorry," over and over again. The Labrador began to howl. If the parrot picked up the rhythm, they'd have a trio.

"Hey, Phil," Ian chimed in, no smile on his face for a change. "What's going on, man?"

So this wasn't normal behavior for Phil. I took a quick glance around me. Gerry, Eric, Becky, and Ian were all staring at the minister with wide, startled eyes. I had a feeling Phil was having a nervous breakdown on fast-forward. And I was the healer in the house.

I looked at Phil's aura, remembering as I did what Kapp had said about Phil's institutionalization as a young man. I could see great bursts of green, blue, and purple in and around his body. And in those colors, I saw and felt a huge sense of despair, combined with loss, confusion, and self-hatred. But there was another set of colors, too, white with gold in a column that began at his crown chakra and softened into the space above his head. That space felt of peace and unconditional love. And it remained untainted by the turmoil below.

"Phil?" I began gently. "Can you hear my voice?"

"Yes," he replied softly, though his eyes remained closed, and he continued to rock in place.

"Phil, may I have your permission to work with you energetically?" I asked. "To help you find your way back to your place of peace?"

"Yes, please!" he cried. "Oh, Lord help me!"

"You have a place of peace, don't you?" I pushed on, not absolutely sure if he was asking me or God for help. Or maybe both of us at once. "A place where you're sure of unconditional love?"

His eyes opened then. They were wide and wild, but looking at me, connecting finally. "Yes, ma'am," he said. "I do. It's God's promise of divine grace."

I paused as the white and gold seemed to brighten in the column that now flowed up to the orange ceiling and beyond it.

"Good," I told him softly. I imagined the blues and greens and purples slowly deflating and draining from his body. "That place of divine grace is your true home, isn't it?"

"It is, ma'am," he agreed, unwrapping his arms from his body. He wasn't rocking anymore. But I was shaking by then. The change was happening very fast, much faster than with my usual clients. I closed my eyes for a moment as he continued, "When I'm with God, all the rest drops away."

"And does it drop away completely?" I prodded, my eyes open again. Because the white and gold had become brilliant, but the blue remained, no longer bursting, but there like a tint on an old photo.

"No, never," he answered honestly, his voice calm. "I am human, and the human part of me is always troubled.

But God soothes me and brings me untold joy. I learned that a long time ago. Sometimes I forget, but then I remember again."

"And now?" I asked.

He looked into my eyes. "I remember. Yes, indeedy, God is with me. I remember." He laughed unexpectedly and looked up at the ceiling. "How could I have forgotten, Lord?"

I tried a smile, but it was strained. Phil had the ability to change states faster than I could move my cane. And there was a part of me that didn't trust his ability. I saw his troubled "human" part, but then I could see his faith before my eyes in shimmering white and gold. Transcendent? Psychotic? Both? My skin tightened with a hint of fear.

"Thank you, ma'am," Phil said gently. "The ways of the Lord can be surprising sometimes. But you are of God, too. Thank you for helping me find my way back."

Phil was comforting me. I could feel it. And it was working.

"Well, thank you—" I began.

"Are you okay?" Eric interrupted me. I was pretty sure he was talking to Phil.

"I'm fine," Phil answered him. "Thanks to this good lady."

"Right," Ian hissed. His low voice sounded strangely angry. Maybe he was afraid. "Can someone explain to me what just happened?"

I felt my face flushing, because I was the healer, and I wasn't sure exactly what had happened. Of course, I wasn't really the healer. Whatever was running through Phil was the healer. But—

"Cally, you give this old dog hope, the way you brought young Phil back to himself," Gerry Cheng put in. "Maybe I'll find my way back, too."

"Oh, Gerry," I said. "I never asked you if you wanted energy work. Please, if you do—"

"No, no." He put up his hand. "Maybe sometime, but I think it's my time to grieve now."

"Try a little tenderness," the parrot sang from above.

"Well, this has been a real party," Ian put in. "Anyone want a drink? Gawd, I do believe I need one."

I stood up then, taking advantage of Ian's change of topic as an excuse to leave. I was still slightly shaken by my experience with Phil. And I was abruptly realizing that I shouldn't have done my work in public. I should have asked the others to leave.

"Thank you so much, Cally," Phil's deep voice rumbled, reassuring me. "I don't know how long it would have taken me if you hadn't jumped in when you did. I was like a man drowning in a spoonful of water. But you lifted my eyes to God."

Phil smiled my way, and in that moment I saw him how Sarah saw him, his large dark eyes intense with happiness, his big body straight and strong. A man you could lean into for support.

I smiled back, a real smile this time. "You're an amazing human being, Phil," I told him honestly. "Thanks for the tour."

He laughed deeply.

It wasn't until I'd said good-bye to everyone and was in my Honda exiting the driveway of Citrus House that I wondered how often Phil Morton broke down. And I wondered just what it was about May's death, or Dutch's, that had upset him so deeply. Dack, I'd probably never know. People always think that medical intuitives are psychic, but I'm not. If I were, I would have known May's murderer on the spot. I was back to square one. I'd checked out May's "nearest and dearest." It was time to go a little farther afield.

By the time I got to downtown Mostaza, I'd decided some shopping was in order. Julie Turner had said John's shop was down here. And there were probably other shop-keepers around who'd known May. I needed to find out more about May North. I'd liked her, but had I really known her? Nope. I might have thought I had, but that was before I'd found out that Dutch Krentz was her brother.

I spotted John's store a block after I'd decided to stop and shop. The sign said World Imports. That had to be his place. I parked and sidled on into the store.

Sure enough, John Turner stood behind the counter, his graying head bent over a wooden box. He held a screw-driver in one hand and seemed engrossed in whatever he was doing.

I looked around the store. Four or five wooden cabinets with dozens of little drawers stood against the nearest wall, flanked by wooden and brass Buddhas and other carved figures. The far wall featured tapestries, gongs, sconces, cedar chests, carved masks, and brass bowls. I even saw another carved door like the one at the Turners' house. There were birdcages hanging from the ceilings and brass lanterns and woven baskets. For a moment, I played with the fantasy of having unlimited money. I liked the chests with the little drawers. I reached out and tugged on the brass pull of one of the drawers. It slid out smoothly from the chest, and I could smell the wood, with a touch of incense. I imagined how the chest would look in my work-room. But what would I use all the little drawers for?

"These were originally used in Asian pharmacies," John informed me from across the room, his quiet tone friendly.

I swiveled around and faced him. I felt the guilt I

always felt in small shops where I couldn't find any price tags. The lack of price tags meant John's wares were out of my price range. And I was here to find out about May, anyway.

"Very nice," I temporized. "What do people put in them?"

"Netsuke collections, buttons, jewelry, hardware." He shrugged. His voice didn't sound as friendly as it had before. Maybe he hadn't recognized me from the back.

"I probably can't afford your stuff," I admitted.

"Probably not," he agreed, his voice softening again. He lowered his gaze. He looked tired. "Are you hear to ask questions about May?"

"I suppose so." I wondered whether he'd heard about Dutch's death yet.

"My wife was closer to May than I was," he told me. "Julie liked her a lot."

"Your son seemed to like her, too," I reminded him.

"Zack hasn't learned about boundaries yet," he replied. "He's just a kid."

"How about you?" I prompted. "Did you like May?"

He half closed his eyes for a few breaths. I could hear a car passing in the street.

"I didn't like her or dislike her," he finally concluded. "I worried about her influence on Zack though."

"Because of her past?"

"No," he answered seriously. "Because of her present. May North collected losers. She thought that was fun. And she thought it was fun to incite kids to rebel. A kid doesn't need any help rebelling, but May always saw herself as a wild woman. She didn't even act like a grown-up most of the time."

I nodded. In an odd way, it was good to hear someone

talk about May who didn't think she was a saint. John seemed pretty levelheaded in his evaluation.

"May got a kick out of annoying people," he went on. "She was a success, and she could afford to do what she felt like. So she annoyed people. That house she built? It was a piece of junk. And she put good money into it. She probably put even more money into getting the planning commission to approve it. She and that Quesada woman. They were friends. Something was going on there. May was trouble. Generally, I avoid trouble when I can. But my wife and son liked her, so I put up with her."

"How about her boarders?" I asked.

"A bunch of losers," he dismissed them.

"No, I meant which one was giving her trouble?" I tried. He looked at me blankly.

"You told me you thought one of May's boarders was giving her trouble," I reminded him.

"Oh, right," he conceded. "It was just something she said."

"What did May say?" I asked impatiently.

"Something about someone being on the street if he didn't straighten up," he offered, shrugging again.

"Who do you think she meant?"

"It could have been any of them," he said slowly, apparently thinking it over. "That doctor. Damn, he's a doctor and he's broke? And that so-called actor hasn't had a part since he moved in. And the minister can barely fill the first pew most days. Maybe she was tired of them. I would be."

Another shopper entered the store, a good-looking woman in her later years.

"How goes it, John?" she asked jovially.

"Great, Wanda," he answered. His voice wasn't as

enthusiastic as hers, but he was trying. *She* was probably a paying customer. I decided to leave him to it.

"See you later, John," I said, and exited the store.

The next shop down was some kind of tea shop, with teas to buy for home use, and a few chairs to drink a cup on the spot. They also had fresh pastries, imported English biscuits, painted teapots, cups, trays, and, incongruously, a host of stuffed animals.

"May I help you?" the woman behind the counter asked. She was a homey-looking woman with brown skin, a shelf for a bosom, and the hint of a British accent.

I considered a pastry and tea. It seemed a long time since I'd eaten.

"May North used to come here, didn't she?" I tried. "She told me she liked one of the teas. Now, what kind was that?"

"May?" the woman asked. And then her dark eyes seemed to light in recognition. "Oh, May!" she exclaimed. "Wasn't that terrible, her killed like that. I could barely believe it when I heard it."

"I know, she was so full of life," I prompted.

"That May, she liked the honey peppermint tea," the woman offered. "Now I remember." She turned behind her and came up with a cellophane-covered box that had East Indian figures on the front. "That and a bit of gossip and giggle. Oh, she made me laugh, doing her imitation of the mayor and such."

I smiled. The mayor? Could the mayor have killed May? That was an interesting thought.

"And her and her husband," the woman added. "Such a sweet couple. It's a shame she passed."

"Any idea who killed her?" I asked.

"What?" the woman replied, eyes widening.

It'd been worth a try. I bought the box of tea and left with a promise to return.

I went into the next store, a clothing store staffed with two young women who were talking about their respective boyfriends. They had never heard of May. Nor had the owner of the health food store on the corner. The man in the bookstore remembered her though. She read everything from science fiction to poetry to medieval mysticism to the greats of literature.

"It was like she was starved for books," he told me. "She was a real addict. Once, I told her she needed to take a *slow* reading course to save money. She thought that was pretty funny."

"She had a good sense of humor," I said.

"She was a riot," he agreed, his eyes clouding. "Damn, I'm gonna miss her."

I didn't ask him who he thought had killed her. I just bought a few used books and left.

I visited a frozen yogurt stand, more clothing stores, a music store, a jewelry store, and a coffee shop. The merchants of Mostaza who remembered May, remembered the same May I did, full of laughter and free with her money. Nothing more, nothing less. No one popped up with any ideas about her death.

I realized I was near to Phil Morton's Church of Divine Love as I walked. So, I walked a little farther. Now that the magic of the session with Phil was wearing off, I wanted to know more about him. I was betting there would be a volunteer at the church.

I was right about the volunteer. A sweet-faced young woman named Zoë came to the little office door on the side of the church when I knocked.

"Hi!" she greeted me enthusiastically. I felt immediately

guilty. "Did you want to know about church services?" I felt even guiltier.

"Actually," I said honestly. "I was wondering about your minister, Phil Morton."

"Oh, Pastor Morton is great," she told me without blinking. "People have been calling all week asking about services since he did that great memorial for Ms. North. And that's really cool 'cause the church was losing money and everything. See, I just volunteer. They can't pay anyone but the pastor, and they can barely pay him. But the board thinks that things are going to get better now. It's like the pastor is some kind of celebrity or something, you know, after that memorial. People are all excited. And he's really cool. He's so handsome and friendly and all. I think people like him. At least, they ought to. I sure do. And my mom says—"

"Zoë," a voice interrupted. "Do we have a visitor?"

Zoë turned around and giggled, looking at Phil Morton, towering behind her.

"I get running at the mouth, sometimes," she whispered.

I smiled at her, trying to think. I hadn't expected Phil to be back. I'd wanted to pump someone *about* him, not talk directly *to* him.

"Hi, Phil," I muttered.

"Cally, is that you?" he asked.

"Yep." I answered, pumping some life into my voice. "I wanted to see how you were feeling." It wasn't a complete lie. I was curious. And concerned, of course, I reminded myself.

"Oh, Cally, I couldn't be better," he assured me. If guilt was cholesterol, I'd have long since had serious heart problems. "Yes, indeedy, God has smiled on me today."

"Well, that's great," I told him, turning. "I guess I'll be going."

"Wait," Phil ordered.

I turned back, my heart thumping. Maybe guilt *was* related to the heart.

"Cally, I sense that you're troubled," Phil told me, his dark eyes serious. "Are you all right? Is there something I can do?"

I almost laughed. Now, he was trying to heal me.

"Thank you, Phil," I told him, considering the true heaviness of my heart. "But I have a lot of thinking to do. Just seeing you is enough for now."

"Just remember," he tried again, his face still concerned. "My door is always open."

"I promise I'll keep it in mind," I assured him. "It was good to see you. And it was nice to meet your friend Zoë," I added.

Zoë giggled again.

We all said our good-byes, and I left the church, controlling the urge to run.

When I'd finally hiked back to my car, I pondered what I'd learned from my field trip. Not much. But there was one nugget. How *had* May pushed her house plans through? Had she involved Sarah Quesada illegally? Dutch had passed the whole thing off as ordinary business. But John Turner had mentioned money, and money was, if not the root of evil, a good motive for murder. Even I knew that.

I headed back to Citrus House. Gerry Cheng had to have known what had gone on with Citrus House. And if I could work up the nerve to ask him, I was pretty sure he'd answer.

Ian showed me into the living room when I got there. Gerry still sat in his orange easy chair. But he looked a little less gray than he had earlier. I said hello and dived in.

"Mr. Cheng . . . Gerry, how did May get the plans for this house approved," I asked.

"It was mostly Dutch's doing," Gerry answered easily. "He just ramrodded it through as a favor to May."

"Dutch could do that?" I pressed.

"Well, Sarah helped, of course," Gerry said. "I mean, May always helped Sarah out after her mother died. Poor woman had cancer. Sarah's mother had been one of May's girls, you know."

SEVENTEEN

"Are you saying that Sarah's mother was a prostitute in May's house?" I asked, still not sure I was hearing Gerry correctly.

Ian snorted and walked out of the room, shaking his head theatrically. He must not have liked my question.

"Yep," Gerry answered me without embarrassment. It was then that I realized *I* was the one who was embarrassed. And I was embarrassed about being embarrassed. "Trudy worked for May in Alaska," he went on. "Trudy Quesada. May talked a lot about her. She worked for May for a long time, and then the poor lady got cancer. May took care of Trudy till the day she died, and she promised to take care of Trudy's daughter, Sarah, too. Sarah didn't have a father, you see. Well, not one who would admit to it. Guess that's part of the reason that Trudy ended up a prostitute. She was disgusted with the regular world. She and May were real good friends. And May kept her promises. May was a good friend to Sarah."

"May was like that," Eric put in mildly. "She helped the people she liked. A lot of people talk about compassion, but she acted on it."

"See, here's the thing, Cally," Gerry told me seriously.

"I know you're wondering about May's being a madam and all. Dang it, everyone did. But see, she figured that prostitution existed, so she'd give her girls the best deal she could. She had her own code about her place. She was a real lady, my May, good and kind. So she ran the business the best way she could. She never hired someone who hadn't been a prostitute already. She didn't allow any men to live off of her girls. When any of her girls got sick or had troubles, she helped them out. She never made anyone do anything they didn't want to. That's the way it was. She used to tell me she was in a bad business, but she made it better than it had been for the women who worked for her. And I believed her. My May wasn't a bad person."

I considered Gerry's words carefully before I spoke.

"I'm certainly no expert on the subject of prostitution," I told him honestly. The closest I'd come to the whole thing was a client whose years in the business left her emotionally disconnected and unstable. "But if May took a bad business and made it better, more power to her." I took a big breath. "I don't think that May was a bad person for having been a madam. I just wonder if her business didn't somehow draw her into tragedy. That's what's important here. I wouldn't presume to judge May's morals. I just want to know whether her profession led to her death."

There was a silence, and I wondered if I'd hurt Gerry's feelings irreparably. But then he said, "That's exactly what I've been wondering. Over and over again, I think of all the bad feelings that May could have stirred up, doing what she did. Someone might not have understood what a class act she was. It's true, Cally, it's true."

"But who?" I asked eagerly. "Did she ever mention any-one who was angry with her or anyone who had something bad happen or—"

Gerry cut me off before I could even finish, shaking his head. "My May kept confidences," he explained. "She didn't talk about the nasty side of her business. That was part of her code, too. Oh, she was real sentimental about her girls. Once in a while she'd talk about them, ones who'd found true love or whatever. And she had a lot of funny stories about things that happened at her house. But she never talked about the serious stuff, the bad stuff. I only knew about Trudy 'cause of Sarah. Now I sure wish she'd told me more. Maybe something *did* happen. But I just don't know."

I swallowed my sigh. Poor Gerry. "Of course," I murmured.

"It was her way of being a lady," he summed up, a little light in his face. But the light was gone in a blink. "I wish I could tell you more."

Ian wandered back into the living room with a glass of something in his hand, which I guessed was alcoholic.

"May was always a lady," he pronounced, raised his glass in a toast, then walked away again.

At least I didn't have to stand up to leave this time. I'd never bothered to sit down.

I said good-bye to Gerry and Eric. Ian was nowhere to be seen.

"Gerry," I added before opening the front door. "I'm really glad I met May. She was a fine woman."

Gerry smiled wanly. "Thank you," he whispered. "Thank you."

I kept that smile in my mind as I left Citrus House for the second time that day. I wanted to talk to Sarah Quesada. May might have kept things confidential, but maybe Sarah's mother hadn't. I just hoped Sarah wasn't in jail.

But Sarah was in when I presented myself at her real estate office in downtown Mostaza.

The office Sarah worked in was a simple redwood-shingled building that looked like a vacation cottage from the outside. It was just a block or so away from John Turner's import store and all the rest of the stores I'd been in earlier. Downtown Mostaza wasn't very big. The inside of the real estate building was filled with desks, computers, and phones. Sarah sat at one of the desks, her round, usually friendly face blank as she stared across the room. I took a peek at her aura, but saw nothing. Aura-wise, she was flatlining.

I walked slowly into her line of vision, not wanting to startle her. Even then, she didn't seem to see me.

"Sarah?" I prompted quietly.

Slowly, Sarah's eyes focused on me.

"Cally?" she said uncertainly. Then her body seemed to come alive, radiating red and yellow. "Cally," she said again. "They think I killed Dutch Krentz. Shoot, it's so crazy. I got mad at him, but I wouldn't kill him. I'm trying to make it here, to be a success. I wouldn't kill someone in a house I was showing. I mean, jeez, how stupid would that be?"

"Of course, you wouldn't," I agreed. She was right. Even if she was ruthless enough to kill, she wouldn't want to implicate herself, would she?

"And they even think I killed May. I loved May. May was . . . was . . ."

"Your mother's friend?" I suggested.

"You know?" she whispered.

"I know," I told her. "Let's go get a cup of tea. I found a great tea place today, not far from here."

Sarah left her office willingly, grabbing her jacket on the way, and checked out with a younger women at the front desk.

"Whoever called my office set me up," she explained, as the door shut behind us. "The receptionist even told the police that someone called, asking what house I was showing today, and what my cell phone number was. At least they can't say I made that up! And then, whoever it was called me with this big song and dance about Phil Morton having an emergency. I looked for him at his church. I called his house. I even called the hospital, but they said no one by that name was registered. And by the time I got back, Dutch was dead and the police were there. Oh man, Cally, this is awful."

"What did the person sound like on the cell phone?" I asked as I steered her down the street toward the tea shop.

"Sorta like the queen of England," Sarah replied earnestly.

"The queen of England called you?"

"No, no!" she protested, her hands flying. "But that's what the person sounded like. You know, all silly British and upper-class." I thought of Ian Oxton, but dismissed him as the perpetrator. It would be as bad a disguise as using his own voice if he did one of his British imitations. Maybe. "It was some kind of goofy, made-up accent, but I didn't realize it at the time. I couldn't even tell if it was a man or a woman. The receptionist said it was the same voice that called at the office."

By the time we'd reached the tea shop, I realized that Sarah had told me all she could about the unknown phone caller. Or all she *would* tell me. What if she had called the receptionist herself?

"So who told you about my mother?" Sarah demanded just as I put my hand on the tea shop's doorknob.

"Gerry Cheng," I answered.

"Oh, Gerry is all right," she said more softly.

I turned the doorknob, and we entered the sweetly scented shop. The same homey women who'd waited on me before was still behind the counter of the tea shop. But there were a few more customers milling around than earlier. One man bought an immense stuffed tiger, and I realized that the stuffed animals probably kept the little shop in business.

"Come back for more tea, then?" the women asked me when it came our turn. I nodded. She added, "Glad to see you, Miss Sarah. You two both knew May, did you?"

I nodded again guiltily. Here I'd been nosing around in a place where Sarah and May had obviously spent affectionate time together. I felt like a Martian at a Shriners' convention.

I let Sarah choose my tea for me. She ordered a couple of raisin scones, too.

"Daphne's a really neat lady," Sarah told me, as we took our tea and scones and sat in a couple of wicker chairs. "She owns this place. May and I used to come here all the time. It's so hard to believe she's gone. And now this thing with Dutch."

I took a sip of tea before speaking. It was spicy, almost peppery. "I hadn't realized you and May were so close," I prompted.

"Well, you know about my mom, right?" she asked. Her face flushed. "I mean about her working for May and all?"

"Uh-huh," I muttered through a bite of the rich scone.

"Well, Mom got sick when I was a teenager. Cancer of the uterus. It metastasized real quick. Oh man, she was sick. May took care of her. And me. May set Mom up with nursing care and all where we lived." Sarah looked down. "And then Mom died. May took care of me after that. She put me through school and everything. When I decided to sell real estate, she was behind me all the way. Said it was my decision." Sarah lifted her head again. Her eyes were damp. "May said everyone did things their own way, 'shake hands, hug, French kiss,' she'd say, 'what the hell?' Shoot, I miss her."

I did, too. But I had questions to ask.

"Listen, Sarah," I began. "I've been wondering if something from May's past was behind her death. And you probably know more about May's past than most people because of your mother."

"My mother?" Sarah questioned.

"Your mother was there," I explained slowly. Sarah was obviously tired. "Your mother knew what went on. Did she ever tell you any stories about May making someone mad?"

Sarah just shook her head. "Mom didn't talk about working for May. I didn't even know what Mom did for May until she was dying. She told me then. I thought she was a waitress before that. I was always asking to go to the restaurant that May owned, but Mom said it was for men only."

"Well, I guess it was," I commented.

Sarah laughed, and I felt my own tension leave my shoulders.

"May used to tease me about the 'restaurant,' too," she confided. "She told me I was a sweet girl. Well, she was one sweet lady, and I don't care what anyone else says."

"Is that why you helped her with the plans for Citrus House?" I asked.

"Yeah," Sarah admitted, her discomfort obvious in her posture. "Me and Dutch. We just made sure her plans were okayed. Dutch . . ."

"Dutch what?" I prompted.

"Cally, promise you won't tell?" she said, looking

around her. No one was listening. The one customer left in the store was talking with Daphne.

"Tell what?" I tried again.

"I knew Dutch, you know, before," she whispered. "He was May's brother. Once in a while he came over to see Mom. I could never stand him. He gave me the creeps the way he looked at me. But May liked him, so Mom was nice to him. But she always made sure I wasn't alone with him. I mean, yuk!"

"Have you told the police?" I asked.

Her eyes widened in panic. "No, Cally!" she hissed. "I can't tell them. They'd think I had some kind of motive. You won't tell, will you?"

"No," I said slowly, wondering if I *should* tell the police.

"If I'd wanted to kill Dutch, I would have done it a long time ago," she assured me. "Even when he threatened me, I knew he wouldn't do anything, 'cause then I'd tell people what he'd really done for a living. He gave me the creeps, but there was no reason for me to kill him."

"How about his trying to mess up your career in real estate?" I pushed.

"No!" she insisted, shaking her head violently. "I worried about that for a while after I slapped him, but I had more on him than he had on me. He wouldn't have really done anything. He just wanted to freak me out. That was the way he was."

I looked into her brown eyes. I couldn't see a lie there. All I saw was the sweet girl that May had known, grown into a woman.

"Hey, Cally," she chirped. "What do you think of Phil Morton?"

All the muscles in my body tightened. Should I tell her

the man she was in love with had a tendency to insanity? She was smiling a dreamy kind of smile.

"He's so sweet," she murmured. "And real intense, you know. I think he could respect someone like me. I'm gonna make money in real estate. I think he'd be fine with that. Some men wouldn't be, you know."

I nodded. No, I couldn't tell her about Phil. I relaxed a little. Phil was so ethical, he'd probably tell her about his mental problems himself. But still . . .

"I think he has his troubles," I admitted cautiously. "But his faith in his religion keeps him going."

"Yeah," she agreed. "He's not faking the religious stuff. I like that."

We talked about Phil for a while longer. Well, Sarah talked about Phil, anyway. I listened. And, finally, all the tea was drunk and the scones eaten. I was just as glad that Sarah hadn't seemed to hear my opinion that Phil was troubled. She'd made up her mind about him before she'd ever asked my opinion in the first place. I just hoped neither Sarah nor Phil was a murderer.

We left the tea shop, and Sarah gave me a big hug.

"Thanks," she said. "Thanks for everything."

When I got to my Honda, I wondered if "everything" included keeping quiet about her relationship with Dutch.

I bent over to open my car door and caught a rearview-mirror glimpse of familiar, reddish brown hair ducking behind a Saab, Roy's Saab.

I made it over to the Saab just as Roy tried to whip open his door for a quick getaway.

But I blocked him with my cane and moved in, grabbing his arm.

"Roy Beaumont!" I accused happily. "You're following me."

"Cally, darlin'," he drawled. "I truly didn't mean for you to see me."

"Why not?" I demanded.

"I'm causin' you this trouble," he explained. "Just by being too close to you. But I can't let you be in danger and not watch over you. You are in danger, darlin', that's the thing. I see it—"

I just put my arms around him and hugged him as tight as I could. And I put my lips to his. He relaxed into a kiss for a minute, but then he withdrew.

"Oh, Cally," he murmured. "I truly want what's best for you. And I'm not it."

"Yes, you are, Roy," I tried.

But as hard as I tried, Roy wouldn't listen. He finally drove off, leaving me alone. And Sarah had asked me for romantic advice. Keerups!

I got into my Honda and drove off toward York's. I needed to talk to my brother. And it was past time for my weekly cane-fu practice.

When I got to York's, his studio was filled with the disabled and the elderly, all doing martial arts appropriate to their abilities. Two women in wheelchairs sparred with canes, whooping as they circled each other. An octogenerian gentleman spun and aimed a lethal kick into the air. Another younger, shaky man breathed in as he stood across from a young woman whose eyes were hidden beneath dark glasses. He raised his arm, and she blocked it with her own.

"Good," York encouraged. "Tom, what do you do now?"

The shaky man turned as the woman pushed toward him, catching her hands at the last minute so she wouldn't fall.

"Lisa," York commanded. "Next time, don't push so hard that you lose your center."

Lisa nodded, and they went at it again.

"Cally!" a man with a cane very like mine, greeted me. He planted his legs firmly and lifted the cane in salute.

I saluted him back, blowing him a kiss, then turned to my brother York.

"You're late," he admonished me, and pulled a stick from the rack behind him. He jabbed it in my direction. I blocked the stick easily and returned with my own downward slash. It would have knocked the stick from anyone's hands but York's. But he moved with the momentum of my slash and twirled his stick from beneath, raising it again. We sparred, and I whispered.

"Dutch was May's sister," I told him.

"What?" he said, and I knocked the stick from his hand.

He dropped to the ground in an instant, rolled away, and came up with the stick again.

"And Sarah's mother worked for May," I added.

York grunted, but I couldn't get past his stick again. Still, he couldn't get past my cane. Not after years of his training.

After a sweaty fifteen minutes, we finally came up for air. The rest of my classmates were leaving, saying good-bye and waving. I smiled and waved back. These were my peers, disabled but determined.

"Cally!" York demanded once they were gone. His face was pale with emotion. "What have you been doing? Have you been visiting those people alone?"

Before I could answer, the door to the studio opened again, and a whole new group filed in. The Lazars had arrived.

"We knew we'd find you here," Melinda called out cheerfully. She deepened her voice. "Lazar radar always knows."

"We've been investigating, of course," Geneva put in. "You never ask for help when you need it. Criminy, someone has to step in."

"And we are that someone," Arnot announced, stretching his arms out dramatically. "Or would it be those someones?"

"Investigating?" I said in a small voice.

"Do you have any objections, Cally?" Geneva demanded. She narrowed her eyes.

"No, no," I murmured unconvincingly. As if I could ever object to anything that Geneva said or did. I stood up as straight as I could. "So, what did you find out?"

"Say, 'pretty please,'" Melinda ordered, giggling.

"Tell," I said instead.

And they told. Arnot had approached Francie Krentz in her art class. He was of the opinion that her art was more interesting than she was. I just hoped he'd visited her before Dutch was killed. Melinda had chatted with Julie Turner after a PTA meeting. She thought Julie was flaky. Was that the pot calling the kettle black! And Geneva had descended on Citrus House in the apt guise of a dress designer that May had hired and failed to keep her appointment with.

"Did you use your real name?" I asked in horror.

"Of course not," Geneva replied. "Give me some credit."

"So what did you find out?" York asked.

Geneva shrugged her shoulders elegantly. "Nothing really," she admitted. "But everyone seemed to miss May terribly."

York and I exchanged a look that asked how to discourage my siblings from useless investigatory efforts. There was no answer. And then I looked at my watch.

"I've got a client," I cried. "I've got to go."

The great thing was that it was true.

My client arrived at my little house minutes after I did. He seemed a simpler client than Phil Morton. His chest pain was heartburn, real heartburn, caused by the diminishing love of his seventeen-year-old son who thought that drugs and the Internet were far more interesting than hiking and bicycling with his father. I'd worked with teenage-related heartburn before, and I worked with it again, settling back into myself as together we eased the pain out of his body through his little fingers.

We both felt better once the session was done.

After he'd left, I walked to the kitchen, followed by my cat, Leona. She and I were both thinking of food.

The doorbell rang. I considered letting it ring without answering but finally dragged myself back to the front door and pulled it open.

Becky Cheng stood on my doorstep. And she was carrying something that caught my attention.

EIGHTEEN

Becky was carrying a large, flat, white box. It might have held a large, flat gun, but it sure smelled like pizza to me. The mingled scents of garlic, tomato, basil, and yeast drifted up tantalizingly. And she was carrying an interesting looking bag, too. Salad? Soup?

"Becky," I greeted her, as my stomach gurgled hopefully. "How are you?"

Leona yowled in disgust and stomped back to the kitchen.

"I needed to speak to you, Ms. Laz—Cally," Becky stated, her plain face serious. "Would this be a good time?"

I felt like telling her it depended on whether she planned on sharing the pizza. But I didn't.

"I was just going to make some dinner," I said instead. "Would you like to join me?"

She smiled, and her plain, oval face was transformed into something of true beauty. "I brought dinner," she told me. "I must be psychic like you."

"I'm not—" I began, but then I saw that she was still smiling. A joke. Becky Cheng had told a joke. I laughed. Pizza and jokes. This wasn't the Becky Cheng I remembered.

"Come on in," I invited, and the two of us walked to the

kitchen together. "How much do I owe you for the pizza?"

"My treat," Becky told me, and sat down at the kitchen table. But Leona harangued me into opening a can of food before I could join my visitor. Becky spoke over Leona's harangue, her voice clear and authoritative. Somewhere from my brain, I pulled out the memory that Becky was a professor. Biology? Glasse State University?

"My father tells me you've been trying to help him," she began. She drew in a breath. "I realize I haven't been very tactful about May. I had no real right to criticize her, but I did. I was upset. And now, of course, I'm terribly sorry."

Leona crouched at her bowl to eat, satisfied at last. And I felt compelled to fill the silence that followed Becky's confession. I'd never make a good interrogator.

"It must be hard when your father marries someone you don't know," I commented.

"Yes, exactly," Becky agreed earnestly. "It wasn't really about May's former profession, or all of the other things I worried about. It was simply the fact that she wasn't my mother."

"Uh-huh," I soothed, eyeing the pizza box as I sat across the table from her.

I didn't have to yowl like a cat. Becky saw my look and opened the box.

"I didn't know if you ate meat," she said brusquely. "So I got a vegetarian, double cheese."

"Oh, yum," I murmured, and rose from the table to grab the plates and cutlery.

"And I got two salads," she announced, opening the bag and pulling out two styrofoam containers. "One's green with Gorgonzola dressing, and the other's white bean, basil, and tomato."

If this was an attempt at bribery, it was certainly a good

one. Once the table was set, we dug in. The pizza was thick with sauce, onions, garlic, olives, mushrooms, eggplant, basil, and gooey cheese. I chewed gratefully and thanked her with my mouth half-full.

"I thought I might be able to give you an objective view of my father and of May," Becky offered after swallowing her first bite.

"Mrumph," I encouraged her.

"My father is a nerd who made it big in technology," she went on. "His success didn't endear people to him, especially since he has poor social skills and is Asian to boot. People even accused him of stealing software. It was ridiculous, but Daddy's never been able to deal with that kind of hostility. He likes technology better than people. I guess I inherited that from him."

I tried to object, but my mouth was completely stuffed with the white bean salad. It was as good as the pizza. So, I just shook my head.

"No, it's true," she insisted. "My mother was the people person. Daddy and I just aren't. We work hard to earn respect. But we can't charm people."

I finally swallowed. "Your father charmed May," I pointed out.

"That's something I've been thinking about," Becky answered slowly. She frowned in consideration. "In some ways, May wasn't all that different from my father. First of all, they both had terrible taste. My mother used to buy my father's clothes. I think he was still wearing them when he met May, then she took over. He couldn't tell the difference. He has no fashion sense at all. And he and May both worked hard, were successful, and were unpopular for their success. Actually, they are . . . were . . . both childlike and vulnerable. They loved their animals. It's hard to explain, but now I realize that they were more alike than different. Now that it's too late."

"Your father knows you love him," I reminded her.

Becky's nostrils flared. "Well, I didn't act very loving the night May died. And I'll always be sorry. But sorry can't change the way I acted. I guess it was because Daddy always told me that he wouldn't remarry. I'm afraid I counted on his promise. And there was his estate. I was sure he was going to leave everything to May. But he wasn't." Becky closed her eyes. Was she trying not to cry?

I took a peek at her aura. I couldn't help it. It was dim, but I thought I could see something that looked like guilt there, and something else that was more like anger. But was it anger at others or herself? I looked more closely—

"I really blew it," she finally muttered. "Now I wish I could tell May I was sorry. She was an odd old bird like my father, and all I did was criticize her." She banged the table with her fist. My adrenaline jumped with the reverberation as Leona ran from the room. "And now Daddy's heartbroken, and the police suspect him. He's defenseless. He's this ill-dressed Asian man who has never learned to deal with people. He can be kind and direct, but he doesn't understand manipulation. He's a sitting duck!"

"Whoa," I stopped her. "I don't think his social skills are so bad. I like him. And I don't believe he killed May."

"But you're honest, Cally," she argued. "You look at people and see what's really there. You—"

"I'm an odd bird myself," I helped her.

Rose tinted Becky's skin. "No, I mean—"

"It's okay," I assured her. "I'm a Lazar. We're all weird. Listen, we just need to sort out the facts so we can figure out who killed May. If we can do that, your father will be fine."

"Do you really think it's possible?" Becky asked. She bent forward, her face intense.

"Of course, it's possible," I answered. I didn't say *probable*. "It's certainly worth trying."

"I apologize for hitting your table," Becky muttered.

"It accepts your apology," I told her.

She smiled. And I wondered if it was also possible that Becky's temper had caused her to kill May. Sure, she would feel guilty if she had. She wasn't a bad person. But anger could have a life of its own.

"So how do we sort the facts?" she prompted.

I reined in my brain and thought about her question.

"Why do *you* think May was killed?" I finally asked.

"A secret," Becky answered readily.

"A secret?" My brain clicked on search. "You mean about Dutch being May's brother?

"Is Dutch May's brother?" Becky replied, looking startled. And she'd used the present tense. I wondered if she knew he was dead yet.

I just nodded.

"Wow, I didn't realize," she admitted. "But that's exactly the kind of thing I mean. May was full of secrets. That was a big element in her way of coping with the world. She gave me a present once. She trimmed the bush behind my apartment into a fish. She did it in the middle of the night. She didn't even tell Daddy." Becky smiled at the recollection, a gentle smile that softened her whole body. "Can you imagine?"

"I can imagine," I assured her. May was a goofball, that was for sure. She might as well have been a Lazar.

"And I knew she was keeping all sorts of secrets. At least she believed that she was keeping secrets. Like her deafness. She thought no one knew."

"Right," I murmured, remembering.

"And her boarders all went to her when they wanted to talk about something confidential. She knew all their secrets. They knew she wouldn't tell. Daddy told me she had money hidden all over the house: under potted plants, behind drawers, in the parrot cage. I opened a can of nuts once. It felt really strange, not like nuts at all, and there were gold coins in the can! Secrets were her motif. And I just keep thinking that it must have been a secret that got her killed."

"But how?" I asked softly.

Becky leaned forward. "What if someone was afraid she was going to divulge their secret?"

"But she wouldn't," I objected. "Would she?"

Becky looked over my head, thinking. "Maybe not. Still, I can imagine her teasing someone, pretending she was going to tell something. She liked to tease."

"Yeah," I said, remembering the party. She'd teased Sarah about something, something that had frightened her. Was it about the planning commission? Keerups, I just couldn't remember. And how about Becky? Had May known Becky's secrets? Or her father's?

"Becky," I began cautiously. "Do you know of any specific secrets that—"

My doorbell rang before I could finish the sentence.

I slammed my cane onto the floor and went stomping toward the door.

I swung it open without ceremony, and without caution.

Warren Kapp was on my doorstep.

"Kapp!" I hissed. "I've got a visitor."

"Hooboy," he whispered, shaking his finger at me. "Someone got out of bed on the wrong side of the dead body this morning."

"Kapp!"

"Is this Warren Kapp?" Becky asked. I jumped. I hadn't heard her walking behind me.

"That would be me," Kapp confirmed, grinning. He bowed.

"My father, Gerry Cheng, has spoken of you," Becky went on. "I'm Becky Cheng. Do you think my father needs an attorney?"

All the playfulness left Kapp's face. "I think he might," he answered gently.

"Would you be that attorney?" Becky pushed. "I know you're the best."

Maybe Becky's father didn't know how to manipulate people, but Becky wasn't bad, I decided.

"I'd be honored," Kapp pronounced. "I know your father's worried, but no one's going to convict an innocent man while Warren Kapp is on the job."

Ugh. I hated it when Kapp referred to himself in the third person.

But Becky's face showed obvious relief. "I'd appreciate it," she said. Then she turned to me. "And I appreciate you talking to me, Cally. It's good to know there are other people who know my father couldn't have killed May."

"Well, I appreciate the pizza," I put in. I didn't want to get into questions of absolute belief in Gerry Cheng's innocence.

"Pizza?" Kapp asked, smiling again.

"If you're good, you can have some," I told him.

"Mother of God, Lazar," he answered. "You know I'm good. I'm more than good."

I lifted my cane. He chuckled tentatively.

Once Becky had gone, Kapp interrogated me with almost as much enthusiasm as he had for the leftover pizza.

He took a giant slice in his hand, ordered, "Tell me

everything about Dutch Krentz's death," then stuffed the whole slice into his mouth.

"How did you know?" I returned the interrogation.

He waved his hands in the air. He'd probably choke if he tried to answer me just then.

I waited, tapping my fingers on the table. "Police," he finally mumbled through a cloud of garlic.

I should have known. Warren Kapp had connections everywhere.

Kapp swallowed and went on, a big grin on his face. "It turns out that Dutch Krentz was May's brother," he informed me.

"I know," I shot back.

"You know?" His face fell. "Dammit, Lazar! How the hell do you know?"

"Connections," I answered, keeping my face straight.

He laughed then. And I laughed with him, remembering just why I like this man so much.

We talked for a while, then he looked at his watch.

"Well, I gotta get going," he announced. "I've got a late date."

"Yeah?" I challenged. "Who with? The president or the governor?"

"With your sister, Geneva," he told me, and stood up quickly.

He was down the hall and out the door before I could even close my gaping mouth. And I had introduced him to Geneva.

I went to bed then. Leona curled up next to me, and I was glad for her company.

Tuesday morning was cold but clear. And I had a stack of clients to see. It was just as well. I'd spent the night dreaming of Dutch Krentz. And he wasn't any more alive in my dreams than he'd been in my waking hours. So I worked.

My first client was a distraught mother whose daughter had moved to India. She'd tried to control her daughter through the use of her own third chakra. It hadn't worked. And now she was angry, and afraid of her own anger. I began by trying to clear her anger from her liver. It wouldn't budge. Why? Because my client was trying to work out her own issues *through* her daughter. Without her daughter, she felt helpless and unsafe. That's when the work really began to hum. What would make it safe for her to stand up for herself and work on her own issues within her own body? Memories of a punitive father as well as her own internalized self-hatred stood in her way, but she had going for her the strength and the intent to do the best for herself and her daughter. After more than an hour of clearing blockages in her meridians and chakras, her own true essence began to shine through. This was what I lived and breathed for. Another half hour later, she felt clear, and I was happily exhausted. I hadn't thought of murder the whole time.

In my ten minutes between clients, I wondered if Roy was right. Maybe I should just stay out of whatever was happening in Mostaza. Still, there was Gerry Cheng.

My second client was the flip side of the coin, a distraught daughter who was trying to ground her mother's fear. I helped her to find her grounding self so she could root herself into the earth. And she began to separate out her mother's fear from her own at the first chakra.

I wondered then if untangling a mystery might be like untangling a client's issues. You look, you probe, you feel what cries out to be known. But how?

My third client was a woman who had drug problems. First, she'd taken speed to control her weight, then she'd continued the drug for the feeling of distance it gave her. Now she was too afraid to go into a rehabilitation program, and her adrenals and kidneys felt as if they were near total failure. The drug kept her in a hypervigilant mode. We began by clearing her fear, then by clearing the secrets she kept from herself in her small-intestine meridian and her fear of public appearance in her kidney meridian. Each clearing was like a layer of an onion, and layer by layer, we worked. She was feeling better by the time we needed to stop, telling me she was ready to try a stint in rehabilitation. But I knew we'd need at least one more session for her to feel that way long enough to really sign up. There were more layers to go.

Layers and layers, I thought as I ate lunch alone afterward. May's death was about layers and layers. Secrecy, fear, anger? Was a murder investigation like clearing a client? It was an addicting thought.

After lunch, I brought out a huge sheet of paper and did a chart. But there were no meridians and chakras on my chart. There were only suspects and their motives, temperaments, and opportunities. I gave up on the opportunity column when I remembered that York and I had been in the back garden that night. I had no way to establish opportunity. Dack. I put down the chart and called Dee-Dee. But I didn't ask Dee-Dee who she thought had murdered May North and Dutch Krentz.

"Dee-Dee?" I asked instead. "Why am I there when these things happen?" And it was then that I noticed I had tears in my eyes. Healer, heal thyself? Nah.

"All beliefs are tested by obstacles, right?" Dee-Dee proposed.

I was still thinking over her proposition when she went on. "Cally, you believe in light and goodness. Is it possible that you have to see these acts of violence and darkness to test your beliefs?"

"I hope not!" I bleated. Moscow couldn't have bleated any louder than I did.

A half hour later I hung up on Dee-Dee, unconvinced by her arguments, but sure that I couldn't hide from this investigation. And another thought had occurred to me during the long conversation. I couldn't heal one part of a client at a time. And I couldn't clear up a murder without seeing all of the suspects together.

I called Gerry Cheng.

"Gerry," I said, after Ian handed the phone over, "I wonder if you could get everyone together at your house who was there the night of May's party?"

"Here?" he mumbled, his voice sounding as if it was coming through water.

"Yes, at Citrus House," I told him, pushing confidence into my own tone by force. "I want to do a reading of the suspects."

"A psychic reading?" he asked, a little life back into his voice.

"Something like that," I tried. "I want to see everyone together."

"I'll try, Cally," he promised. "I'll try." He paused, and his voice came through loud and clear. "Dang it, I'll do more than try! I'll make sure they come."

Yes! I told myself when I hung up the phone.

It rang a minute later.

"Is this Cally Lazar?" a familiar voice asked. But I couldn't quite place it.

"Yeah," I muttered, hoping I hadn't just admitted my identity to a telephone solicitor.

"Oh, goody. This is Francie Krentz," the voice informed me cheerily. "I wanted to know if I could book you for a session." Then she giggled.

NINETEEN

"A session?" I replied, stunned. Francie Krentz wanted a session? Hadn't her husband just been killed? And I'd heard her giggle. I was sure of it.

"You have a healing practice, don't you, Cally?" she reminded me, her voice still cheerful. "I wanted to talk to you about it when you visited, but Dutch kept interrupting. He does that, you know. Always interrupting me. You wouldn't believe it."

I just hoped he wasn't still interrupting her. As of twenty-four hours ago, give or take a few hours, Dutch was supposed to be dead.

"Francie," I began softly. "About Dutch. Have the police been to see you?"

"Of course they have, Cally," she told me. "I'm his widow. They had to tell me. They could have done a better job, but they're insensitive oafs, except for the chief, what's-his-name. They should know that I'm a highly emotional woman. They scared the dogs, you know. My babies are such *little* dogs, so high-strung. Poor sweeties. Anyway, I thought I'd call and see if you could fit me in. I've heard wonderful things about your work. You're very special."

"Did you want to come in *today*?" I asked, still feeling as if I was missing something.

"Oh, that would be wonderful! Do you think I could?"

"Well, I just finished the rest of my clients for the day," I thought aloud. And I needed a little time to get a bullet-proof vest, I added silently. "How about two o'clock?"

"Oh, goody!" Francie exclaimed. "I'll be there at two."

That was scary.

"Do you need directions?" I asked.

"Oh, no," she answered, and giggled again.

That was even scarier.

After Francie hung up, I paused for a moment, my heart pounding. Who should I call? Roy? Dee-Dee? Kapp? Joan? York, I decided. I just hoped he was available.

I punched out the numbers and held my breath until he answered.

"York, can you come over right away?"

"Of course," he answered.

That's why I'd called York. He didn't even stop to ask *why* I needed him. But I told him anyway.

"Francie Krentz called and asked for a session today. She's acting weird. I want to do the session, but I don't want to risk my life. I thought maybe you could sit in the kitchen and keep your ears open. I'll tell her you're there. What do you think?"

"I'm on my way," he told me.

York would be my bulletproof vest. I closed my eyes and bowed my head, thanking the powers that be for my brother. Then I prepared for my next client of the day.

By the time York showed up, I'd added a little something to my usual session paraphernalia: a bell.

"If she does anything hostile, I'll ring the bell," I told him . . . "or I'll scream."

York nodded seriously and took a seat at my kitchen table. I handed him a cup of tea and a package of dairy-free cookies I kept stocked especially for him.

"Have you had other suspects over here when you were alone?" he demanded.

"Yeah," I answered, hearing the squirm in my own voice.

"So what's different about Francie?"

"She giggled, York," I told him, realizing how ridiculous my words sounded even as I spoke. "Her husband died, and she giggled."

"Okay," he muttered. I couldn't tell if I'd convinced him my fear of Francie Krentz had a solid foundation or if he was just humoring me. But it didn't really matter. He was staying. "Have a cookie," I ordered.

The bell rang a few cookies later.

I got Francie settled in on my massage table in my former living room. She was dressed in a full-length yellow tunic with long tendrils of multicolored yarn that reminded me of her dangling curls. I wanted to frisk her, but I didn't. She was there as a client. Still. . . .

"My brother York's in the kitchen," I told her. Her small eyes widened slightly. "But our work here is confidential. Don't worry."

"He can't hear us, can he?" she whispered.

"Not unless we're really loud," I assured her. "It's one room away."

"Oh, good. I'm very sensitive, you know. It goes with my artistic temperament. Dutch is always making fun of my artistic leanings, but I really am an artist."

"Of course you are," I soothed, wondering why she was still using the present tense to talk about Dutch. "I saw some of your work, remember?"

"Oh, how silly of me!" She giggled. "My memory can be so bad. But the mundane passes by me sometimes."

"Your artistic temperament?" I suggested.

"Oh, yes, Cally! You do understand, don't you?"

I nodded. I could see some of the colors of Francie's aura by then, peeking out, mixing and dancing. Was there a mixed message in them? Impatience twined with fear and self-pity. But I didn't see grief, not yet.

"You know that Dutch is dead, don't you?" I asked, laying my hand on hers gently.

"Oh, yes," she replied. "He's such an old pirate, always up to something. It's just like him to die in a gruesome way. I'm delicate. He should have protected me."

I tried to let her words pass by me, to focus on the energy instead. The self-pity was getting stronger, and yes, there was grief. And there was anger. But those energies were still dancing, still mixing with all sorts of emotions. Before Francie could feel better, she needed to really feel, to feel one thing at a time. But that was obviously too painful for her to do on her own. I imagined the strand of grief I saw separating out and flowing through her thumbs.

"I lost him a long time ago," Francie blurted out. "I loved him so much when we met. I thought I was so lucky. But Cally, he was cruel, really cruel. I thought he loved me, but he didn't. How can I mourn a man I didn't love anymore?"

The grief was moving.

"Do you think he loved you in his own way?" I asked her softly.

"Oh, Cally!" Her eyes filled. "I don't know. He hit me, Cally. He hit me. And he made fun of me. He shouldn't have done that."

"No, he shouldn't have," I agreed, shocked in spite of myself. Dutch was a hitter, of course.

"And now he's gone, and I don't know if he really loved me." Her voice rose in pitch. "I don't know!"

I put my arms around her as she keened, comforting her in one of the oldest healing forms, the hug. Francie clung to me like a child would cling to her mother.

I looked up as she held on and saw York peering through a crack in the doorway. I glared at him and shook my head. He disappeared from the crack.

"Dutch told me I was beautiful when he courted me," Francie murmured through her tears. "He admired my art and my clothes. He said he could see that I was special. The first time he hit me, I couldn't believe it. But then it happened again and again. Oh Cally, did he really love me, at least at first?"

"I'm sure he did," I told her, hoping I wasn't a liar. Dutch must have felt something for Francie. He'd married her. He must have felt what at least passed as love for him. "You know his abuse wasn't your fault," I added.

Francie let go of me then and lay back down on the massage table, her eyes closed. I could see grief flowing cleanly, with self-pity not far behind, blocking the stomach meridian.

"Do you get stomachaches, Francie?" I asked.

"Oh, yes, I do," she answered, her eyes popping open. "Terrible, terrible stomachaches. My health is very fragile."

I worked on clearing her stomach meridian as she continued talking.

"No one ever really appreciated me," she complained, her voice tired and fragile now. "My parents never understood that I was special. Even my first husband just wanted to be taken care of. He was an invalid. He died. I inherited the bulk of his estate. Dutch always acted like I married Howard for his money. But I didn't. And now I find out how Dutch made his money! He was one to talk."

Slowly, her stomach meridian cleared and flowed, self-pity pouring out of her.

"Being understood is really important to me," she went on. "I'm deeply emotional. I'm searching for my truest self. And people come in with their big boots and stomp all over me. Dutch acted like he understood, but then he made fun of me. He actually preferred May . . . his sister, they tell me now, to me. That woman was unbelievably coarse, and he thought she was brave. That hurt, Cally. That really hurt."

"I'm sure it did," I answered, taking in a breath. I reminded myself that it wasn't the time to argue about May. Criticism wasn't a helpful healing modality, even implied criticism.

"No one really understands me," Francie reminded me. I didn't correct her. "And now Dutch has abandoned me."

Francie calmed as the session went on, speaking of her life of disappointment and despair as I helped her let the despair out. But the layers seemed endless. Finally, I drew the session to a close.

"Oh, Cally," Francie murmured. "I do feel just a little bit better. You really are a gem. I knew it the moment I met you. I can tell these things, you know."

"You have an artistic temperament," I said.

And she didn't giggle. She was back in her body. Success.

Once Francie had gone, I stretched my arms into the air and breathed in deeply.

York came into the room, as quiet as a sneaky cat.

"Are you okay?" he asked.

"I'm great," I told him. "I don't know why I thought she was dangerous."

"Dack," he growled. "How can you stand working with someone like that?"

I dropped my arms. "York, were you listening?" I demanded. "You weren't supposed to be listening. Not unless I used the bell or screamed."

"What if you hadn't had time to scream?" he queried, and I knew he'd listened the entire time.

"I've never heard anyone so self-absorbed," he told me. "Doesn't she ever think about other people?"

"York, she's a human being," I argued. "She is what she is. She really feels all those things. And she's supposed to express her feelings. And we shouldn't even be having this discussion."

"Right," he conceded. "As long as you're okay."

I hugged him. "Thanks, big brother," I said.

When York left, he told me to take care of myself. And I knew he meant it literally.

Pretty soon, I was back at my kitchen table. York had left a few of the dairy-free cookies in the package. I sniffed them. Peanut butter, carob, and coconut. I told myself he wouldn't want them to go to waste, and began munching as I wrote up my client notes on Francie.

With the session over, I could ask myself if Francie's words had been those of a woman who might have murdered her husband and her husband's sister. I doubted it. What York didn't know was that many of my clients were self-absorbed, especially in a setting where revealing one's real self was encouraged. Self-absorbed didn't mean murderous. In fact, I wondered if Francie was *too* self-absorbed for the competence necessary to murder.

I was still thinking about her when the phone rang.

Gerry Cheng was on the line, and his voice sounded clear and crisp, businesslike.

"We've decided on tomorrow evening for the get-together," he told me. "The boys here are going to make the calls once we decide on the time. I just wanted to make sure you were going to be available."

"I'll be there," I promised him, warmed by the new confidence in his tone.

"I thought I'd make it a potluck," he went on, "have everyone bring a little food. Maybe you'll be able to tell something from what they bring?"

"Maybe," I answered, wishing it was that easy. Beans into bullets? Freudian analysis? "I'll bring tabouli salad."

"May wants this, Cally," he suddenly whispered, and I felt a chill. Was she guiding the party?

"Well then, we'll do it," I answered finally. "For May."

"For May," he agreed, and hung up not long after.

I reached into my shelf and pulled down two cartons of prepackaged tabouli mix. I dutifully poured water over the contents of the cartons and added oil and lemon juice. I chopped parsley and tomatoes and threw them in. The flavor would be better if the ingredients marinated overnight. I'd add avocado the next day.

As my hands worked, I asked myself what I really expected to do tomorrow night. Was I raising Gerry Cheng's hopes too high? Was I putting myself in danger? Duh, did my cat like tuna?

By the time I'd finished the salad and put it in the refrigerator, I was feeling the way everyone had been telling me to feel: afraid.

When my doorbell rang, I was even more afraid. Gerry Cheng had probably already told the murderer that I would be exposing him or her the following night. Maybe the murderer was here for a preemptive strike. I grabbed my cane and crept up on the door, quietly turning the doorknob, then flinging it open at the last minute, ready to—

My friend Joan Hussein stood on my doorstep, her lush, doe-eyed beauty belied by her smirk.

I lowered my cane slowly, nonchalantly. I tried to do the same to my racing pulse.

"So, are you going to ask me in, or are you going to beat me into quitting law first?" she asked.

I raised my cane again in answer, hoping my smile was as nasty as Kapp's on a bad day.

"God, Cally. Sometimes, I just don't believe you. You put yourself into all this danger, then you scare the tar out of yourself."

I looked down at the floor innocently.

"Tar?" I muttered. "I don't see any tar."

Joan leaned her head back and laughed. Then she hugged her way into my house by force.

We sat down on the stuffed chairs in the client room.

"I've got a friend in the prosecutor's office," she told me without further fuss. "She told me the police are seriously considering Gerry Cheng for his wife's murder—"

"But—"

She held up her hand. "I'm only reporting. Don't shoot the messenger. They think they could make a case. He's the deceased's husband. He inherits. He knew who her brother was. He's distrusted in his own industry. He'll make a poor witness. He was in an interracial marriage—"

"But—"

"Don't be an innocent, Cally," she admonished. "This is the real world. Racism counts. They can use it if they don't overplay their hand."

"But Gerry Cheng didn't do it," I argued. "Don't they care—"

"Are you absolutely sure of that?" she challenged.

"No," I admitted. "That's why I'm trying to find out who *did* do it. Gerry's daughter was here last night. She said pretty much the same things as you did. You just missed the fact that Gerry has poor taste in clothing."

"Guess I didn't notice," she commented dryly. "I've never met the man."

"Then why—"

"I'm telling you the way things stand," she answered before I could finish. "You need to stay away from these people, Cally. First off, you've got a murderer out there who's killed twice. Second off, you've got some yahoos after Cheng. Third off—"

Joan never did get to her third point because the phone rang. It was Sarah Quesada on the line.

"I asked him out, Cally!" Sarah shouted triumphantly into my ear. "And he agreed to a date. Isn't that great?"

"Um," I began.

"He is so cool. We're supposed to go out to dinner, but I was thinking of making it at my own place. I mean, shoot, he doesn't have any money. Whaddaya think?"

"Tonight?" I asked. What if Phil was the murderer?

"Yeah, tonight. I'm thinking about baked ham, but he might be a vegetarian or something, so maybe a quiche."

It was a good twenty minutes before I got Sarah off the phone. And Joan was still waiting when I hung up the receiver.

"I gotta find out who did it," I told her, thinking about Sarah and Phil. Should I have told Sarah about Phil's bouts with insanity?

"Cally, you have to watch yourself," Joan warned. "It doesn't take Roy to tell you dark things are at work here. Don't get involved—"

"I already am," I told her. "Thanks to Kapp," I added.

Joan squinted her beautiful eyes angrily. And the phone rang again.

"Cally, Phil told me all about his mental problems," Sarah announced before even saying hello. "Don't you worry. I'm not worried."

Sometimes, it was hard to tell who was supposed to be psychic, I thought as I hung up the second time.

"So, you were lecturing me?" I said to Joan.

She laughed then and stuck her arm in mine.

"Let's go out for an early dinner," she suggested. "Then I'll really lecture you."

I got my jacket and left with Joan.

We walked all the way down my driveway to the street where Joan had parked. Joan liked to walk. She and the goats were soul mates.

I spotted Roy's Saab first, parked a couple of spaces behind Joan's Honda. I stomped toward it. Roy wasn't inside. I looked around and circled to the other side of the Saab. A crumpled body lay there. A wiry, crumpled body with reddish brown hair.

TWENTY

"Roy!" I screamed, running toward him. There was no mistaking his crumpled body, the body I'd lain beside for seven years. I threw myself on the ground next to him, reaching out my hand.

"Cally," someone said. Was that Joan? "Let me handle this."

I touched his arm. It was warm, flopped out to one side. But the back of his head was bleeding, and his eyes were closed.

"Roy!" I tried again. "Are you all right? Please, be all right." I'd done this. I hadn't listened to Roy, and now he was—

Joan's hand tugged at my shoulder and I ignored it.

I covered Roy's body with my own and held on to him. "I'm sorry, Roy," I whispered, wondering if he could hear me. "I'm sorry. I see the darkness now—"

Joan pulled at my shoulder more insistently.

But I held on to Roy. He was warm. Maybe he was alive. Please let him be alive.

Joan knelt next to me. She grabbed Roy's arm and pressed her fingertips to his inner wrist.

"He has a pulse, Cally," she announced softly.

"What?" I asked, still holding his unmoving body.

"Cally, listen to me," Joan ordered. "Roy is not dead. He's unconscious. He has a pulse."

I held on for a second more, then remembered that you weren't supposed to move unconscious people. You probably weren't supposed to jump on them either.

I got up carefully, looking at Joan for the first time since I'd seen Roy.

"He's alive?" I asked, seeking the truth in her large, lustrous eyes.

"Dead men don't have pulses," she reminded me. I think someone just knocked him out."

"Oh, poor Roy!" I was on the ground again, though this time, I didn't straddle his body. I just looked at him. And amazingly, I saw his chest move. He was breathing!

"An ambulance," I announced, my mouth moving faster than my brain. "We gotta get an ambulance."

"I know, Cally," Joan said slowly. I knew that voice. It was the one *I* used with hysterical clients. "I have a cell phone in my car. I'll call it in. You stay with Roy. Can you do that, Cally?"

I wanted to scream at her to hurry, but I just nodded.

"I'll only be a minute," she told me, and ran back to the space where her car was parked.

I put my hand gently on Roy's shoulder, just hoping that I couldn't hurt him by touching. I felt his warmth, and it comforted me. I took off my glasses.

"Roy," I told him. "You're going to be all right. I love you Roy. I love you very much. The lightness of our love can replace this darkness. Roy, you'll be better again, then we can be together. I know they say people can still hear while they're unconscious, so I just want to tell you how much I love you. Leona misses you. And the goats do, too.

Remember the day we went to the park and the ducks followed us?" I could feel the tears coursing down my face, but I kept talking, trying to keep from choking. "And remember when Moscow got out and butted the solicitor?"

I leaned down and kissed the side of his neck. I was afraid to touch his head.

"Be well, Roy," I ordered. "Be well, and know you are loved—"

"They're coming," Joan whispered from my side. "The paramedics will be in the ambulance. Roy's going to get the help he needs."

"Thank you," I whispered back, taking my spare hand and reaching behind me to touch Joan. I ended up squeezing her leg, but she understood. What would I have done without her?

"Roy," I began again. "Joan's called for help, and they're coming. You're going to be all right. You're going to be fine."

"Cally," Joan asked. "Was Roy following you? I thought I saw his car when I parked, but I decided it must have been someone else's when I didn't see him in it."

"I think he's been keeping an eye on me," I told her. "He won't get close to me, but he's been watching out for me." My voice clogged with tears again.

"So someone saw he was your watchdog and decided to get him out of the way?" she theorized.

"Maybe. But then, why didn't they attack me?"

"Because you had visitors?" she suggested.

"Yeah," I said slowly, thinking it over. People had been in and out of my house all day.

"Dack, Joan," I groaned. "Maybe they knocked out Roy and went up the hill to find me and saw that the two of us were together. You may have saved my life."

Joan frowned. "I didn't see any strangers lurking, but then, I didn't see Roy either. Maybe it all happened earlier. Maybe they knocked Roy out, went up the hill, and saw . . . saw who?"

"York," I thought out loud. "York was here earlier, and clients. But that would mean Roy's been lying here for a long time. Oh, I hope not." My brain buzzed back to Roy-panic. "Roy, you'll be all right. Help is coming—"

"Can you see his aura?" Joan asked.

I opened my mouth and closed it again. Why hadn't I thought of that? I looked and saw a dim aura pulsating. And it wasn't black. It was violet and purple with streamers of crystalline green. Was that the green of love?

"Roy, I love you," I said again. The green streamed stronger.

I imagined all the love I had entering Roy's wounded body, healing him, soothing him—

The siren of an ambulance sounded in the distance. I kept thinking healing love.

Then the ambulance arrived with the pandemonium of busy paramedics and radio chatter. They climbed over Roy's sprawled body, checking him out, talking in words I didn't understand. Then they lifted him onto a stretcher.

"May I ride with him to the hospital?" I asked a uniformed woman.

"Are you a relative?"

"No, but—"

"You'll have to meet us there," she said.

They slid Roy into the ambulance, closed the doors, and sirened down the road.

I looked at Joan.

"I'll take you," she offered. And I knew better than to argue. She patted my hand as she drove just over the speed limit to Glasse General Hospital. Even in my shock, I felt the familiar warmth that the goodness of a friend could bring to my body. And my cold body needed it.

I don't know how much time we spent in the hospital waiting room. The time seemed endless, as children screamed and relatives paced and newcomers begged for attention. Joan asked for information, then sat next to me in one of the chairs in a row that was permanently attached to the floor. We might have been on a bus, only it wasn't moving. It even smelled like a bus, but that was probably the scent of people.

"They say they'll let you know when they have him stabilized," Joan informed me. There was a television set hanging from the ceiling at the end of the room, and my eyes kept drifting up to watch the pixel beings that flitted across the screen.

"Cally, are you okay?" Joan finally asked. It wasn't a rhetorical question, but a real one. And I found that I could answer.

"I am, Joan," I answered. "You can go home. I'm going to stay with Roy as long as I can."

I could see Joan's eyes consider me and find me fit. That felt good. I grabbed her hand and squeezed it.

"The people at the desk have your name," she let me know. "They'll call you when Roy is ready to see you. It won't help to bug them any more. They're overwhelmed already. But they promised they *will* call you."

She stood up, hesitating.

"Joan," I told her, "you've done way more than I can ever thank you for. You're the best. And I'm okay now. You can go home." I stood and hugged her, sinking into the rush of friendship once more. "Thank you," I whispered.

And Joan left. I sat back down, my eyes drifting up to the television again.

But I tore my eyes away so that I could look inward. I meditated, going to the place where my healing worked, imagining Roy whole and well. An infinity later, I was infused with the light of peace. I kept myself there in the light and brought Roy in with me. Roy, healthy and happy. I imagined his wounds healing quickly, normal bodily functions returning.

"Ms. Cally Lazar," I heard from above me, and I opened my eyes. But the speaker was not a doctor. He was a uniformed police officer, brown-skinned and diffident.

"I'm from the Estados Police Department," he announced. "You found Roy Beaumont?"

I nodded. "Is he okay?" I asked.

The officer blushed. "I don't know. The doctors are busy." Then he pulled out his notebook. "Do you have any idea what happened to him, Ms. Lazar?" he asked.

By the time I'd finished filling the officer in, he was sitting next to me where Joan had been, his notebook overflowing.

"So, you think the Mostaza Police Department should be informed," he summed up.

I nodded again. My throat was sore from talking. My whole body felt sore, as if *I'd* been in an accident. I had a feeling I looked like I'd been in an accident, too. I reached up and ran my hand through the curls on the top of my head. There was nothing I could do about my braid.

"You'll stay here?" he asked as he moved away from me. I decided he'd been taught to give orders, but the training hadn't taken.

I smiled at him and promised I'd stay in the hospital until the Mostaza police showed up.

He smiled back, a real smile. I wondered how long he'd last as a police officer.

I was back in meditation land when Chief Upwood arrived.

He cleared his throat politely, but loudly, and I opened my eyes again. The chief's childlike, heart-shaped face held an expression of concern. I wondered if it was genuine.

"I've talked to the fine officer from your town of Estados," he began. "He tells me that your significant other, Roy Beaumont, might have been attacked while trying to guard you from the murderer of May North and Dutch Krentz."

"That's right," I agreed. "But I don't know if Roy saw anything. He was unconscious when I found him." I pointed my chin at the nursing station. "I don't know if he's conscious again. They're supposed to call me when he's stabilized."

"Well, my goodness," Chief Upwood chirped. "I'm sure we ought to be able to see the young man."

He turned and strode up to the nursing station. Yeah, right, I thought, and closed my eyes again.

And then, finally, I heard my name called out.

"Cally Lazar," came over the loudspeaker. "Cally Lazar."

I rushed up to the nursing station.

"That her?" a harassed-looking woman asked Chief Upwood.

He smiled sweetly and nodded.

"Room 410B," she said. "Don't wear him out."

So the chief and I took the elevator up to the fourth floor.

"Did she say how Roy was doing?" I demanded.

"Apparently well enough to see us," he answered. "She said she didn't have a report yet."

"Then how did you—" I began, but I didn't push it. I was going to see Roy. I didn't care how the chief had accomplished the meeting.

The elevator pinged, and we went down the hall toward

410B. There was another nursing station on the way. Chief Upwood stopped to talk to the nurse there. I didn't. I went running toward Roy's room.

The first bed in the room held an elderly man whose benign expression seemed to radiate transcendence. But he wasn't Roy. I peered around the curtain that divided the room in half.

Roy lay in bed, his head bandaged, his eyes closed in what might have been sleep or just pure exhaustion.

"Roy?" I whispered tentatively.

His eyes fluttered open. And then he saw me. A smile spread across his pale, bony face, lighting up his freckles.

"Roy!" I yelped, and ran toward him, embracing him fervently but awkwardly over the raised rail of his hospital bed.

"Cally, darlin'," he murmured dreamily. Was he medicated or just in shock? "I thought I heard you. You told me everything was gonna be all right, and it is. You always bring me light."

"Oh, Roy," I mumbled through new tears. "I thought I'd lost you."

"You'll never lose me, darlin'," he said. He smiled and let his eyes close again. "Never. We're always together. That's why I fret so. So hard to love with the darkness all around. But I can't seem to not love you."

His voice stopped. I heard Chief Upwood walk in and slide the curtain back.

"Well," he announced heartily. "Your young man is lucky. No concussion, they tell me. Hurt his ribs worse than his head, but they'll heal."

I jumped back from the side of the bed. His ribs? I remembered holding him when I'd first found him. Criminy!

"Roy, I didn't hurt your ribs when I hugged you, did I?" I asked.

"No, darlin'," he answered me softly, his eyes open again. "Your touch is so fine, so healing. Did I tell you that? I felt you workin' on me; I felt the light of your soul. Oh, foot, I shouldn't be going on. We have a visitor."

I turned to the chief.

"Mr. Beaumont," the chief introduced himself. "I'm Chief Upwood from the Mostaza Police Department. If you're up to it, I'd like to ask you a few questions in private."

"Yes, sir," Roy responded. My Kentucky boy was always polite. But I wasn't.

"Is it okay if I stay here, too?" I asked the chief.

Chief Upwood thought for a moment. I know he was wondering if I'd been the one to hurt Roy. His eyes seemed to weigh the facts and find me not guilty.

"I'd appreciate it if you'd be good enough to help me talk to your friend," he pronounced finally. "I think it would be helpful for you to stay."

So I pulled up a chair on one side of Roy's bed and reached over the rail to hold his hand, and the chief pulled up a chair on the other side of his bed and cleared his throat.

"Mr. Beaumont," The chief began.

Roy pulled his gaze from mine and looked at the chief.

"Tell me what happened to you today in your own words," the chief suggested. "Start at the beginning."

"Well, sir," Roy tried. "I guess I'd have to start by saying that I was keeping an eye on Cally, Ms. Lazar, when I ran into trouble—"

"Keeping an eye on?" the chief interrupted.

"Um . . ." Roy faltered. A blush colored his bony face. "I had this idea that if I watched Cally wherever she went, I'd keep whoever it was who murdered Mrs. North and Mr. Krentz away from her. I suppose I didn't do such a good job."

"And so, you parked at the bottom of Ms. Lazar's driveway?"

"Yes, sir. I parked there, and got out of the car and watched people come and go. Cally has a very successful business, you know. I kept out of sight as much as I could, ducking when people were coming and all. I remember seeing her brother York leave after some woman in a goofy kind of getup, then I believe I saw her friend Joan drive up and walk up the driveway, but my mind's all kinda muddled up around it. Next thing I knew, I was in here and so worried about Cally. I was frettin' something terrible. But the nurse said Cally was here, waiting for me. And it seemed as if I could feel her here."

Roy turned to me, and I blinked my eyes at him the way I did at my cat when I want to smile without using my mouth. He blinked back Leona-style, his golden eyes shining. I breathed in and let the moment take me.

"Ms. Lazar, when did your friend Joan arrive at your house?" the chief asked, his eyes on me now.

"I, uh . . ." I started over again. "About a half an hour to an hour before we found Roy," I told him.

"Did you or your friend see anyone—"

"No," I told him, ready for the question. "Joan and I talked about it. Neither of us saw anyone lurking."

"Mr. Beaumont, before you were hit, did you see anything or anyone that could give us a clue to the identity of your assailant?" the chief asked. Actually, he seemed to be begging.

"No, sir. I wished I could tell you something, because I believe this person must have been the same one mixed up in your murders. But I didn't see anything. I was probably standing by my car when the person came up. They must have been quiet, I imagine, or I would have heard something.

Or maybe I did and just don't remember. I'm afraid I just don't know."

Still, the chief stayed and stayed, asking us both questions over and over again.

Finally, a smiling young woman came into the room, pushing a cart with dinner trays. Roy's held soup, a tuna sandwich, potato chips, a slice of lemon cream pie, and a cup of herbal tea. I wondered if it would be better or worse than airplane food.

"Well, I'll leave you two alone," the chief said, and stood up. Maybe it was the unwholesome smell of the soup.

"Do you think I can spend the night here with Roy?" I asked him. I added in a whisper, "For safety's sake. I don't want anyone coming after Roy again."

Chief Upwood smiled and told me he'd take care of it. And I believed him.

Roy insisted on splitting his dinner with me. He refused to eat until I did. If it had been anyone else besides Roy, I would have suspected that he was using me as a taster. But Roy would no more have eaten dinner without sharing than he would have used obscenities. It was beyond him.

I'd just finished my half of the tuna sandwich and chips when I remembered that I'd scheduled an appointment that evening. I went to the nursing station to find a phone, passing Roy's elderly roommate and introducing myself on the way.

"Glad to know you, the name's Pete," he informed me. "You got a good-hearted boy in there."

"Thanks, Pete," I muttered. "I think so, too."

And then Pete closed his eyes. I wondered if they put tranquilizers in the food. I was feeling drowsy, too.

The nurse at the station was a pinched-looking woman, but her voice was kind and musical.

"You have some kind of spell over that handsome police

chief?" she asked me. "He said to give you all the privileges he might have. Said you could spend the night if you want. Said young love was a beautiful thing."

I felt my own blush. "I, uh, I don't know," I answered.

She laughed and directed me to the closest pay phone. I caught my client for the night and told her I was at the hospital with a friend. She murmured sympathetically, and I trotted on back to Roy's room. Young love? I hoped so.

But when I got back to Roy's room he was asleep, his tray on the night table with half a piece of pie left. I ate it and judged it on a par with airplane fare. Only airplanes smelled better than hospitals. Then I sat in a chair and feasted my eyes on Roy's sleeping form.

My own eyes were just starting to drift closed when the visitors began.

Dee-Dee was first, along with Joan. They whispered their way into the room.

"Oh, Cally," Dee-Dee murmured, and wrapped her arms around me. "We snuck past the nurse. We've come to take you home."

"I'm spending the night," I told her.

"You're what!" Dee-Dee yelped.

"Pipe down," Joan hissed. "The nurse will hear you."

Dee-Dee and I argued in whispers. Roy woke up somewhere in the middle of our argument, said, "Dee-Dee, Joan, watch out for Cally," and fell asleep again.

York was next. He wouldn't say, but I was fairly certain that Dee-Dee had called him. He wanted to guard the room if I insisted on staying with Roy.

Pete from across the curtain told him not to worry, that he'd keep an eye on us, but that didn't seem to move York. What did move him was the nurse who came in and shoved him out. She was lucky he let her.

I was almost asleep in my chair again when I got my next visitor, Phil Morton.

"How'd you even know I was here?" I asked him. So much for Roy's safety in the hospital.

"I was doing my rounds on this floor when I spoke to Nurse Lawrence," he explained. "I often come for evening rounds here. Got a lot of patients on this ward that need a kind word. And the nurse mentioned a Cally who was spending the night with her wounded boyfriend in 410B. I thought I'd peek in, and it was you. I just wondered if there was anything I could do to help."

I looked at him and reminded myself that chances were he wasn't our murderer.

"Didn't you have a date with Sarah, tonight?" I demanded.

"Oh, my," he replied, looking at his feet. "I did indeed. That's why I'm so late on my rounds."

"Do you like her, Phil?" I asked.

He bobbed his head up and down. "She's a kind and generous woman," he told me. "I don't know what she sees in me, though."

"Oh, Phil," I said, my tight muscles letting go. "She sees a kind and generous man."

"Oh, my!" he exclaimed, and looked up at the ceiling. I thought I heard Roy rustle in his bed.

Phil changed the subject to Gerry's potluck and let me know I was expected at seven o'clock the following evening. I was still smiling when he walked out of the room.

"Is Sarah nice?" Roy asked me softly once Phil was gone.

"Very nice," I told him. "But not as nice as you."

"Oh, Cally," he murmured. "I just wish the darkness would go away. I really do, darlin'."

And so did I.

I fell asleep in my chair sometime after midnight, finally immune to the periodic check-ins of the night nurse. I dreamed of my mother, then of my mother and Roy. They were talking, and there was danger nearby. But they couldn't hear me when I tried to warn them.

I jolted out of my dream to find my aching body in a hospital chair. Someone had draped a blanket over me during the night.

I looked over at Roy's bed, eager to see his face, eager to see how he was. But Roy wasn't in his bed.

TWENTY-ONE

"Roy?" I tried, my voice shaky. "Roy, where are you?" I looked at my watch. It was eight in the morning. Roy couldn't be gone.

I padded over to the bathroom and peeked through the doorway. Roy wasn't there. But I tiptoed in anyway, closed the door, and used the facilities. Never search for a missing person on a full bladder, I remembered. If someone hadn't said it, they should have.

When I came out of the bathroom, I remembered something else: Roy had a roommate. I craned my neck around the edge of the curtain and saw Pete staring back at me.

"Where's Roy?" I asked, taking a step into Pete's territory.

"Roy's gone," he told me gently. "He checked himself out about a half an hour ago. He didn't want to wake you up."

"What?!" I yelled.

I shouldn't have yelled. A nurse came rushing in, a new nurse I hadn't met.

"What are you doing here?" she demanded.

"I'm . . . I'm with Roy Beaumont," I answered.

"Who is—"

"The man who should be in this bed," I informed her. "Roy Beaumont, your patient."

"410B checked himself out this morning," she told me. "Now, I'm going to have to ask you to leave—"

"She's visiting me," Pete declared, cutting her off.

"It's too early for visiting hours—"

"This is important," Pete insisted. "If you don't think so, call Chief Upwood of the Mostaza Police Department."

The nurse threw up her hands in disgust. "Fine," she muttered. "Just fine." And she stomped out of the room.

I grabbed my cane, ready to stomp out behind her. But Pete stopped me with a word.

"Wait," he ordered gently. I turned his way. "Roy asked me to talk to you before you left."

"He did?"

Pete nodded. "He told me you'd be upset. But I had a good talk with Roy. I think you ought to know about it."

"What did you talk about?" I asked tentatively.

"The darkness," he answered.

"Oh, criminy," I whispered, and grabbed a chair.

"You see," Pete began, after having assured me sixteen different ways that Roy's physical condition was fine. "I know about the darkness."

"Do you see it, too?" I asked.

"No." Pete smiled, his tranquil features almost translucent in the artificial light of the room. I didn't think Pete had long to live. "My wife Theresa saw it."

"What does it mean?" I demanded, holding the sides of my chair.

"We never really figured it out for sure," he told me. I opened my mouth. He held up a finger for silence.

"When we first met, Theresa and I thought we would marry. We were very much in love. But then she began to see darkness between us. She'd been raised in South America. At first, I thought she was just being superstitious, a result of a different culture. But after a while, I could see the darkness, too. Not with my eyes, mind you, but with my body. I didn't know what to make of it. But Theresa did, at least she believed she did. She was afraid, like your Roy, that the darkness would bring *me* harm, so she broke off our engagement. We each went our own ways and eventually married other people." He paused, and I heard the busy morning sounds of the hospital coming from the doorway. "My first wife died in a car accident before a year was out. Theresa's husband died of cancer not much later. Theresa and I met again after some time had passed, and we decided to start over. Theresa still saw the darkness, but we both figured there was no escaping fate. Everyone has their share of darkness. So we married. We had four decades together before Theresa passed away. It'll be a year, next Friday."

"You loved her," I said, feeling the goose bumps on my arms.

"That I did," he agreed. "That I did. And I still do."

"And you told Roy?" I asked softly, wondering at this magical, fragile man. My own heart hurt, and yet I could feel the lightness of his joy.

"I told Roy. I don't know how much he heard or understood."

"We all have our share of darkness," I murmured. Was this what Roy and I had to learn? I, that darkness was part of life? Roy, that there was no running from fate?

"Thank you," I told Pete.

"Theresa would have said there was a reason you and Roy ended up in this hospital room with me. I'm glad if I've helped any." He was beginning to doze off again, his eyelids drooping. "Theresa? I'll never know what would have happened if we'd just married when we first wanted to. Or maybe I will." He chuckled, his voice dreamy. "Soon, maybe I will."

I got up out of my chair and whispered another thank-you to Pete. Then I bent over and placed a light kiss on his forehead.

He muttered, "Theresa," and I walked out of the room into the hospital hallway.

The hallway was filled with nurses, doctors, technicians, aides, and janitors. They were all moving briskly along. The world was different out there than it was in the room with Pete. Was it more real or did it just feel that way? I wondered for a moment if Pete would still be in the room if I went back. I felt as if I could have just imagined him. But I didn't go back.

I wanted to find Roy and talk over what Pete had said. And it wasn't just that. I *had* to find Roy. Because whoever had knocked Roy out might be considering killing him now.

I'd taken the elevator to the lobby by the time I realized I didn't have a car. And I noticed something else in the relative cleanliness and calm of the front lobby. I didn't smell very fresh after a night in a hospital chair. I needed a shower, not to mention a toothbrush and hairbrush. Dack.

"Cally, yoo-hoo!" I heard.

I turned and saw Dee-Dee running after me.

"Whoa," she said, her small body vibrating with energy as she caught up with me. "I went up to the hospital room, but Pete told me you'd left."

"Roy's gone, too," I whispered urgently.

"Yeah," she confirmed. "He was well enough to leave. That's so cool."

"No," I contradicted her. "That's not cool. Whoever hit

Roy could be afraid he'll recognize them. What if they come after him again?"

Dee-Dee grinned.

"What?" I tried.

"I'm not supposed to tell you," she began slowly.

"Tell me!" I hissed.

"Roy's with Ben. Ben's taking care of him for a while. You're not supposed to visit."

"But why—" I stopped myself. If I visited, I might lead the murderer right to Roy. And Dee-Dee's sweetie, Ben, was a good choice for a bodyguard. He worked in repatterning body movement. He was three hundred pounds of serene bulk, muscle, and love. And he was Roy's friend.

"Okay," I agreed finally.

"Okay?" Dee-Dee repeated, tilting her head. "Don't you want to bop me with your cane or something?"

I realized I was holding my cane way too high and lowered it.

"Thank you, Dee-Dee," I said dutifully.

I brought you a present," she told me, presenting a paper grocery bag with a flourish.

I looked inside the bag cautiously. Dee-Dee was a truly spiritual woman, a hypnotherapist, a friend, and . . . a woman with a taste for practical jokes. And a saint, I added mentally when I saw what was in the bag: a change of clothing, including underwear, toothpaste, brushes, and my own soap. I got to be a human again!

"Roy gave me the key to your place," she told me. "I hope that was cool."

"Very, very cool," I assured her, and hugged her mightily, smelly self and all.

After a trip to the public restroom off the lobby, I was sponge-bathed, brushed, coifed, and dressed in matching clothes that smelled ever so slightly of laundry detergent.

"Lookin' good," Dee-Dee assured me when I walked out into the lobby again.

"It's the thing about the clothes matching," I told her. "I hadn't thought about that before."

She tilted her head back and laughed. I laughed with her.

"Kapp's meeting us here," she told me. I stopped laughing.

Kapp was waiting in the hospital cafeteria. I ignored him as I loaded my tray with scrambled eggs, raisin toast, yogurt, and a fruit cup. I added a bowl of granola and some green tea. I was dressed, and I was hungry.

There weren't many civilians in the cafeteria. A couple of security guards were sitting together. There was a table with what looked like nurses. But mostly people sat alone at their tables, gulping coffee and stuffing down breakfast. They weren't there to socialize; they were there to eat.

"Lazar," Kapp greeted me, standing as I sat down.

"Kapp," I returned his greeting, then attacked my food, crunching into the toast first, because I was having mixed feelings about Kapp. He had recommended me to Gerry Cheng as someone who could figure out murder. And somehow, that had led to Roy's being hurt. I stirred the granola into the yogurt and mixed in some fruit. It was true that Kapp had played a very small part in the events that had brought me to the hospital. My own arrogance and curiosity had been the major factors. I took a sip of tea. But still—

Kapp cleared his throat. "Sorry to hear about Roy," he offered.

I choked on my tea.

Kapp had apologized! And about Roy, who he liked

about as much as I liked dental work. I looked at him closely and saw genuine regret on his bulldog face. For once, he looked his age.

"It's okay, Kapp," I told him once I could speak again. "It's not your fault."

"If it'll make you happy, Joan reamed me out royally last night," he added. "Mother of God, she's good."

I smiled. Life was coming back into his face.

"I'm happy," I assured him. And I was. I had friends. Whatever darkness I had to face, I had the light of friends to help me.

"Do you still want to find the murderer, Lazar?" he asked. It was a serious question.

"Yes," I answered without thinking. How else would I ever feel safe again?

"Damn, I knew you wouldn't give up!" he shouted.

"Shush, Kapp," I hissed, surveying the room. But no one had even looked up. These guys were probably used to melodrama with breakfast.

"But—" he began.

"Enough," I cut in. "I suppose you've got more information to share."

Kapp looked at Dee-Dee, raising his brows over his glasses. "Psychic," he muttered. "Holy Mary, the woman's psychic."

"You say that like it's a bad thing," Dee-Dee put in.

Kapp glared at her as I snorted through my scrambled eggs. Then he began his information download.

"Becky Cheng," he whispered. "She used to teach at Ross University. But she wasn't rehired her fourth year, along with a bunch of other nonwhite teachers who'd been brought on board during affirmative action days. She made a big fuss, instituted an antidiscrimination suit. They paid her off big-time. Then she went to teach at Glasse State University."

"Is she a good teacher?" I asked.

Kapp shrugged. "No student complaints that I know of."

"What else?" I demanded.

"Ian Oxton," Kapp gave me. "The police had been watching Citrus House even before May North died. Ian Oxton's a druggie. They think he might be a distributor, too."

"What kind of drugs?" Dee-Dee asked, frowning.

"Cocaine, grass. Nothing unusual." Kapp smiled like a shark. "But there's a doctor in the house, too. No one's come up with anything on Eric Ford, but they'd sure like to."

"And . . ." I prodded. Kapp had that look. He still had more to tell.

"John Turner and Dutch Krentz were buddies. People who've been interviewed said they hung out together, sailed, golfed—"

"Guy stuff," Dee-Dee summed up. "What's the crime in that?"

"Just that neither of them mentioned any relationship when *they* were interviewed."

I tried to remember if the police had even asked about our relationships with other people in the group of suspects. I gave up. It seemed to be a century ago. I couldn't remember.

"But the biggie is . . ." Kapp leaned forward over the table.

I leaned forward, too.

"Yeah?" I whispered.

"Francie Krentz."

Then he just leaned back in his chair and smiled.

"What about Francie Krentz?" I demanded, trying not to raise my voice.

"Well," Kapp began slowly, lazily. I used my cane to tap him on the shin under the table. His voice sped up. "Remember how I told you there wasn't much on Francie? She married a rich, older man, and he died? Well, there wasn't anything *officially* on the incident, but unofficially, there was a lot of talk. A connection of mine dug up some folks from the town Francie and her husband lived in. These folks were of the opinion that there was something fishy about the whole thing. Francie was her husband's practical nurse before she married him. Hooboy. What kind of marriage was she expecting from an invalid?"

I pondered that one. Maybe they played chess together. Or read. Or talked. Or something. It didn't just have to be about money.

"Francie Krentz was investigated when her first husband died," Kapp went on. "His kids said she killed him, that she used her nursing skills to help his heart attack along. But there was no proof, so the investigation was dropped."

"Well?" I asked as Kapp leaned back again. "Do you think she killed her first husband?"

"Nah," Kapp dismissed his own case. "The kids were probably just royally huffed that she inherited."

"That's it?" I pushed.

"I said 'probably,' Counselor," he reminded me.

"Oh," I said. I looked at my watch. I had a client in twenty minutes.

"Dee-Dee, can you drop me at my house?" I asked.

"Sure thing, boss," she replied.

"Thanks, Kapp, for all the information about Howard's death," I offered as I stood.

"Howard?" he objected, glaring. "Who told you her first husband's name was Howard?"

"Connections," I whispered. "Connections, Kapp."

Kapp's face reddened. I was glad we were already at a hospital.

"I'll get you later, Lazar," he hissed as we left, waving his cane. But when I turned back at the door, he was smiling again.

"Did Francie tell you?" Dee-Dee guessed once we were in her old Mustang, heading toward my house.

"Yep," I confirmed. "Connections, like I said."

When she dropped me off, Dee-Dee promised me she'd keep an eye on Roy, then she was revving the engine of her car.

"Go for it, Cally!" she shouted, and took off.

I fed the goats and the cat and spent the rest of the morning on two clients, one with angry liver issues and the other with every issue under the sun, a real renaissance man of troubles. I was just glad I hadn't booked three. I could have used some time on the massage table myself.

So I did my morning meditation in the afternoon and ate a quick lunch involving fresh bread and stale peanut butter. I had places to go and people to bug before I went to Gerry Cheng's potluck in the evening.

I thought about Francie. Was it ethical to visit a client as a suspect? It was, only if I didn't use the information I gleaned while she'd been on my table, I decided. Maybe. Or only if I didn't use anything against her unless she had actually killed Dutch and May? I figured Howard was in the category of the karmic statute of limitations. Finally, I just got in my Honda and drove to her house in Mostaza.

But Francie wasn't home. I knocked on the door of the graying redwood house. But instead of footsteps, I heard little claws clacking and yipping to end the world. But no Francie.

I got back in my car, wondering if Francie's absence

was the answer to my ethical questioning. Still, John Turner hadn't been a client, and I was betting I'd find him at his import store.

I bet right. World Imports was open when I got there. I walked in, smelling cedar and incense and wondering how to approach Dutch's old buddy. Would John Turner be in mourning? He was talking to a customer, another man about his age.

"I collect antique watches," the man was saying. He grabbed the brass pull of one the many drawers in a tall cabinet and yanked. I winced. I liked that cabinet. Couldn't he be more gentle?

"There are twenty-six drawers in this chest," John Turner told the man, his voice bland, nonjudgmental.

"Quality," the customer pronounced. "Quality is everything."

"Quality," John repeated like a therapist.

"How much?" the customer demanded.

"Six thousand dollars."

The customer flinched.

"Let me think about it," he said.

"Certainly," John agreed. He turned from his customer and saw me in the doorway.

"Ms. Lazar?" he greeted me, walking my way.

"Is this a good time?" I whispered.

He shrugged, his symmetrical face cool and reserved. I didn't see mourning there, but then, I didn't see anything.

The customer who'd been inspecting the cabinet shoved past me.

"I'll think it over," he mumbled, and was out the door.

John Turner smiled for a moment as if amused. Maybe he was amused.

"So, Ms. Lazar," he said politely. "Did you want to buy a chest?"

"I'd love to," I told him. "But your price tag has too many zeroes for me."

He let out a small bark of laughter. "It had too many zeroes for Mr. Quality, too." He shook his head. "So I suppose you want to ask me more questions."

"Well, yeah," I admitted. "I heard you were a friend of Dutch Krentz's. I thought you might be able to tell me something about him."

He looked over my shoulder for a moment before speaking. I looked, too, but I didn't see anything there.

"First off, let me give you a tip, Ms. Lazar. Dutch Krentz was not what I would call a friend. We played an occasional game of golf, sailed together a couple of times, but he and I didn't have much in common. And his wife was enough to put me off visiting forever. She was bothering Julie about 'doing lunch' so much that Julie had stopped answering her calls."

I guessed John wasn't in mourning.

"Do you have any ideas who might have wanted to kill Dutch?" I pushed.

John smiled ever so slightly. "His lovely wife," he suggested, then turned back to the interior of his store.

I'd been dismissed.

"See you at Gerry's tonight?" I said.

"I doubt it," he replied quietly.

I drove to Citrus House after I left John Turner's store, hoping to see Ian Oxton. Ian was in, though it seemed that everyone else was out.

"Cally!" Ian sang when he opened the door. He pulled me into the orange living room with a quick tug, and asked, "Shall we dance?"

"Um . . . no," I answered, moving out of his grip with a move that York had taught me many years ago.

But Ian was undeterred by his lack of a willing partner, humming and twirling to a very different drummer by himself.

"Ian," I began, then realized that asking him about drugs came under the category of stupid questions.

I just told him good-bye and walked out the still open door.

Once I got back in my Honda, I realized I had nowhere else to go but home. And once I was home, my bed looked very appealing. An uncomfortable overnight in a hospital chair doesn't count as a good night's sleep. I lay down, telling myself I'd rest for a fifteen minutes. I woke up a few hours later.

I had just enough time to shower and chop some avocado for the tabouli before heading back to Citrus House. Actually, not enough time, but I took it anyway.

The circular driveway was full when I got there. Yes! Gerry Cheng had done his job. Now, it was my turn.

Ian Oxton was once again in full butler regalia when he opened the door. His long, lean face looked haggard but no longer stoned.

"Ms. Lazar," he said with a bow. "Please come in. Your audience awaits."

I opened my mouth to say something about our meeting earlier that day, but the black Labrador retriever was jumping up and licking my face before I could.

And Francie had taken center stage anyway. She stood in the middle of the room, across from Phil Morton.

"I told you, I don't believe you!" she shouted, her round face red and streaming with perspiration. So much for my healing work. "It's just too awful."

Gerry Cheng stood behind Phil. And I saw Becky, Eric, York, and Sarah circling around the three. Only the Turners seemed to be missing from the crowd.

"Now, Ms. Krentz," Phil soothed. "I know you wouldn't want to be unfair. You've had some shocks recently, and—"

"My husband was not a brother to that woman!" Francie insisted. "I've thought and I've thought, and Dutch wouldn't have condoned her disgusting behavior—"

"Mrs. Krentz," Gerry Cheng broke in, his angry voice almost unrecognizable. "I must ask you to leave our house immediately."

TWENTY-TWO

"But, I didn't mean—" Francie began, turning to Gerry.

"I don't care what you *meant* to say," he insisted. His cheekbones stood out sharply in his usually placid face. He could have been an aging Mongol warrior. "What you *have* done is insult the memory of my sweet and dear wife. There is no excuse. You are in her house. I ask you again to leave."

Francie put her head in her hands and began to sob.

"Didn't you hear my father ask you to leave?" Becky Cheng demanded, at her father's side, her hand on his shoulder. But Gerry's resolve was visibly retreating in the face of Francie's tears.

"Shoot, how can you come here and say such awful stuff?" Sarah put in. Then her voice softened along with her brown eyes. "What's the matter with you?" she asked. It wasn't a rhetorical question.

"Hussy!" the parrot added from its perch.

"I don't know!" Francie wailed. "Dutch is dead, and I don't understand anything. I'm sorry. I know I shouldn't have said anything about May. I just don't understand why Dutch loved her so much. He loved her more than me!"

"Francie," Phil tried again, stooping over the small woman, his brow furrowed. "May I call you Francie?"

"I . . . I, yes, you can," she mumbled through her hands.

"You lost your husband," he stated. "It doesn't seem fair to you, so you've said some unkind things tonight. Put them to right, Francie. Let goodness be your guide."

There was a pause as Francie lifted her head from her hands. She stood a little straighter.

"I . . . I apologize, Gerry," she offered tentatively. "I'm highly sensitive, emotional. Too emotional, I guess. Sometimes, I say things I shouldn't. I'll leave now. I'm very sorry. Please forgive me. Your wife was a very strong woman, very attractive."

"Of course," Gerry said awkwardly. He turned his head away. "You're welcome to stay—"

"No, no," she murmured. "I've done too much damage already. I don't know what I was thinking. I'll go."

The only relief in the silence was the sound of two of the dogs playing in the kitchen. Then Ian slammed a closet door and approached Francie.

"Your coat, madam?" Ian offered, holding out a purple velvet cloak that could have been made for a magician. Francie took the cloak and wrapped it around her shoulders, keeping her eyes straight ahead as she left the house. I stepped back into the shadows, out of sight, before she passed me. I didn't want to embarrass her more than she already had embarrassed herself. Despite her bad behavior, I felt sorry for Francie Krentz. Even after May's death, Francie couldn't compete with her ghost.

"I should talk to her," Phil whispered to Gerry. "Is that all right with you, sir?"

"Gosh dang, son!" Gerry exclaimed. "Of course it's all right. She's out of her mind with grief."

Phil scooted out the door, and I let out a breath. Someone would comfort Francie. And Gerry had forgiven her.

I put my tabouli on the buffet table as Becky started in.

"That woman had no right to speak that way," she declared. "How could she come into your house and—"

"It's May's house, honey," Gerry put in. "And Francie isn't thinking right. She said so herself."

Becky flinched at the implied reprimand. "I'm sorry, Daddy," she tried.

"I think she was jealous," Eric suggested, his voice booming unexpectedly off the walls. He lowered his volume. "She said it herself, that her husband loved May more than her. She shouldn't have said those nasty things about May, but I understand why she did, in a way."

"The old love farce," Ian offered. "Dutch loved May. May loved Gerry. Francie loved Dutch. And no one loved Francie."

"Francie loved Francie," York offered scornfully.

"York," I objected. "Have a little sympathy."

"I don't think she even realized how mean she was being," Sarah piped in.

York sighed. "Our sympathies should be for Gerry," he pointed out. "And for May—"

"Hello, everyone," a new voice broke in. I shifted my gaze and saw Julie Turner, carrying an enameled tureen in her hands. "I can only stay for a minute," she told us. "I just thought I'd come by to tell you how much I . . . I admired May."

"Well, thanks, Julie," Gerry said. "Are you sure you wouldn't like a drink or a bite to eat?"

"Oh, gosh," she muttered, her big blue eyes widening. "That'd be really neat, but I don't want to leave Zack alone. So I'd better get going."

She walked to the buffet table and set down the tureen. "I made pumpkin soup. I hope you guys enjoy it."

"It sounds great," Gerry assured her. He took her hand for a moment. Julie's eyes misted up.

She swiveled around and walked quickly out the front door. I surveyed the room, looking at who was left from the night of the original party. Gerry, his daughter, and two lodgers. York, Sarah, and myself. The dogs, cats, and the parrot. Pathetic.

Phil came back in the door. The count was up to' three lodgers. But what was I going to observe in the absence of Francie and the three Turners? How had Nero Wolfe always induced *all* the suspects to attend his get-togethers?

Gerry turned to me as if he'd heard my thought.

"Cally, are we enough for your reading?"

"I can always try," I told him, attempting nonchalance. "But why don't we eat first?"

Actually, I'd been hoping that the interactions between the suspects might tell me more about them than their auras. But as I filled my plate with tabouli, corn bread, guacamole, spinach lasagna, and carrot cake, I started taking peeks. I'd get to the soup later.

I tried York first, not that I believed my brother was a true suspect. But York had always been hard for me to read. I theorized that he shielded himself in some way unconsciously as part of his martial arts training. That evening, I saw the faintest haloing of yellow around his first chakra. It wasn't even close to the intensity of the color I'd seen emanating from him on the night of May's death. But in that haloing, I saw his fear and wish to protect both himself and me. I looked away as he glared my way. York was far too sensitive to miss the peek.

I sat down on a short neon orange sofa and probed the others, searching and wondering. What would a murderer's aura look like? Would I know it if I saw it? Anger, fear, guilt? I saw those reflected around me, and yet none of them screamed out murderer to me. Sarah's predominant hue that evening was a kind of pink that often came from a wish to hide from bad things, a self-protective haze, with hints of suppressed feelings floating underneath.

I took a bite of lasagna. It was rich with cheese and sauce. Phil was the most interesting, aura-wise. His lower body was enveloped in the murky blue of mourning and separation I'd seen before, but instead of the previous white and gold in his upper chakras, I now saw the violet of religious certainty.

And Becky and her father, Gerry, were case studies of family patterns, their matching bursts of turquoise and chartreuse, and spikes of orange exhibiting a mixture of frustration, anger, loss, guilt, and fear overlaid with the paler yellow of intellect. I felt around more closely, but found nothing that seemed abnormal, as if there was a normal state to compare theirs to. I took another bite of lasagna in frustration.

Ian's auric essence was made, not surprisingly, of silky rose red sensuality and taxicab yellow impatience with a touch of hot red anger, while Eric was mostly a sea of blue and green loneliness and separation, though he shared a wisp of the violet religious certainty that Phil had in such abundance.

Who was a murderer? No one? Anyone? Why had I even suggested this exercise?

The colors of auras that I'd worked so hard to read for so many years were just clues. Green emanating from one person might be love or loss, from another, healing or frustration. It took time to really feel what they meant for an individual, hours not minutes. Location on the body, interaction with chakras, intensity, or quality of color could help pinpoint their meaning, but even these markers weren't absolute. And people changed constantly, their auras situation-dependent. I concentrated more deeply, closing my eyes and reaching out with my energetic antennae for a hint of murderousness, a tug of insatiable rage, a flash of unreasoning insanity, anything. And I found nothing.

I ate the rest of my meal just listening with my ears and watching with my eyes.

"I'm thinking of taking up topiary," Becky Cheng announced. "You know, to show some appreciation of May's work. I thought I could begin by trimming her menagerie in the back, then maybe I'll try a little something on my own. Maybe just an egg or something."

"That would be really neat," Sarah enthused, munching on corn bread and spilling crumbs as she spoke. "One of the things that makes this property really special is the topiary."

Gerry nodded wordlessly, his eyes and mind somewhere else. His plate had food on it, but he wasn't eating.

"I've been thinking of branching out, too," Eric put in.

"Oh, gawd! Branching out?" Ian laughed. "Is that a topiary joke?"

"No!" Eric yelped, his face reddening under his beard. "I meant as an eye doctor. I've been working on eye exercises to improve sight without glasses or surgery. I'm trying them myself first. If I can improve my own vision, I figure I can help other people."

"Let me know if it works," I told him. Glasses were almost as much a part of my life as my cane was.

"Well," Ian said, then cleared his throat. "Not to be boring or anything, but I've been seriously thinking about rehab. May was always on me to do something about, you know, my substance problems. And I just think I might."

"Good for you," Phil cheered him on. "You've got to have a positive attitude. And you've got it. Put your trust in the divine, and you'll be halfway there."

"Thank you, my man," Ian murmured, bowing his head in Phil's direction. "Thank you."

"How about you, Gerry?" Sarah asked. "You making any plans—"

Gerry shook his head. "I . . ." he tried. "May and I . . . oh, dang." And he began to cry.

"Oh, shoot," Sarah burst out. "Jeez, I'm sorry."

"No, no," Gerry insisted through his tears.

I drank my water, looking anywhere but at poor Gerry, who was trying so hard to compose himself.

"Time to go?" York whispered hopefully in my ear.

"Yep," I answered, and stood up from the sofa.

"Gerry," I murmured in the gentlest tone I could manage. "Thank you so much for inviting me this evening."

"Are you going?" he demanded, a look of alarm blending with the misery on his face. I hadn't done my job yet.

"I'm afraid so," I told him.

"But—"

"I'll call you," I assured him. "I need some time to think."

"Oh, sure you do," he answered after a minute. "Sorry I'm such a mess. I'm just an old dog, I suppose."

"No," I insisted.

And then he insisted some more. And I insisted some more. And then, York got in the act.

It was at least fifteen minutes more before York and I finally left.

My brother and I let the door of Citrus House shut behind us before we started in.

"What'd you see?" he asked in whisper.

"Nothing," I whispered back. "Or too much. I don't know. Nothing useful, as far as I can tell." I shivered. It was cold outside.

"Well, criminy," he told me. "Half the people weren't even here. I mean, look at the Turners. Julie shows up and leaves. I could understand if the kid didn't come, but how about her husband?"

"I think he feels that he and his family shouldn't be forced to involve themselves," I guessed. "They weren't that close to May, and they weren't related. I can't really blame him."

"Well, I can," York insisted. "Gerry's lost his wife, and they can't even come over to help. But then they're respectable types, not outsiders like May and Gerry—"

"And us," I finished for him.

A little bit of his tension evaporated.

"Yeah, like us." He shook his head. "I guess that's what I liked about May. She was such an oddball, she could have passed for a Lazar."

I gave York a hug and smiled up at him. "She'll take that as a compliment," I promised him.

He hugged me back, then released me. I turned to go to my car.

"Are you okay tonight, Cally?" York asked.

"What do you mean?" I asked back.

"Well, you know you can always call or come over," he said, not really answering me.

"Late date?" I guessed.

"Maybe," he conceded. "But promise you'll come get me if you need me."

"I promise," I told him, and I meant it.

I was driving home when I got to thinking about families. We Lazars were all alike in more ways than I liked to think. We all shared the sharp features, for one. No Lazar had the full lips and wide blue eyes that May had. Or Julie. Without realizing, I superimposed their faces in my mind. They could have been mother and daughter. Saucer blue eyes, lush lips, and high cheekbones. Criminy! Could it be? Julie looked as much like May as I looked like Geneva. Dack, even Zack looked like May. My hands tightened on the steering wheel. No, I was letting my imagination run away with me. But I hadn't guessed that Dutch was May's brother, either. And he had those wide blue eyes, too.

I turned onto the road that would take me home. Okay, what if Julie had been May's daughter? That wasn't exactly a motive for murder. Or was it? It was a secret. Maybe Julie hadn't wanted the PTA to know that she was May's daughter. And she'd been arguing with May at the party, I suddenly remembered. Still. I shook my head. Even if Julie had been May's daughter, I couldn't imagine her killing her own mother. And her grief over May's death seemed genuine.

I still hadn't made up my mind by the time I got home. I stomped into my house and headed straight for the telephone. Kapp could find out if Julie was related to May. Kapp could find out anything. I dialed his phone and got an answering machine.

I cursed as I hung up the phone. He was probably out with my sister Geneva.

Julie? Julie bringing over pumpkin soup and looking misty when Gerry took her hand. Did Gerry know? I went to the phone again. But I couldn't pick it up. Gerry didn't need a phone call just then. Not unless I was ready to tell him the murderer's name.

York, I decided. I needed to try this one on York. And I needed to talk to him in person.

The drive to York's place seemed endless. My mind was doing its version of a cat chasing its own tail. Julie. May. Julie? Julie! But May? Julie. And Dutch. He was her uncle! I tried to think of something else as I drove up the long narrow road that led to York's studio and home.

I parked next to York's familiar Subaru and an unfamiliar BMW. I remembered our earlier conversation. Did my brother have company?

I decided I'd play it safe. I had a key to York's studio, but I rang the bell instead. I'd almost turned back to my car by the time I heard his elevator creaking down to the ground floor. When he flung open the studio door, he was dressed in blue jeans as usual, but wore a shortened kimono that had Geneva's stamp on it. And he was barefoot. He had to be cold, standing there in the doorway.

"Cally?" he asked, looking at me.

"Hey, York," I said, hoping for a laugh. "Have you forgotten your own sister?"

"No, sorry about that," he muttered, glancing back at the building that housed his studio and living quarters. He wasn't laughing. And he still hadn't invited me in. He *did* have company. No turning back now.

"Julie," I whispered.

"Julie?"

"Think of May," I suggested. "Think of Julie. And their looks. What do you see?"

He frowned for a few breaths. Then he looked into my eyes.

"Dack," he erupted quietly. "They're related."

"Yes!" I shouted exuberantly in the cold night. "You see it, too."

"I can't believe I missed it before," he complained. "But what does it mean?"

"I don't know," I admitted, my exuberance gone. "And I'm not sure how to find out."

York frowned again.

"Come on in," he told me. "I have to put on some warmer clothes."

So the two of us walked into his studio and took the elevator up to his living quarters. He left me in his kitchen.

A tall man with a beard and glasses joined me there.

"Hi, I'm Bill," he greeted me, holding out his hand.

"I'm Cally, York's sister," I greeted him back, shaking his outstretched hand.

We both sat down at the kitchen table and tried to think of something to say. I didn't want to ask him if he'd just met York, or worse yet, to tell him that we were searching for a murderer. Bill broke the stalemate.

"I met York at a martial arts symposium," he told me. "I teach tai chi."

"Oh, who did you study with?" I asked, having learned the protocol years ago from York.

We were still tracing Bill's lineage when York got back. He was wearing a sweater and running shoes.

"Are you ready?" he asked me.

"Ready for what?" I asked him back.

"To talk to Julie."

"Now?" I squeaked. Julie's relation to May was a great theory, but somehow I didn't feel like testing it at night. Not right away—

"Now," York insisted.

"But what about your guest?"

"Bill," York said, turning, "you can take care of yourself until I get back, okay? You know where the tea is."

"Sure," Bill answered.

"Fine." York turned back to me. "Cally," he said. "Focus. And . . ."

"And what?"

"And be ready to use your cane," he answered.

TWENTY-THREE

We took York's Subaru. We'd gone about three yards down his driveway when I asked him why he thought I'd need my cane.

"Julie Turner's in danger," he answered quietly.

"What?" I demanded.

"May died. Dutch died. Julie's next," York pronounced, as if the logical steps were obvious.

"Oh, come on, why would someone want to kill a whole family?"

York just stared straight ahead, his gaunt features tense as he drove.

"Maybe they just happen to look alike," I threw out hopefully.

York remained silent. My pulse went up another notch.

"Look, let's go ask Gerry about this," I suggested. "I'll bet he knows if Julie's related to May."

"Gerry might be the one who's killing them," York answered.

The hairs went up all over my body. Gerry was the whole reason I was trying to find out who killed May and Dutch. Gerry couldn't—

"Who knows how he benefits financially from Dutch's or Julie's deaths?" York interrupted my thought.

"No, that just doesn't make sense," I argued, the long-repressed lawyer in me surfacing. "May died first. If Dutch or Julie inherited, they would have already done it."

"What if Dutch or Julie left their money to May or her heir, and her heir was Gerry?" York proposed.

"But they had their own families!" I objected. I could hear the impatience in my own voice. And the fear.

"I didn't say Gerry did it," York put in. "I just said we can't ignore the possibility."

"Okay," I tried, forcing calm into my voice. "Let's say someone is trying to kill May and her relatives, and that someone isn't Gerry. Who is it?"

That discussion took us the rest of the way to the Turners'. But we still hadn't reached any conclusions by the time we'd driven down the exclusive Mostaza drive where May had lived, and parked in front of the Turners' mission-style adobe home.

"Keep your focus," York ordered as he knocked on the carved wooden door I'd knocked on only two days before.

Julie answered the door, opening it all of six inches and peering through the gap.

"Mr. Lazar?" she murmured, her high-pitched voice hazy as if she'd been sleeping. "Cally?"

"May we come in, Ms. Turner?" York asked.

"Oh, of course," she agreed, opening the door wide. "John's not home yet, but he'll be here any moment."

I wondered if she was warning us that the cavalry was on the way. I wouldn't blame her. As far as she knew, we might be murderers.

"It was really you we wanted to speak to anyway," York told her gently.

"Me?" she questioned, her big blue eyes widening till they were even larger. It was then that I realized why neither York nor I had noticed Julie's resemblance to May earlier. It was all there, in the eyes and lush mouth and cheekbones. But Julie's hair was black where May's had been silver. And May's big blue eyes had been shaped by wit and living, while Julie's were still childlike.

"Mom?" a voice called out from behind Julie, Zack's voice.

"It's just visitors, honey," she returned his call. "You keep studying till your dad gets home." Then she turned back to us. "Gosh, I haven't even invited you in. I don't know what I'm thinking. Please, come in."

We did, and once again I smelled the faintly exotic scents of cedar and incense. Julie sat us down in carved chairs, then pulled up her own chair and sat across from us.

"Oh, my," she began. "I can't imagine what you want to talk to me about. I mean, I know communication is very important. Meaningful dialogue and all. But I don't know—"

"Are you May North's daughter?" York interrupted.

Julie stopped speaking and just stared in our direction for a moment of silence. Then her blue eyes filled with tears.

"It's all right, Julie," I told her, resisting the impulse to wrap my arm around her. "It's just that you look so much like May—"

"I am!" Julie wailed. "May was my mother!"

York sent me a sidelong glance that I couldn't interpret.

"I miss her so much," Julie sobbed. "But I couldn't even grieve for her properly. I'd been pretending I wasn't her daughter so long. Oh, Cally, it's been so hard. I know everyone wonders why I'm so upset, but I can't tell them. I can't even tell them . . ." She pressed her hands to her temples and cried even harder.

"But why couldn't you tell?" I asked.

"I grew up in boarding schools," Julie murmured, her voice thickened by her tears. "May thought it was best. See, I always called her May, even when I was little. Not 'Mom.' I never knew who my father was. Maybe May didn't either. It was awful at her place. It was, you know, a house of prostitution. I can hardly say it. The women were crass, and Uncle Dutch was scary, always pestering me like he wanted to, you know, do something to me, too. And May didn't seem to understand how bad it was. Maybe she couldn't do it and let herself know. But she knew I hated what she did, so she agreed that she would never publicly acknowledge me as her daughter. And she didn't. She even gave me my inheritance way before she died, so no one would know where the money came from. She loved me in her own way. And when we moved to Mostaza, she followed us. And then Uncle Dutch moved here, too. I . . . I . . ." Julie faltered again.

"Why were you angry with May the night of the party?" York asked in the gap in the waterfall of her words.

I wondered if his glance had meant he was changing his theory. Did he now think Julie had killed her mother?

"May waved at Zack in the nude," she answered, her tears suddenly gone. "How could she do that? I had to protect Zack. And our respectability. John thinks respectability is really important, you know. So I went to her party to tell her not to do that stuff anymore. But she just thought I was funny. She never took me seriously. No one takes me seriously—"

"Did you kill her?" I asked softly. I had to ask.

"No!" Julie's eyes filled again. "I wouldn't kill May. She was my mother. You can't think that I'd kill her—"

"Maybe I killed her," John Turner said quietly.

Julie gasped, her beautiful face stretched into fear now.

I saw John standing at the kitchen door. I wondered how long he'd been listening. I had been focused, but on the wrong person. I'd been listening to Julie while her husband came in the back door. And John Turner was holding a gun.

John stepped into the living room, his tread as light as York's. It was no wonder I hadn't heard him. And his usually bland face was smiling.

He walked our way calmly, cautiously, holding a gun out in front of him, stopping a yard away from us.

"Here you are, accusing my poor wife of murder," he went on mildly. "And you're ignoring me. See this house?" He used his gun to point our attention around the living room. "How do you think I made the money for all this, dealing in imports? How about drugs? Hmm . . . now there's a thought. What if I was a drug dealer in the golden triangle, *then* entered the respectable world of imports? What if I killed complete strangers in Vietnam? How hard would it be to kill again for business purposes? If I'd kill complete strangers and other drug dealers, don't you think I'd kill to protect my own wife?" His smile disappeared now. "No one bothers my family. I own my family."

Julie stared at her husband. Was she actually seeing him for the first time?

"May couldn't leave well enough alone," John told us. "She had to move here and pester Zack. It was too much for Julie."

I didn't know you were a drug dealer," Julie whispered.

"Well, I didn't know your mother was a whore, not until

after we were married," he retorted. He laughed angrily. "All I did for respectability. You were perfect: beautiful, well dressed, soft-spoken, educated. A young widow with a young son. And then I found out your mother was a whore. I almost killed her the first time you told me."

"My mother wasn't a whore!" Julie cried. "She was a madam. And I loved her."

"Well, how do you think people would look at me?" John asked her mildly, as if the question was of minor academic interest. "Me with my PTA wife and perfect son. How do you think they'd look at me if they knew my mother-in-law was a whore?"

"But—" Julie tried. It was useless. Mr. Silent was on a roll.

"I worked hard to earn my money and get respect. I don't deal in drugs anymore. May wanted to ruin all of that for you . . . and for me. As bad as my mother was, at least she didn't—"

"I thought your mother was a housewife," Julie interjected.

"Well, she wasn't," John said angrily. "She was a whore, just like yours."

"But—"

"It was a pleasure to kill May," John plowed on, the anger gone from his voice. "The woman had no shame."

"Oh, John," Julie sobbed. "You didn't know her."

I saw Zack out of the corner of my eye, making his way quietly into the room as his stepfather continued to speak.

"And Dutch thought he knew who did it," John said. "He thought it was Julie. He threatened to tell the police all about their relationship if I didn't pay him off." John smiled again. "It was a pleasure offing him, too, all the times he'd messed with us. Him a friend? He was a loser, always going

on about how well he did in business, when he just used his
sister to get rich. He practically blackmailed me into hanging out with him, hinting about how interesting it'd be if
people knew who was related to May in town, how we were
practically brothers-in-law. Blah, blah, blah. Dutch tried to
hurt Julie, and no one hurts Julie, you hear me? Or Zack.
They're mine."

He owned his family, I remembered. He didn't love
them, he owned them.

"Dad," Zack chimed in.

John whirled around.

"Did you kill David?" Zack asked.

"You mean that stupid kid who was making fun of you
all the time?" his stepfather asked back.

Zack nodded.

John chuckled.

"Of course, son," he cooed. "I said I take care of my
family. I went to talk to that kid. He threatened me, do you
believe it? Said he'd tell people I molested him if I made
trouble. Little sociopath. So I planned it. Hit-and-run, no
one ever even thought of me."

Zack's blue eyes widened, but he said nothing. He just
turned his eyes on his mother briefly, his glance protective
but powerless. I wondered how long Zack had known
about his stepfather. Longer than his mother had?

"You were my prowler on the hill, that night, weren't
you?" I asked.

John frowned. "I thought you might know something,"
he admitted. "I thought that you might be psychic. That's
what May had said. But I decided that the way your goats
protected you was a sign, a sign that you didn't know anyway. You would have told the police if you had. Still, I
should have killed you that night, killed your goats." My

heart clenched, but I wanted to keep him talking. He obliged me.

"I almost got you yesterday," he announced. "Gerry called me about his damned potluck, said you were going to finger the murderer. So I went to your place. I saw that weirdo who was always following you. I hit him from behind. Once he went down, I kicked him in the ribs for good measure." At that, my hand made a fist, but I willed myself to keep still. "I was trying to figure out how to get in your house when you came out with that big woman. So I snuck away. You didn't even see me. No one ever does."

"And you," he accused, turning his eyes to York. "Some martial artist you are. You don't even own a gun. I checked your whole house, not even a slingshot."

"Weren't you afraid of the police?" I questioned.

"No," he answered, baring his teeth again. "I have an excellent paper trail. I'm a respectable businessman, the only son of a wealthy family." He tilted back his head and laughed then. "They weren't my real family, of course. My mother *was* a whore. But my paper is good enough for the authorities."

"But you—" I began.

He motioned me to be quiet with his gun.

"Sorry, Ms. Lazar, but I have to think," he explained. "You two," he mused, "are murderers, I believe. The two of you in it together. My family will back me. They'd better." He looked at Julie and Zack. They seemed to shrink. "You broke into our house. I caught you and stopped you. No, even better." He waved his gun in an extravagant gesture. "I'll set it up to look like Francie killed you—"

His gun was still pointed away from us when I knocked it out of his hand with my cane. And then York was on him. John Turner was wrong. York *was* a martial artist.

TWENTY-FOUR

It was Saturday afternoon, and we were all outside among the topiary of Citrus House. The sun was shining in the winter's sky. And York had something near a smile on his face. He hadn't broken any of John Turner's bones when he'd jumped him, but he'd certainly succeeded in subduing him.

"So Julie is taking back her name now, the one her mother gave her," Gerry announced to his rapt audience. His skin had lost its gray tones. I still saw grief in his aura, but also a growing peace. "Juliette North," he enunciated carefully. "She's having it legally changed. And Zack wants to change his last name, too. He hasn't decided whether to use his real father's name or North. Anything but Turner."

"Is Julie staying in Mostaza?" Dee-Dee asked.

Dee-Dee, Joan, and Kapp had shown up for the get-together, as well as the three boarders, Gerry's daughter, and Sarah Quesada. Francie Krentz had even made a token appearance, leaving a small bonsai tree "for May," she'd said, then left. I was proud of her gesture. And then there was Roy. Roy was there, Roy who'd arrived at my house the moment he was sure I was safe from him, safe from his darkness, safe from murder. I leaned back into his arms, smelling his familiar scent and feeling the warmth and pulse of his body rhythms.

"Julie's not sure yet, but she's getting stronger every day," Gerry answered. "She's acting like May's daughter now. She's not afraid anymore. May would be happy."

May would be happy. As if to punctuate the thought, the mop dog yipped from where he was chasing the Labrador retriever and dachshund around the leafy giraffe, oblivious to the solemnity of the occasion.

I breathed in. The cool air felt good in my lungs. In a way York had been right when we'd driven to the Turners' house that night. Julie had been in terrible danger. If she had gone along with her husband, knowing what he'd done, she'd have lost her . . . something. Her goodness? Her soul? Her identity? Something. But if she hadn't gone along with him, she might have lost her life and her son's. I shook my head, glad once more that she hadn't had to make that decision.

"But why did John confess?" Sarah Quesada asked. "Jeez, he didn't have to." She stood with her arm around Phil Morton's waist. The two of them looked natural there together, as if they'd always been a couple.

"Because we already knew who Julie's mother was," I explained. "That was it for him. Julie's mother had been a madam. To John Turner, that was worse than murder. His mother had been a prostitute. That was his hot button. There was nothing, not drugs, not murder, nothing as bad as prostitution to him. Once we knew about May's relationship to Julie, we had to die anyway."

"And he was tired of Julie mourning her mother," York added. His tone softened. "He was tired of playing a role all the time, too, I think. He wanted to shock Julie into accepting his reality. He was lonely in his way. He'd created an artificial persona, and he couldn't ever step out of it."

"Priorities a little skewed, what?" Ian pronounced in his best British accent.

"Hear, hear!" I seconded his assessment. And yet, there was a tiny part of me that felt sorry for John Turner. What kind of person can only be safe as someone else?

"Julie's not ashamed of being May's daughter anymore," Gerry said proudly. Becky squeezed his hand, and he smiled. He looked over at the small cardboard table set up outside, with an orange tablecloth and a few trays of crackers and cheese as well as a crystal punch bowl filled with the remains of an orange juice and sparkling water concoction that brought summer into the winter day.

"I'm going to get some more punch," Gerry told us, and went inside the house, carrying the almost empty bowl.

Then Kapp cleared his throat. All eyes turned to him, knowing he'd been waiting for a chance to recite the gory details.

"When Julie followed May up the stairs that night, she hadn't known that her husband, John, was right behind her," Kapp whispered. As we listened, we imagined. "He stood back in the shadows of the hallway and listened as Julie argued with May. She wanted May to stay away from Zack, but May just laughed. She told Julie to lighten up, that nothing really wrong had happened. Julie pleaded. She even cried. But May just turned her back on Julie while she looked for more jewelry on her dresser. And May never stopped talking. She really wanted her daughter to hear what she was saying: that it didn't matter how a thing looked, just what it *was*. But Julie had left. She'd heard May's opinion before. Only May didn't hear Julie leave. She continued lecturing her daughter as John Turner came in."

"She was deaf," Eric reminded us.

Kapp ignored him, going on with his story. "So John just stepped up and killed May from behind as May continued to try to convince the person she thought was Julie that the appearance of respectability wasn't important. It was a matter of seconds for John to do his work. And then he left the room, too."

I imagined John Turner twisting the gold chains around May's neck. And for a moment, I almost wished that York had broken some bones. I breathed in and found some light, a glimmer of compassion. John Turner was going to have enough problems now, if he hadn't before. I just hoped it was possible for him to find some peace eventually.

"Julie claims she didn't even know her husband had followed her," Kapp went on.

"I believe her," York put in. "John Turner knew how to walk lightly."

Kapp cleared his throat again. The rest was *his* story. "Then later, Dutch told Julie he knew she'd killed her mother and was going to tell. Holy Mother, what an idiot! Because Julie was more than a little upset by his accusation and his threat. So she turned around and told her husband, John, hoping John would protect her somehow. And then John killed Dutch, too. If Dutch had gone to the police, he might have told them that Julie was May's daughter. That was enough for John. So John set up the killing at the house Sarah was showing. Dutch was only too glad to accompany John there. Dutch thought they were going there to make trouble for Sarah." Kapp paused, his audience in his hand. "At that point, Julie began to worry. Even from her cocoon of denial, she wondered about the coincidence of each person she argued with dying, not to mention the kid that was nasty to Zack."

"I think Zack had already figured it out," I interjected. "But what could he say about his 'dad'?"

"Especially a dad who might kill his own stepson," Kapp added.

The back door slammed, and Gerry returned with a full punch bowl sloshing in his hands as he walked toward the card table.

"Beautiful day," Kapp commented. I smiled at my friend's fledgling sensitivity.

"Shoot, Gerry!" Sarah demanded. "Why didn't you tell the authorities that Julie was May's daughter?" *Her* sensitivity needed a little work.

"May loved her 'Juliette,'" Gerry explained with a little sigh. "She wouldn't have wanted her daughter bothered. May settled most of her money on Julie years ago in a trust, so Julie wouldn't be embarrassed by the connection coming up when May died. She'd settled some money on Dutch, too, and their brother, Axel—"

My mind made a gymnastic leap. "Dack, did May and Dutch and Axel *all* speak German?" I asked abruptly.

"Sure," Gerry answered me. "German was the language the three of them grew up with."

"So, Dutch had probably been talking to his brother, Axel, the time I heard him speaking German on the phone."

Gerry thought for a moment, then nodded.

"It makes sense," he confirmed. "Axel called me. He must have called Dutch. He wanted to know if there was more money he could get his hands on. He was the blackest sheep of the family. He sponged off of May and Dutch even after she gave him all that money."

"An even blacker sheep than Dutch?" Ian questioned,

eyebrows raised. "Oooh, he is definitely someone I don't want to meet."

"I couldn't believe Julie would have killed May," Gerry went on, as if he hadn't heard Ian. "I didn't take John into account." He shook his head. "Dang, I hardly noticed John."

"That's because John wasn't John," Ian reminded him, his voice without affectation now. "He was really James Thompson. He had a long and successful career as a drug importer. And then, just as the police were closing in on him, he disappeared. And poof, John Turner was born."

"I just wish he'd never met Julie," Gerry whispered.

"Drug dealers, gawd!" Ian exclaimed. He paused, then said quietly, "I'm going into rehab next week."

There was a stunned silence, then a flurry of congratulations. Ian Oxton was serious.

"May would have been glad," Gerry told him.

"I know," Ian replied, blushing and turning his head away.

"I wonder why I never saw anything in John's aura?" I mumbled, seeing in *Ian's* aura that for once, he wanted to be out of the spotlight. "Not a hint."

"He was a sociopath, darlin'," Roy piped in unexpectedly. "He spent his whole life tamping down his real self, until no one could see him, not even energetically. That's why he was so successful, you see. He was the man who wasn't really there." I snuggled closer to Roy's chest. Roy had told me he was considering what his hospital roommate, Pete, had told him of his own experience with the darkness. Maybe there was no escape. Maybe we should be together. He was still "thinking on it." I'd already made up *my* mind.

York looked at Roy and me and seemed to smile and

frown at the same time. "John Turner owned his family,"
York summed up. "May and Dutch threatened his family,
but worse, they threatened his respectability. It was a threat
he wasn't willing to allow. So he killed two people."

I pulled Roy's arms around me, not wanting to think of
John Turner anymore.

"Still," Phil put in gently, "all beings have the potential
for good. John Turner carried out evil acts, God help him.
But maybe he can make amends someday."

There was a silence. Were we all thinking of Gerry?
How could John *ever* make amends to Gerry?

"The air is clear," Gerry pronounced, smiling as he
turned his face up to the blue expanse. "The sun is shining.
Let's think of May. Let's celebrate!"

I felt the thin rays of the sun expanding in my heart.

"A toast!" Ian shouted.

"A toast!" a handful of voices, including my own,
answered.

Gerry ladled out the punch into paper cups. Phil passed
the cups around, bowing as each of us reached out to
accept our portion.

"Please lift your glasses," Phil ordered.

"May, the effervescent lady of orange," I added softly,
and each of us lifted our glasses to the light of the clear
winter sky.

"To May!" we chorused, and we drank of sparkling
orange juice.

The debut in the mystery series
with great karma—

Body of Intuition

by

Claire Daniels

Alternative healer Cally Lazar's sensory skills help
her soothe her clients' auras. But once in a while,
what she finds will make her jump out of her skin.

0-425-18740-3

THE KARMA CRIME MYSTERIES ARE:

"A HOLISTIC PRESCRIPTION FOR FUN.
ENJOYABLE SIDE EFFECTS INCLUDE LAUGHTER."
—LYNNE MURRAY

"A DELIGHT."
—JANE DEAN OF MURDER MOST COZY

"ORIGINAL, INNOVATIVE, AND UNIQUE."
—JANET A. RUDOLPH, EDITOR OF
MYSTERY READERS JOURNAL

Available wherever books are sold or
to order, please call 1-800-788-6262

B164

LOVE MYSTERY?

From cozy mysteries to procedurals,
we've got it all. Satisfy your cravings with our monthly
newsletters designed and edited specifically for fans of who-
dunits. With two newsletters to choose from, you'll be sure to
get it all. Be sure to check back each month or sign up for
free monthly in-box delivery at

www.penguin.com

Berkley Prime Crime

Berkley publishes the premier writers of mysteries.
Get the latest on your
favorties:
Susan Wittig Albert, Margaret Coel, Earlene
Fowler, Randy Wayne White, Simon Brett, and
many more fresh faces.

Signet

From the Grand Dame of mystery,
Agatha Christie, to debut authors,
Signet mysteries offer something for every reader.

*Sign up and sleep with
one eye open!*

B112